P9-BYC-351

truest

JACKIE LEA SOMMERS

KT
Katherine Tegen Books
An Imprint of HarperCollinsPublishers

Katherine Tegen Books is an imprint of HarperCollins Publishers.

www.epicreads.com

Library of Congress Cataloging-in-Publication Data
Sommers, Jackie Lea.
Truest / Jackie Lea Sommers. — First edition.
pages cm
Summary: "Westlin Beck's summer is turned upside down when the Hart twins move to town: aggravating, intriguing, and quirky Silas and his mysteriously ill sister, Laurel"— Provided by publisher.
ISBN 978-0-06-234825-8 (hardback)
[1. Friendship—Fiction. 2. Twins—Fiction. 3. Brothers and sisters—Fiction. 4. Sick—Fiction. 5. Family life—Minnesota—Fiction. 6. Minnesota—Fiction.] I. Title.
PZ7.1.S675Tru 2015 2014047919
[Fic]—dc23 CIP
AC

Typography by Jenna Stempel
15 16 17 18 19 PC/RRDH 10 9 8 7 6 5 4 3 2 1
❖
First Edition

For Emma, Ava, Elsie, and Owen, four PKs I love even more than Westlin Beck.

And also for Cindy Woerner, whose conversations fueled this story, and for Kristin Luehr, who rescued it twice.

one

The swans on Green Lake looked like tiny icebergs, only it was the first weekend of my summer vacation. One hundred feet from where I sat in the car, they lay quiet claim to the lake, as if it were their inheritance.

"Here? Really? I thought we were going to Gordon's," I accused, now staring out the windshield from the passenger's seat at the sprawling Tudor-style home that was definitely *not* the senior living center.

"We are," Dad said. "After this." He rooted around in the backseat for his portable communion set, a black leather case with "In Remembrance" embossed on the cover in gold. "Ready?"

"Can I stay in the car?"

"West," my dad said, his voice thick with disapproval. I

grumbled as I undid my seat belt.

At the front door, Dad rang the doorbell. Inside, a voice yelled, "Got it!" After the sound of approaching footsteps, the door opened, and in its frame stood a boy my age.

He was *tall*—maybe six foot two or three—and thin, with a perfect jawline and beautiful peach lips. His hair was a thick, dark mop that fell into his cheerful eyes. They looked at my dad expectantly, as if he'd come a-caroling.

Then he saw me.

In an instant, he went from ten-thousand-watt cheer to shadowy disappointment. My ears grew hot in humiliation. Did I have something in my teeth? I ran my tongue over them to check—all good.

Dad was as distracted as ever and noticed none of it. "Hey there. You must be Silas," he said, shaking the boy's hand. "Pastor Kerry Beck. This is my daughter West." I offered a little wave, but he ignored me.

"Good to meet you, sir," said Silas, the smile returning—and seeming genuine enough—for my father. He held the door open for us, saying, "Come on in. Mom! Dad!"

As I walked in past him, he dropped his gaze, refusing to even *look* at me. His threadbare T-shirt read, "PRACTICE SAFE LUNCH: Use a Condiment." It seemed completely out of place inside this storybook house.

"Sunroom is this way," he said, leading me and Dad down a hallway, past the kitchen, and through the dining and living rooms, which were being updated to modern perfection. Thomas and Joanie Griggs, the former occupants, had called it quits on Minnesota winters and moved south two or three years ago. Rumor had it "the old Griggs house" had a rooftop patio with a fire pit the size of a hot tub.

A rich house for rich snobs, apparently—I'd expect nothing less from Heaton Ridge, the expensive thumb of our mitten-shaped town.

Anyway, why should I care if the hot new guy was a jerk? I had a boyfriend.

Still, Silas's obvious disappointment irritated me. What had he been expecting?

The sunroom turned out to be more like a conservatory—glass-paned walls *and* ceiling, vaulted and with white beams. This house couldn't have been more different from our family's humble little parsonage. A white rug made of something suspiciously like polar bear fur covered the pale floor and lay beneath a matching set of white wicker furniture. Sitting on the couch was a princess.

I stared. The girl, who also looked about my age, offered only a faint smile as we entered the room. Her hair was the color of golden honey, and with the afternoon sun shining down through the glass ceiling, she glowed like an angel. She had the same perfect peach lips as Silas (a *sister*, I realized), beautiful cheekbones, dramatic eyebrows, and a pale oval face. It took me several moments to notice she was wearing her pajamas.

"Hi, Pastor Beck," said a man, stepping from behind us into the sunroom along with his wife. He nodded toward his daughter. "This here is—"

"Laurel," said the girl, holding out her hand to shake my father's, although she made no move to stand up. She turned toward me. "Hi," she said, still only the slightest of smiles on her face. Her eyes looked deep into mine, not unkindly—but *fierce*. And only for a moment. Then they seemed to fade somehow, as if a light inside her had turned off.

It gave me goose bumps.

"West," I muttered. "Nice to meet you."

Everything was too quiet in this eerie glass room—but then a hand on my shoulder broke the tension. "West, good to meet you," their mom said. "Teresa Hart. This is my husband, Glen." Noticing Silas's T-shirt, she rolled her eyes. "You couldn't have changed?" Silas laughed and kissed his mom on the cheek, making her grin. "Silas, go show West around."

I glanced at my dad, hoping he'd object—after all, he had strict rules about when and where my boyfriend, Elliot, was allowed in our house—but he only smiled in a *have fun* sort of way. Silas looked as horrified as I felt, and that pissed me off even more.

"We can just stay . . . ," Silas began, but his mother said, "Shoo."

Annoyed, he nodded in the direction we'd come from. Great. He wasn't even going to speak to me.

The carpet that lined the stairs was thick, luxurious. Every step felt like *this—family—is—so—rich*. I asked, "So, how long have you guys been in Green Lake?"

He sighed, and for a second I thought maybe he'd just ignore me. But then he said, "Couple weeks? We moved from Fairbanks."

"Alaska?" I asked, dumbfounded. "Why'd you move to Minnesota?"

"My mom grew up here." We passed an open door, the second on the left. "This is my room."

I paused in the doorway. The room smelled like *boy*—and a little like feet, which I assumed came from the beat-up Nikes that were tucked halfway under the bed. It was messy inside, a welcome respite from the perfection of everything else I'd seen—some shirts and jeans lying on the floor, and a pair of boxers, from which I quickly looked away. A song I didn't know was playing from an ancient CD player, and there was a small TV in the corner of the room. Beside the TV was an empty frozen-pizza box with some pieces of crust on it. Silas's nightstand was piled high with a mix of *Runner's World* magazines, notebooks, and novels. Beside his closet was a huge bookcase, double-lined with books.

"You wanna see the roof?" he mumbled from the doorway, looking in on the chaos.

But I was in his room already, the bookcase drawing me in like a tractor beam, my hand automatically reaching for the spines. Rather, reaching for *a* spine—*Collier* by Donovan Trick, my favorite book, favorite writer. I pulled it off the shelf, noticing the telltale signs of devotion: well-worn cover, cracked spine, three or four makeshift bookmarks marking favorite pages.

"Is this y—?" I started to ask.

"Be right back," he muttered before disappearing down the hall.

"Um," I said aloud to no one, "okay."

Being alone in his bedroom was awkward, but I wasn't sure where else to go in this unfamiliar house. I looked down at the book in my hands and opened it; there was an inscription on the inside cover.

> *Silas,*
>
> *"Stories are our most august arms against the darkness."*
>
> *We know you know that.*
>
> *Love, Mom and Dad*

Silas slipped back into the room. "Do you listen to *August Arms*?" I asked, turning to look at him. His hair was all wet, and his T-shirt was soaked around the collar.

"Is that a band?" he asked, looking everywhere around the room but at me.

"No, it's a radio show I like." I put the book back. "Are you okay?"

"I'm fine. You read much?" Silas asked, sitting down on the edge of his bed. Posters hung on the wall behind it. One said "NOTICE" in official-looking red letters across the top, and beneath it were the words "Thank you for noticing this notice. Your noting it has been noted." Beside it was a poster of an orange looking in horror at a glass of orange juice and saying, "Mom??" In the corner of the room was a full-sized cardboard cutout of Darth Vader.

Silas followed my gaze. "At night, Vader joins me in bed and puts his head on my chest," he joked. "Falling asleep to the sound of his ventilated breathing is very soothing, actually."

"I'll bet," I said dryly. I hadn't answered his question—nor was I going to. What business was it of his whether I "read much"? And why were his hair and shirt all wet? Why the jokes after he'd been so unapproachable? I couldn't nail down his mood.

"Poetry's my thing, I guess," he offered.

"*You* read poetry?" I asked, narrowing my eyes in skepticism.

"'Poets are the unacknowledged legislators of the world,'" he said, like a total asshat.

"Enchanting," I said.

"I'm not just being a tool," Silas said. "Shelley wrote that." He paused, then added, "The English Romantic poet?"

"I know who he is," I said. Well, I *sort of* knew who he was, at least.

Then, in the most baffling move in the history of mankind, Silas grinned—that same goofy, cheerful grin I'd seen at the front door—and my heart turned a traitorous cartwheel.

I had to look away.

I struggled to regain the ground I'd lost to that grin. Faking confidence, I sat down beside him, then immediately doubted myself but tried not to show it. "So what's with Laurel?" I asked, careful not to let my shoulder get too near to his. "Can she walk?"

He frowned. He had a tiny freckle on his left cheek. "*Yes*. She's *fine*."

"Oh," I said, retreating. "Sorry. We just usually bring communion to—sorry. I thought that maybe she—"

"She's *fine*," he repeated with a scowl. "Small towns," he spat out, then bit back whatever he was going to say next.

"I should go," I said, starting to get up.

"No, don't." He clutched my shoulder so that I stayed seated. I wrenched it away from him. "Sorry," he mumbled.

I glared at him, and he seemed to soften. "Sorry," he said again, his mouth a worried knot until he maneuvered it into a forced smile. "Laurel—she's my twin sister. It was really good of your dad—and you—to bring over communion. Body and the Blood. Good conversation."

"Conversation?" I asked. "With my dad?"

"With God," he said, without explanation.

I'd never thought of it that way before. To me, it tasted like crackers and juice.

"How old are you?" I asked him, suspiciously. No one my age talked that way.

"Seventeen. You?"

"Seventeen."

I looked hard at Silas Hart. His cheekbones were like Laurel's, his eyebrows aggressive and his eyes just as alive as his sister's had looked hollow. "What?" he asked, but this time his voice had a playful, almost teasing, tone. He knocked his knee against mine.

"Nothing," I said, standing up and moving away from him. On the other side of the room, I leaned my back against his bookcase. "Your mom grew up here?"

"Yeah, Teresa Mayhew, if that means anything to you. My grandparents are—"

"Arty and Lillian?"

"Yeah. Wow."

I shrugged. "They sit behind us in church. Your grandpa gives out gum to the Sunday school kids. Your grandma . . . is usually upset over something."

Silas laughed. "Sounds about right."

"Here's your first lesson in small town life: every last name means something. Thomas means you're adopted; Boggs, you're homeschooled; Travers, you raise cattle. Arty and Lil are the only Mayhews still around, but the name still has a reputation for being athletic."

Silas raised his eyebrows. "My mom and aunt were both

state track stars. That's actually a little creepy, you know."

"It's Green Lake."

"Wink!" my dad called up the stairs. "Ready to go?"

Yes.

No.

Maybe?

"Coming!"

Silas followed me out, asking, "Did he just call you 'Wink'?"

I ignored him.

At the bottom of the stairs, Mr. and Mrs. Hart were saying good-bye to my dad. I glanced back down the hall in the direction of the sunroom, wanting to see Laurel again, but the couch was now empty.

"Silas, good to meet you today. We'll see you at church next week?" asked my dad, shaking Silas's hand again.

"Yes, sir," Silas promised with a grin, "or I'll have Oma Lil to answer to."

He was charming my father, who laughed and said, "Nobody wants that! Glad you got to meet Westlin. Maybe she can show you what's fun in Green Lake."

"There's nothing fun in Green Lake," I countered. Then I smiled at Mrs. Hart to show her I was joking, even though I wasn't.

"Actually, I need to find a decent summer job," Silas said. "No fun for me."

"West here makes pretty good money detailing cars in the

summer, and she's short a business partner and needing some help," my dad said. His words were a double blow: first, a bitter reminder that my best friend, Trudy, had left just yesterday, abandoning me for summer camp; and second, Dad's offer to Silas to take her place. I glared at Dad—but only for a second. Pastors' kids aren't supposed to glare.

Silas looked equally reluctant, but Dad said, "A divine appointment!"

How do you tell the pastor to *shut the hell up*?

He and Mr. and Mrs. Hart all looked at me.

"You interested?" I squeaked out against my will.

"Sure," Silas said, sounding anything but.

"Okay, well, I have a detailing tomorrow morning at nine. We're in the parsonage by the community church. You should wear junky clothes."

Silas pointed to his condiments T-shirt with a smirk. "I'll be there at five to."

two

After the calamitous transaction with Silas, I gave my dad the silent treatment all the way to Legacy House, though he never seemed to notice. But my mood changed when Gordon answered his apartment door. Dark glasses on, he looked like an elderly Ray Charles with an even brighter smile.

"Welcome, welcome, Pastor Beck!" he said. "West? You there?"

"I'm here, Gordon." I tugged gently on his sleeve. Gordon is, among many things, blind, ninety-something, and, as a retired university professor, the smartest man I know. I'm pretty sure his doctorate was in American history, but as far as I'm concerned, he has a PhD in Everything.

"Come on in," his warm voice welcomed us, then he walked confidently—though a little stooped—back into his living room and sat down in his rocker, turning off his radio on the way, which was—as always—tuned to the station that hosted *August Arms.* The whole room smelled like cherry pipe tobacco and peppermints, the latter of which Gordon kept in tiny bowls all over the apartment. I helped myself to one.

Gordon lives in the "senior apartments" half of Legacy House meant for those who manage mostly on their own. The other half is for assisted living—smaller rooms, a twenty-four-hour nursing staff, and a lot less freedom. I didn't like to think of Gordon moving to the other side, though Dad said it was only a matter of time.

Gordon's apartment is one of my favorite places: everything is always in its perfect spot, which allows him to move around freely—the couch, the coffee table, Gordon's own rocker—and the walls have *no decorations.* Our house, the parsonage next to the church building, looks like Pinterest barfed all over it.

Instead, Gordon's walls are lined with bookcases.

"How have you been, Gordon?" my dad asked, his upbeat voice not matching the tired look on his face. He set his little portable communion set on the coffee table and opened it up, taking out the container of grape juice and pouring some into a tiny disposable cup.

"I'm going to snoop around your shelves, Gordon, okay?" I said, standing up and walking to the nearest bookcase—a colossal mahogany one that seemed to house at least twenty Steinbeck novels, along with a collection of books about military weaponry.

"Oh, sure, sure, Westie. Help yourself. Always learning, Pastor Beck. Always learning," Gordon said as my dad took the older man's dark hands, opened them, and placed a cup in one and a wafer in the other. "Just started teaching myself Spanish online. And listening to the Narnia CDs my great-granddaughter bought for me. Always dreaming about heaven and seeing Mavis again. *El señor, prisa el día.*" Gordon raised the miniature cup as if he were toasting God, then put it to his lips. He ate the bread and was silent for a moment.

Dad's cell phone rang. He looked at it. "Oh, I'm so sorry, Gordon. I'll just take this in the hallway."

Gordon was unfazed. He began packing and lighting his pipe with a practiced hand, putting out the match in a little jar of water. He drew on his pipe, then let out the cherry-scented smoke, asking, "Westie, will I see you much this summer? I mean, of course, *figuratively*."

I laughed and turned from where I was running my fingers over the spines of the books. One of my teachers had told me *East of Eden* was a must-read. "Of course! You can't get rid of me."

"Nor would I want to," he said, grinning. "Car detailing again this summer?"

"I guess," I said, my voice withering. "Trudy bailed on me to be a counselor-in-training at an adrenaline junkie camp in Wisconsin," I groused, pulling *East of Eden* off the shelf.

I pictured us in summers past: detailing cars and talking about all the things we couldn't with anyone else, like ghosts and periods and whether our friend Whit was drinking too much since his dad died. We grew up together, me and Trudy. My mom did day care for her when we were little, so she was sort of like my first sister, before my actual sister, Libby, came along. Tru and I spent those early years building castles in the sandbox and making up plays and organizing the church hymnals in exchange for candy money. We were never ones to be athletic, and our parents were politely asked to withdraw us from T-ball when we made a habit of making dandelion chains in the outfield instead of watching for fly balls.

Trudy and I were the least likely candidates to spend a summer at adventure camp, so when she told me about her plans, it felt like a betrayal. We rarely fought—barring the incident when we were four and she sat under the kitchen table, systematically breaking my crayons—and even though this wasn't a fight *per se*, her absence hurt me. A lot.

Before Gordon asked any more questions, I added, "Not only that, but Elliot's dad hired him on at the farm, so it's like he's gone, too. And"—I lowered my voice, even though I knew Dad couldn't hear me from the hall—"now Dad brokered some partnership with this moody new kid in town. It's just not how I pictured this summer going. Can I borrow *East of Eden*?"

"Thou mayest," he said, which didn't make sense until a

few days later, when I'd read most of the book. "And haven't you learned anything from *August Arms* and all your reading, Westie?" Gordon asked. "With a setup like that—static in the air?—lightning is bound to strike."

That evening, I took the family car out to the Thomas farm to see Elliot. There are six Thomas kids, all adopted from the Philippines, and all but Tara—Elliot's oldest sister who was in college and studying abroad for the summer—were always running around the farm in pleasant chaos.

Lorelei and Laney, the two youngest at five and seven, mobbed me when I stepped out of the car. "Did you come to babysit?" Lorelei asked. "Why didn't you bring Libby?"

"Let's make popcorn!" added Laney. "With Red Hots!"

I gave them both hugs. "I think it's almost your bedtime. Where's Elliot?"

Greg, thirteen, pulled up on a four-wheeler. "Elliot's inside showering; he just finished milking."

"Mom's inside too!" said Lorelei, taking one of my hands. Laney grabbed the other, and the two of them ushered me indoors.

"Elliot!" Laney shouted down the stairs to her brother. "West is here—but she's not babysitting and didn't bring Libby and won't make popcorn!"

I giggled as they dragged me into the kitchen, where their mother was. "Hi, Mrs. Thomas!" I said. She had been my sixth-grade teacher, and I'd never gotten used to calling her anything else.

"West!" she said, wiping up flour from the island, where she'd been making bread. "So good to see you! Enjoying the first weekend of summer?"

I pulled a stool up to the island and paused before I answered.

She laughed. "I know, I know—it'd be a lot easier if Elliot wasn't working full-time for his dad, right?"

"Bingo."

"I heard there was a pretty girl upstairs," Elliot said, appearing in the kitchen doorway, his hair wet and his T-shirt clinging to him. His little sisters giggled, one on either side of me. I had been dating Elliot for nearly two years—to the town, he was a football god; to me, an unassuming boyfriend, modest and mellow in spite of the attention lavished on him for years.

"There is," I answered. "Your mom's a total knockout."

Mrs. Thomas rolled her eyes and shooed us out of the kitchen.

Elliot and I went downstairs to his bedroom, stunningly clean in comparison to Silas's—and, admittedly, my own. Elliot lay on his back on his bed, and I lay on my stomach beside him.

He and I have known each other forever. In second grade we got "married" under the monkey bars at recess—or would have, anyway, if Mark Whitby hadn't tattled on us, making the playground attendants come over and break things up before we'd kissed. Still, I did make off with the ring he'd gotten from a gumball machine, and wore it for at least a week before it turned my finger green.

I still kept the ring—cheap, soft metal etched to give the illusion of sparkle—in the desk drawer in my room, though I hadn't taken it out since the night sophomore year when Elliot had *finally* kissed me at the end of Trudy's dock, eight years after a young playground "minister" had pronounced us husband and wife. I'd tried it on again that night, and since it was one-size-fits-all, I had to widen it only a little to make it fit.

"How was your day?" he asked now, his head turned toward me.

"You are not going to believe this," I said, picking at my nail polish, which was chipping off, "but Dad found a detailing partner for me today, and he's kind of an asshole."

"Wait, what? Who?"

I grinned at the barrage of questions. "Silas Hart. He's new to town. His mom is Arty and Lillian Mayhew's daughter."

"Holy shit, really? I think my dad dated her in high school."

"No way."

"I think so. Teresa?"

I nodded. "Well, she's back," I said, "and she brought her kids with—they're in our grade. Silas is really . . . moody or something, and Laurel—that's the sister—seems just weird."

"Your dad asked him to help you detail?"

I nodded, pouting.

"Can you get out of it?"

"Maybe. I can try. I wish *you* were helping me."

Elliot exhaled deeply. "I know. I feel bad about it, West, especially with Trudy gone. Just remember, working all summer for my dad, I should save enough to buy a car. That'll be nice, right? We can go out whenever we want this fall, without having to track down a vehicle or bum rides off Whit."

"True," I said. "I just feel like I'm never going to see you."

"You're seeing me right now, right?" he said, propping himself up on one elbow and tucking the hair that had come loose from my ponytail behind my ear with his other hand.

"I guess. I just already know how this is gonna go: you'll either be on the farm or in the weight room."

"You can join me in the tractor sometime," he offered.

"Oh, golly gee," I teased. "Fun!"

He smiled. "Come here, you."

Elliot slung an arm around my waist and pulled my back against his chest. He kissed me softly behind the ear, then at my jaw, then on my neck. I turned over, took his face in my hands, and kissed him on the mouth. His hands wandered underneath my shirt. "Hey now," I warned.

He grinned against my lips. "Don't you want to?"

I kissed him again, then sat up in his bed. "Here? With your mom upstairs? She was my sex-ed teacher, you know."

"Maybe she can come down and give us pointers," he teased, still lying down, his eyes dark and hooded.

I hit him in the chest. "Gross!"

I knew he wouldn't pressure me. Even on prom night, when I'd backed out of our plans, he didn't complain. I'd told my parents we were going to the post-prom lock-in, but instead we got a hotel room. Elliot had told me at dinner about his plans to work for his dad that summer, and that news—combined with my nerves—made me crabby and doubtful. When we'd changed out of our prom clothes and were sitting side by side on the hotel bed, I'd admitted I wasn't ready.

Disappointed, Elliot had begun, "Do you know—?"

"Know what, Elliot?" I'd snapped, trying not to cry. "That a million other girls would consider themselves lucky to be in my situation?"

He'd frowned and spat out, "God, don't keep pushing me into that shitty jock box! You know I hate that."

I was quiet—embarrassed and a little regretful, even though it was my decision. I didn't even know exactly *why* I was backing down: something to do with timing and fear and discord and—*ugh*—my dad.

"West," Elliot had said, standing up and pulling me to my feet, "listen: *I'm* the lucky one here." Then he'd kissed me on the cheek, grabbed our overnight bags, held out his hand to me, and together we left the hotel and spent the rest of the night at the lock-in.

"Not tonight," I said to him now, there in his bedroom, then leaned down to kiss his lips again. "I have to go."

Elliot rolled his eyes. "Time for your date with Sullivan Knox?"

"Yup."

"I hate that damn radio show," he said, sitting up beside me.

"I know."

"It's so pointless."

"It's the *opposite* of pointless. It's . . . pointful."

We both grinned. This kind of back-and-forth was so routine it felt like reciting lines. Whenever Trudy heard us arguing over *August Arms*, she'd say, "You fight like an old married couple," and Elliot would smile and I would laugh because I knew we were both thinking of "I do" beneath the monkey bars.

He teased, "Okay, fine. Radio, have fun. Detailing, no fun. Got it?"

"Deal," I said, grinning, then ruefully added, "I already miss you."

Elliot kissed the top of my head. "Look," he said, "Marcy and Bridget are still around—call them up, go to the beach! Read a thousand books. Go bug Whit when he's working at the mini-mart; make sure he's keeping out of trouble. I'll see you whenever I can—I'm not going anywhere."

three

I woke up to the sound of my little brother, Shea, pitching a fit over how much sugar he could put on his cereal. "Think you could be any louder?" I complained on my way down the stairs from my bedroom.

Shea and Libby, seven and twelve, were both sitting at the breakfast bar, eating generic Cheerios, which—in Shea's defense—taste like crap unless you add a ton of sugar. Mom was at the kitchen table, which was covered in her scrapbooking materials. The three of them look like a trio, all sandy blond and blue-eyed. But I look like my dad: eyes and hair like dark chocolate.

"Where's Dad?" I asked, pouring some orange juice.

"Jim Roberts found out last night that he lost his job. Dad went over to talk to him," said Mom.

"Oh. That sucks."

"Don't say 'sucks,'" Mom said. "I'm sure it will all work out. 'When the Lord closes a door, somewhere he opens a window.'"

"Is that from the Psalms?" Shea asked, milk dripping from his chin.

"It's from *The Sound of Music*, moron," said Libby.

"Libby, don't say 'moron.'"

Mom. She's the prototypical pastor's wife, a smiling martyr for God because she signed on for a life of pot roasts. She gets sort of swallowed up by my dad's overwhelming personality: everyone in Green Lake knows and likes my father.

"How long is Dad gonna be gone?" I'd been hoping for some info before Silas arrived this morning.

"Hmmm?" Mom asked. "He'll probably be home for lunch and then go over to his office for the afternoon."

It felt like I was always asking when Dad would be around. If he wasn't off visiting or consoling parishioners, then he was in his office, studying or preparing a sermon, or else counseling young couples or answering questions from the people who would drop by the church building, looking for advice or prayer. With only a handful of churches in our town, he stayed busy; meanwhile, we got the leftovers: migraine-routed Dad, needing dark, soundless rest.

Inside our house, an exhausted husband and father. Outside it, a minister in perpetual motion, Green Lake's hero, *a good man*.

Mom held up a couple of pieces of nearly identical scrapbooking paper, trying to choose which was best. "Your dad mentioned Lillian Mayhew's daughter moved into the old Griggs house and that her grandson is going to help with your detailing this summer, yeah?"

"Yep. His name is Silas. And listen up, Shea—I don't want you bugging us when he comes over, all right?" Libby was shy and generally wary of all boys except for Chuck Justice, this teenage pop singer she was obsessed with. Shea, on the other hand, was the princeling of awkward questions. Just the other night at dinner, he'd looked up from his spaghetti and, with furrowed brow, asked, "What's a *whore*?"

"Do you have *two* boyfriends now?" Shea asked, making faces at himself in the reflection of his spoon.

"No," I stressed. "Seriously, Shea? Does that make any sense?"

He only shrugged.

"Just don't bug us, okay? We'll have plenty of work to do without having to deal with any crap from you."

"Don't say 'crap,'" said Mom, choosing the light gray over the light gray. I took my OJ outside to the front steps.

Silas showed up that morning on a bike, wearing mesh shorts, Tevas, and a T-shirt that said, "South Korea has Seoul." His thick hair was damp and had a tiny bit of curl to it. I felt a little plain with my stick-straight brown hair pulled back into a basic ponytail. Jerk or not, he looked like an adventure with skin on.

"Morning," I said, without moving from my spot on the steps. "You look tired."

"Vader rocked my world last night," he joked with a wicked grin.

My first thought was *multiple personality disorder.*

He seemed like a different person from yesterday, more relaxed, less standoffish. His eyes—dark like an oil spill—took in everything as if he expected the things around him to make him laugh.

"So?" he asked, nodding toward the bin of cleaning supplies sitting in my driveway.

"Have you ever detailed a car before?" I asked him, standing up and joining him in the short driveway. When he shook his head, I said, "Okay, listen. I've been doing this for four years, and if you screw up and make me lose my customers, I . . . I don't know what I'll do, but it won't be pretty. The most important thing you have to know is this: do not use a vinyl product on leather seats. Repeat after me: *I will not use a vinyl product on leather seats.*"

Silas put his right hand on his heart and held his left up as if he were swearing in at court: "I will not use a vinyl product on leather seats."

"Okay, good," I said. "Don Travers—he's on the city council with Dad—is going to be here in a couple minutes; then you're going to have to listen closely and work fast—but be thorough. If you do well, I'll let you be my apprentice this summer—"

"—partner," he interrupted.

"Apprentice," I repeated firmly. "In which case, we make a hundred bucks a car and split it sixty-forty. A couple times, we'll need to take a cut from the total to restock supplies. Not too shabby, is it? Of course, we do only about two or three cars a week. Makes for an easy summer." I thought of Elliot, how he'd been up since dawn and would be every day this week.

"You split it sixty-forty with your friend too?"

"No. Trudy and I split our profits down the middle. But *you* are not *her*."

"Thank God."

"What's that supposed to mean?"

"Nothing." Silas appeared to be doing the math in his head.

I eyed him suspiciously. "What do you need a job for, anyway?" I asked. "Your family is loaded."

He laughed, even as I clapped my hand over my mouth. "I need to get out of the house. And I buy a lot of stuff my parents think is crap," he said. "Or maybe you think *they* bought my 'Your Mom's a Horcrux' T-shirt?"

I stifled a laugh as Don Travers pulled his car into my driveway and parked.

Don was nearly as tall as Silas, though not as thin. "Hi, West," he said, getting out, along with Judy, who waved at my mom through the front window. "We're going to get breakfast at Mikey's and then go run some errands. Hardware store. Red Owl. Three hours enough time, you think? We've got plans in St. Cloud this afternoon."

"For sure," I said. "Although I've gotta teach the new guy here the ropes." I nodded toward Silas, who grinned and shrugged as if he were helpless. "Silas Hart," I told Don. "He's Arty and Lillian's grandson."

"No kidding!" Don said, clearly pleased. "You're not Teresa's son?"

"That's me," said Silas, still with that same grin that annoyed and excited me.

"Teresa Mayhew was a freshman my senior year. I was the captain of the track team, and I couldn't catch her," Don said. "I guess I thought she was in Florida."

"For a while," said Silas. "Alaska most recently. Now back in the motherland."

"Can't do better than Green Lake," said Judy.

Don added, "You'll catch on quick to life here."

"I hope so, Mr. Travers. How are the cows?" By which he proved that he already was.

Silas was just as sharp at learning to detail, a star pupil. I was impressed but also sort of irritated. "We start on the inside," I said. "Inside out. And everything has to be thorough, like I said. It's called 'detailing' for a reason."

"What are you, the dictator of detailing?"

I glared at him. "Do you want this gig or not? Because I don't need your help, you know."

Silas grinned. "Whatever. You just told Mr. and Mrs. Travers their car would be done in three hours. It would take you at least five on your own."

He was right.

"Fine," I said. "First, we take out the floor mats and vacuum like crazy. Move the seats around—"

"—does that mean you want me to stay and help?" he interrupted.

"—as much as we can to get everything. Then we wash the floor mats and clean the hard surfaces inside. We use cans of compressed air to get into the dashboard crevices, and we clean the vent grilles with Q-tips. And you already know about the seats."

Silas crossed his arms in front of him.

"Well?" I said. "Let's get started."

He didn't move.

"What now?" I asked.

He still had that persistent grin on his face. "I'm waiting for you to admit you need my help."

"You are *so* annoying," I complained.

"And you are *so* bossy," he retaliated.

I waited.

He waited.

Finally I grumbled, "I'd appreciate your help today."

"And we'll split everything fifty-fifty?"

"Fine. Gosh."

Silas's smile could have split the earth in two. "I will not use a vinyl product on leather seats," he recited.

"You'd better not!" I said, turning away so he wouldn't see my smile.

We got to work, and I examined his efforts like a drill sergeant. "The goal is to blow them away," I said. "Nope, stop. See how this is an aftermarket tint? We can only use the ammonia-based glass cleaner on factory-tinted glass. For this we'll actually use seltzer and then dry it with crumpled newspapers to keep it from streaking."

"Got it," he said, returning to the stockpile of supplies on the lawn. "How did you learn all this stuff?" He found a bottle of seltzer and soaked part of a cloth with it and began to work on the interior windshield from the driver's seat.

I was in the passenger seat, meticulously cleaning the various ins and outs of the dashboard. "Online forums mostly. In eighth grade, Trudy—she's my best friend, but she's at camp this summer—Trudy and I wanted something we could do together, and the Red Owl always rehires the college students who come home for the summer, so it's hard to get work there. We thought about detasseling, but Tru has allergies. We couldn't get a job in St. Cloud because we couldn't drive yet, so we sort of stumbled into this. It works great—we have no supervisors, we get paid in cash, and the whole time we'd just talk about boys and books and plans. Let's switch sides," I said, since we'd each finished our respective jobs on either side of the cab. Before I could move out of my side, all six feet plus of Silas crawled over the center console and into my space, his knee pressing into the seat near my hip, his arm around the seat's headrest so that our faces were only inches apart.

"Hi," he said, looking right into my eyes.

I quickly scooted myself over to the driver's seat. I swallowed hard, and my heart did that annoying cartwheel thing again. I wondered if . . . if he was making fun of me. Like, if he was aware of how attractive he was and was kind of teasing me by flirtatiously invading my space the way he just had. Maybe he was the kind of boy who felt powerful by making girls blush.

"Listen," I growled, my throat getting hot. "I have a boyfriend."

"How nice for you," he said patronizingly. "And *I* have a girlfriend."

"You do?"

"Mmm-hmmm."

"Well . . . just . . . just . . . don't do that."

"I was only switching sides with you. Don't get your panties in a twist." He was wiping down the right side of the windshield and had assumed the egotistic hauteur of the day before—only, I thought I caught sight of a tiny, crooked grin on his face.

It infuriated me.

Taking quick, seething breaths through my nose, I sat back in the driver's seat and told myself to calm down. He was just some ridiculous, moody, strange whack-job from Alaska who was trying to get under my skin. *Don't let him.*

"Look, can we work together in peace?" I asked quietly. "Is that possible? Do you know how to act like a normal person and not be such an asshole?"

He laughed. He actually laughed.

But it didn't sound mean or patronizing. It sounded apologetic.

Which also irritated me. It's harder to hate someone with a conscience.

"Let's start over, okay?" I said, squeezing my eyes shut and shaking my head as if to erase everything that had gone before. I looked at Silas, and he nodded. "How long did you live in Alaska?"

"About three years," he said. "My mom was an aerospace engineering professor at UAF and did consulting for the Kodiak Launch Complex. My dad taught astronomy."

"Did you like it there?"

"Yes. I loved it. The *last* thing I wanted to do was move to Minnesota."

"Why did you guys move?"

Silas paused. "Well, Mom got a pretty good offer to teach at the University of Minnesota." He pursed his lips, obviously debating whether to say what came next. Then suddenly his face relaxed and he said, "Yeah." That was it. I wanted to coax him into telling me more, but I remembered his frown when I'd asked about his sister the day before. We were finally speaking without hostility, so I didn't press him.

"That's cool that your mom's from here."

"Yeah," he said again, "I'm still getting used to how everyone here seems to know everyone else."

"And everyone else's business too," I added. "You'll see."

He pressed his lips together thoughtfully. When he noticed I was looking, he gave me another one of those forced grins. I picked up the Windex, sprayed the plastic covering the odometer, and cleaned it with a cloth, the ammonia yanking at my sinuses. "So, what's it like in Alaska? Isn't it twenty-four hours of sun in the summer and twenty-four hours of darkness in the winter?"

"Not in Fairbanks," he said. "In Barrow, yeah. That's as north as you can go. In the winter, the sun doesn't rise there for over two months." He shook his head, incredulous. "But still, even in Fairbanks, we would have only about four hours of sunlight in a winter day. Of course, in the summer, there's only about four hours of darkness, and then after the sun sets, it's still bright enough to do regular stuff."

Silas and I each stepped out of the cab, closed our respective doors, and began to wash the outside of the car. "Start from the top down," I instructed. No matter what I thought about Silas Hart, it was a treat to watch his lean, strong frame as his long arms reached easily over the roof of the car to wash it. His height was going to be an asset in this job. "Sounds like it would be hard to sleep," I said. The slippery, soapy lather smelled like cherry foam.

He laughed a little. "It's trippy. I'll be honest. Fairbanks has this summer solstice celebration, and the whole town stays out super late. We have a baseball game that starts at ten thirty at night, and we don't even use any artificial lights. Stores stay open later. Last year, a couple of my friends and I headed out to Cleary Summit, about twenty miles outside town, and stayed there for hours watching the sun. We camped out, and Beth did this long-exposure photography thing and ended up with a picture of the Chatanika River Valley with about a dozen suns in the background."

I wondered if Beth was his girlfriend but couldn't think of how to ask.

The hose and high-pressure sprayer attachment I used to clean out the wheel wells made a loud, rhythmic trill against the metal, so I spoke louder when I asked, "So, what about winter then?"

"Winter is kind of a beast," Silas admitted. "The temperature is moody, depending on where the wind is coming from. So it goes from just an average cold down to, like, *cold*-cold and back up again. And meanwhile, it's dark out and *purple*. The sun sets before school's out. *That* is a terrible feeling." He laughed a little. "I literally could not go running in daylight because the sun didn't come up until three hours after school started. I kinda hated it. Laurel *really* hated it." Again, he looked as if he was going to say more. He chewed on the inside of his mouth, still undergoing some internal debate.

I remembered the Nikes peeking out from under his bed. "You run?" I asked, immediately regretting giving him the easy way out.

"What?" he asked, as if distracted. "Yeah, I love it. Like mother, like son, I guess. I run my best and hardest when I'm frustrated . . . which is why it's great to have *Laurel* as a sister. No one more frustrating than her." He grinned at me, lips pursed mischievously, eyebrows raised—an oddly suggestive look, as if he'd just made some outrageous or even salacious proposal.

"I refuse to believe that until you meet Libby and Shea," I said. "They're twelve and seven and watching us through the window right now."

Silas looked over at the window and waved. My siblings ducked out of sight. I pictured them giggling on the floor.

"What are you doing after this? Wanna get lunch?" he asked, pushing his thick hair out of his eyes.

"Not really. Your moods are kind of giving me whiplash here," I confessed.

"I'll behave. Promise."

The afternoon stretched out before me, empty of friends and responsibilities. If I could just get through the day, I could call Elliot and Trudy later on to catch up.

Silas held up three fingers—Scout's honor—squinting at the sun in his eyes. "I promise," he repeated.

"You're annoying," I said again.

"Is that a yes?"

"Fine, whatever."

"Is *that* a yes?"

"Yes."

four

We went to the Red Owl—which has technically been a SuperValu since before I was born, though no one in Green Lake calls it that—and bought pop and apples, along with a bag of cinnamon-roasted almonds and some sandwiches from the tiny deli section, then biked to the park that brushed up against the pointer finger of the town. We ate lunch on the swing set near the lake.

Just the sight of the playground made me ache for Trudy, who had accompanied me to these swings since the days when we'd buy Pop Rocks and magazines with our allowance money and listen to the carbonated candy fizzle on our tongues while we debated the merits of various teen stars. I smiled thinking of the Pop Rocks and how, when you'd crunch down on them, it sounded like all your teeth were breaking.

"My turn to ask the questions," said Silas, polishing his apple on his shirt. "Tell me what you like to do."

"I read a lot," I said, my feet dragging in the sand beneath them as I bit into my apple—Gala, sweet.

"I knew it. Like what?" Silas grinned as he took a bite of his own.

"Kind of everything. Contemporary, historical, fantasy, sci-fi."

"Nice. Have you read C. S. Lewis's space trilogy?"

"Like a million times," I said.

Silas's eyes grew wide with childlike excitement. "I'm making Laurel read it this summer!" he said, waving around the hand that held his apple. "He has total command of language. Gosh, such great alliteration. There's this part with all these *k* sounds . . . stops you like a king in the road."

I smiled at him, a little skeptically.

"What?" he asked, eyes wide and beatific, and I burst out laughing.

"I've just never heard anyone talk affectionately about plosives."

Another grin from him. That same walloping one that made me stagger. It was wide and warm and in his eyes as much as on his lips. It was playful and had just the smallest hint of mischief. The gulf between this boy and the one who'd been so cold the day before spread wider, confusing me.

"So, you read," he said. "What else?"

"I also have this weird penchant for Australian authors."

"No, I mean, what else do you like to *do*?"

Oh. That.

"Mmm, I don't know," I said, munching on my apple, trying to appear thoughtful—but really, frantically searching for a response. I hated questions like this; while they gave definition to other people, they reminded me that my outline was fuzzy and gray. What *did* I like to do? I didn't play sports or music, didn't follow fashion, had no crazy obsessions, wasn't extreme in any way. Around town I was known as "Pastor Beck's daughter" or "Elliot Thomas's girlfriend." Stories were my one real love, and Silas had just asked what else I did besides read.

I stretched to fill in my own embarrassing blanks: "Um, I listen to the radio. Avoid thinking about college. Con people into telling me their secrets."

"How do you do that?"

"With my long eyelashes," I said, batting them at him. "Now spill your guts."

He laughed, then looked at me through narrowed eyes. "You know, you're all right."

"I'm so glad I have your approval," I said, half annoyed that he was allowed to issue this verdict and half grateful it was—sort of—positive. "Daily validation, check! So, what about you?"

"Oh, I write," he said, tossing his apple core toward a garbage bin about fifteen feet away. It went in easily. "Yesssss."

"Epic adventures of danger and daring?" I teased, glad to

redirect the focus onto him as I opened the bag of almonds. He let me shake some into his open palm.

"Nah, I'm no good."

The humility shocked me.

"I'm a seventeen-year-old poet; what do you expect? My poems are shit."

"Favorite poet?" I asked.

"Billy Collins," he said. "Though when I read his stuff, I want to light myself on fire."

"I guess I should be happy I stand on the *reader* side of literature," I said, savoring the sugary crunch in my mouth. "The *writer* side sounds like masochism."

He looked at me, eyes wide in understanding. "Absolutely. Why do you avoid thinking about college?"

"I guess I don't know what to do with my life," I said. Then, before he could ask any more questions, I held up the bag of nuts. "Actually, I just had an epiphany. I think I'm gonna major in almonds."

"You're such a dork," he said—and there was that grin again.

That evening was a perfect Minnesota June night, cool and breezy, and Cedar Street was quiet except for the sound of Jody Perkins riding his lawn mower home from the bar. We waved to each other as I wondered what Tru was doing that moment at camp. Probably trying to corral middle schoolers into quieting down in the cabin. I wondered how Trudy was handling living with a herd of young females all summer—especially with Ami Nissweller along for the ride. Ami, a self-proclaimed chess nerd and a bit of a hanger-on, had always annoyed Tru, who, when finding out that Ami would be working at Camp Summit too, announced, "She's checkmated me!"

I called Elliot's cell from my front steps that night as the sun streaked the sky with pink. He answered, either on or near a tractor, the sound of the motor a thunderous drone.

"I miss you," I said, trying to speak loud enough for him to hear over the noise.

"What's that?"

"I miss you," I said louder, hoping my siblings wouldn't hear me from inside. *"I spent the day with the new kid, and he's really annoying—but he was too good at detailing to not—"*

"—West? Are you still there?"

"I'M STILL HERE!" I almost bellowed, cupping my hands around my phone, my voice only slightly quieter than a shout. "CAN YOU HEAR—"

"—West? I'm going to have to call you later."

"OKAY," I roared. *"I MISS YOU."*

"What's that?"

I hung up. It was useless.

When I tried calling Trudy, the call went straight to voice mail.

This is the story of my summer, I thought.

I tuned into *August Arms* through my phone while my mom herded my siblings to bed inside. Dad was still gone; apparently, he'd come home for lunch, but then advanced like a knight back into the dark world to fight sin and sadness.

I felt laden with loneliness. The summer had only just started.

But then, Sullivan Knox's voice punctured the night. The host of *August Arms* had one of those deep, slightly overbearing radio voices that could fill any space. It was husky and articulate, and it used clever inflection to add depth to every story. I loved it best at night, when the world seemed smaller and it was easier to convince myself that Sully and I were having a conversation: curious people talking of curious things, things that were so *other* from anything Green Lake had to offer, anything *I* had to offer. So, even though I could listen online at any time, I always tried to listen to the live show when it aired each night. Elliot thought it was silly—and Trudy too, a little—and, heck, maybe even I did. But not enough to change.

August Arms usually centered its stories on a theme, which lasted an evening or a week or sometimes a month, and tonight's common thread was secrecy: an architect who led three separate lives; Arthur Dimmesdale from *The Scarlet Letter*, and the Sacrament of Penance.

As usual, each story was fascinating—but tonight they were heavy too, just like the pressing scent of the blooming crab apple trees on our street. I couldn't help but think of Silas from earlier that day: how he'd cut his answer short when I'd asked why they'd moved, the peculiar way his voice had sounded when he said Laurel had "*really* hated" the polar twilight, as if those two words were the title page for an entire novel. What was he not telling me?

With *August Arms* as my sound track, alone on my porch, I embraced my inner stalker and looked each of the Hart twins up online. Neither of them had high privacy settings, so I was able to see quite a bit. Silas's social media looked exactly as I'd expected: he had lots of friends and was tagged in about a million photos, which I looked through one by one. Silas crossing the finish line at a cross-country meet, Silas in a row of guys all in tuxedos, Silas and Laurel blowing out candles on identical cakes that said, "Happy 17th!"

I even found the time-lapse photo of the midnight sun he had mentioned briefly. Beth Öster, the photographer, *was* his girlfriend and had a stark beauty afforded by her low-bridged nose, dark hair, rosy cheeks, and unexpectedly blue eyes that peeked out from under a parka hood. She had tagged each sun as a different friend. Silas was the sun beside her sun.

When I looked up Laurel, though, it was a different story. There was still a good sample of friends and photos, but she'd obviously not been online much in the past year. People had been posting things like "When are you coming back to school?" and "Hope you're okay—call me!" and "I miss you" quite a bit in December and January—but those posts had dwindled in the past six months. She must be sick, I thought. But why would that be a secret? Her pictures were mostly from dance performances—Laurel in tap shoes, Laurel in a red Latin dress, Laurel in ballet slippers as Odette from *Swan Lake*. They'd all been uploaded years ago.

My phone rang. "Hey!" I said, glad Elliot had called back.

"Hey!" he said. "Sorry about before. I just put the tractor away."

"It's okay. How was your day? When can I see you?"

"Come over."

"What? Right now?"

"Yeah!" he said. "Your show's over, right?"

"Yeah. But it's pretty late."

"My parents won't care."

"Mine will," I complained. I didn't mention that I was also a little worried about what might happen, um, *physically* if I went over there so late. I hated myself for asking, "How about tomorrow?"

"I'm lifting with the team tomorrow night from six to eight. I can stop at your place on my way into the weight room."

"Okay," I said, my voice small with loneliness and longing.

"How was detailing with the asshole today?" Elliot asked.

"He's annoying."

"Good."

"Thanks a lot," I said, laughing a little.

Elliot's grin was obvious—even over the phone. "You know what I mean."

I took a deep breath and let it out. "Yeah. I do."

When our family car finally crept down Cedar and parked in the driveway, I said good night to Elliot. Dad emerged, his whole body showing signs of deep fatigue. He smiled when he saw me on the porch. "Wanna chat?" I asked softly, patting the space beside me.

"In the morning, okay, Wink? Spent the morning with Jim Roberts and tonight at the hospital with the Talcotts. My head's about to explode."

"Yeah," I said, disappointed. "Okay. Sleep well."

I stared through the screen door after my dad as he trudged off toward his dark bedroom.

five

My dad was long gone by the time I woke up the next morning. I'd mostly expected it.

"Billy Collins, you say?" Gordon asked when I arrived at his door, *East of Eden* in hand. "I have a few of his collections, over there on the middle shelf of the barrister—just go ahead and lift the knob. The whole glass front panel swings out and tucks right back into the shelf. See anything there?"

The whole bookcase was dedicated to poetry. Langston Hughes and John Keats. Robert Frost. Emily Dickinson, Walt Whitman, and John Donne. I saw a few books by Billy Collins and pulled one off the shelf.

"Gordon, why do you keep so many books around if you can't see the pages anymore?" The cover had a tiny dog howling on a shore. The sky was yellow and pink, and the sea a dark inky blue and teal and the green-gray of battle gear.

"They're just good company," he said simply.

"We could sell them online, you know? And sign you up for an audiobook account."

"Ahh," he said, "but then you wouldn't come visit me as often."

He grinned while he said it, but it occurred to me that maybe Gordon got lonely here in his little apartment. He had kids—and a small army of grandkids and great-grandkids. I stopped by only a few times each month. "Gordon—" I started.

"Read something aloud, would you? I like when you read, Westie."

I opened up to a poem called "The First Dream," about a man puzzling over such an experience. Then the poem took a turn, wondering if maybe the first dreamer was a woman. The young woman in the poem seemed so sad; even her posture told its own story. My voice curved like her shoulders and turned soft and slow, bowed with understanding as I read:

"you might have gone down as the first person
to ever fall in love with the sadness of another."

"Beautiful," said Gordon, pipe now between his teeth, dark glasses on, looking like some jazz hepcat. "Mmm. Beautiful. Yes?"

"Yes," I agreed, glad I didn't have to admit it to Silas. Which made little to no sense.

"Have you ever fallen in love with another person's sadness, Betsy?"

Betsy. He'd done this once or twice before, and I'd thought I'd misheard him saying "Westie," but this time it was really clear. I knew one of his great-granddaughters—the one who visited him most often but who'd been studying in Spain the prior year—was named Elizabeth.

"West?" He repeated his question.

I thought of the girl in the poem—but also of Laurel, pristine even in pajamas, and my mini obsession with her. "Would you think I'm awful if I said yes?"

He said, "Not awful, merely human."

When I left, Gordon loaned me the book of poetry. Instead of going home, I bypassed my house, crossed the parking lot between it and the church, and slipped inside the building.

My dad was talking to someone in his office, so I tiptoed past and made my way to the unmarked door at the end of the hall, which I unlocked with the key I almost always kept in my pocket. When I heard voices in the nearby fellowship hall, my heart gave a panicked little start and I opened the door and closed it softly behind me, hearing the lock click.

I exhaled deeply in relief. If anyone found out I had the key . . . well, it's not that I would necessarily get in *trouble*, but I would lose my best secret. There was something almost magical about having a clandestine hideaway; I didn't even tell *Trudy*, too worried or maybe selfish to break such a spell.

Besides that, pastors' kids have to share *everything*. I wanted just one thing, one place.

It was four flights to the top of the bell tower. Four flights to my cozy but sparse little sanctuary. An air mattress, some blankets and books, and a camping lantern lay scattered in the space where the tower bells, long since removed, used to be. The space is small but open and has this incredible terra-cotta checkerboard floor, rough stone walls, and wooden beams.

There are four arched belfry windows, one on each wall. They have no glass in them, but decorative bars keep birds out, and the window ledges are wide enough to sit in safely. I leaned out over the one that faced my house and saw my dad marching across the parking lot toward home.

I huffed in disappointment. A part of me wanted to race down the staircase to talk with him, but I was still breathing hard from my trek *up* the stairs and the book of poems in my hands was making its own demands.

It was a lovely morning, the breeze carrying the sweetness of the crab apples through the open windows and the cold stone walls keeping the tower cool enough to enjoy. I lay stomach-down on the air mattress and read through the poems. I liked them all, but kept returning to the one I'd read at Gordon's about the sad dreamer-girl. All I could think of was Laurel Hart, looking so sad and so regal at the same time, sitting bolt upright in that wicker seat, the sunlight pouring in as if it were vapors filling the room.

I lay staring at the stone ceiling, relishing my time alone before returning home. Then I made my way down the stairs, listened at the door for any sound in the hallway, and stepped out, feeling my pocket for my key before letting the door lock behind me.

When I walked into the house, Shea called out, "Someone called for you. It's a *boooooy*!"

"Elliot?" I asked Mom, wondering why he'd called the landline instead of my cell.

She shook her head. "Silas Hart. His number is on the counter."

Silas? Well, that was interesting.

"Is Dad home?" I asked.

"He just left for St. Cloud. There's a book he needs for Sunday."

"Dang it."

"Don't say 'dang.' Sandwich?" She nodded toward one on a plate on the counter.

"Thanks," I said, grabbing the plate and Silas's number, taking both upstairs to my room. I kicked some dirty clothes out of the way and sat on the floor with my back against my bed, which was covered in *Camp Rock* sheets I'd outgrown years ago but kept anyway since boys aren't allowed in my room. Besides, Trudy still used her *High School Musical* comforter.

Trudy. I decided I'd call her first, and in doing so, I noticed on my cell that I *had* actually missed a call from Elliot. I left Tru a quick message, then listened to Elliot's voice mail, while munching on the Pinterest-inspired sandwich Mom had made—strawberry jam and cream cheese, cut into the shape of a heart. I grinned as I listened to him ramble on about his morning. "Still okay if I stop by tonight? Say yes."

I texted him: YES!

His reply was immediate: Can't wait. <3

I replied: Whit will never let you live it down if he finds out you're texting me hearts.

Elliot texted back: <3 <3 <3 <3 <3

My smile felt a mile wide—till I remembered I needed to call Silas.

"Hi, it's West—West Beck," I said after he'd picked up. "What's up?" I set Gordon's Billy Collins book on top of a stack of books on my nightstand, hoping to revisit it again before bed that night. Irrationally, I had the thought that Silas would know I was touching the book, so I withdrew my hand.

"I'm bored. Want to come over and watch *WARegon Trail*?"

"Come again?"

"*WARegon Trail*. It's a TV show—I have the first three seasons."

"There are three seasons?" I asked skeptically.

"There are *five*."

I hesitated. "It's not really my thing."

"How do you know it's not your thing? Have you even seen this show before?"

"No, but—"

"No, but you'd rather be bored and lie around your house all day? If you come over, I'll let you insult my bad taste in television all you want without repercussion."

"Um, now you just *admitted* that the show is bad."

"My offer to insult me ends in five, four, three, two . . ."

"Fine." It seemed to be my motto these days.

I biked out to Heaton Ridge for the first time ever. Crossing the bridge, I was shocked to see just how far down it was to the river. I hadn't noticed in the car; on a bicycle, it was a different story.

At the old Griggs house, the giant oak door was open, but the screen door was still closed, letting a breeze into the house. I rang the doorbell and listened. "Laurel!" I heard Silas yell. "Can you get the door?"

From where I stood on the porch, I could see into the house, the long hallway toward the sunroom on the left, the set of stairs heading upstairs on the right. I expected to see Laurel emerge from the sunroom, but no one came into the hallway or down the stairs. I waited for what felt like forever, not sure if I should ring the doorbell again or try the handle.

"Laurel?" I heard, shouted as if from upstairs. *"Did you get it?"*

Nothing.

"LAUREL! JUST GET THE DAMN DOOR!"

My pulse skyrocketed. I swallowed uncomfortably, not sure

what the right move was. The voice seemed so disconnected from the grinning boy on the swings yesterday. But then again, he was just yelling at his sister. Fighting with siblings was familiar territory to me.

Get yourself together, I told myself, and then did what I figured was really my best option: I tried the handle and, finding the door unlocked, let myself in. "Silas?" I called up the stairs. "It's West. Can I come up?"

"Hey!" he said, appearing at the top of the stairs in a shirt that plainly declared, "YOU HAD ME AT BACON." He tucked what looked like a tiny Moleskine notebook into the back pocket of his jeans. "Come on up. I was trying to make my room more presentable."

"And how did that go?" I joked, climbing the stairs.

"Uhhh, let's watch in the den instead," he answered, grinning and directing me into the room across the hall from his. It was small and cozy, one wall full of a built-in entertainment center, the other three covered in family photos.

Silas moved to the far wall to put a disc into the player, and I looked around the room: wood floor, couch lining the wall shared by the den and the hall, a papasan in the one available corner. The shelves surrounding the TV screen held movies and various knickknacks like a weird silver sphere on a stand, a replica antique telescope, and brass pagoda bookends pressed against a set of encyclopedias.

I wasn't quite sure where to sit. Sitting on the papasan

would make it look like I was afraid of Silas. Also, I had tipped over Trudy's papasan more than once—usually from laughing, but *still.* I supposed I could sit on the floor, but that seemed so awkward. I knew I was overthinking it when Silas turned around, grabbed the remote from the coffee table, crashed onto the couch, and patted the space beside him. "Stay awhile," he joked.

I sat beside him, picked up a navy decorative pillow, which had a constellation stitched onto it, and placed it firmly between us. Then, together we watched two episodes of *WARegon Trail*, which featured five pioneer families in covered wagons retracing the historic journey from Missouri to Oregon. There was dysentery, cholera, oxen—and zombies. Oh, and the pioneer men carried AK-47s.

"It's like *Little House on the Prairie* had a child with Quentin Tarantino's nightmares," I said, examining the DVD case, which was in grayscale except for the red bloodstains that were "splashed" across it. "The blood and guts of these episodes seems a little . . . what's the word?"

Silas to the rescue: "Exaggerated? Superfluous? Gratuitous?"

I smiled. "Yeah, something like that. What are you, a human thesaurus?"

"I'll take that as a compliment," he said. "Praise. Flattery."

"I get it."

"Commendation."

"Yup."

"Hey," said Silas, suddenly looking a little sheepish, "sorry to make you wait on the porch earlier." He rolled his eyes, put the pillow separating us on his lap, and picked at a light gray thread coming loose from the Big Dipper.

"It's fine," I said. "No big deal." But I was still curious.

He sighed, then announced in this very slightly contemptuous and disembodied voice, "Laurel is having an asshole day." *WARegon Trail* played on in the background; Silas clicked the mute button on the remote control, leaving us in silence.

"Oh," I said, a little shocked at this blunt revelation. "Does that . . . does that happen often?"

Silas let his head fall back against the couch. Staring up at the den ceiling, he said, "No. I guess not."

I hesitated, remembering the way he'd reacted when I'd first asked about Laurel. Did I dare press him? *He* was the one who had brought it up this time—so maybe it was okay. I chose my words carefully, mostly just repeating his: "What does it mean for Laurel to have an asshole day?"

He shook his head in frustration. "She's just moody," he said.

Like hell she is, I thought. "Does she—" I started to ask.

"One more episode?" Silas interrupted, effectively ending our conversation about his sister.

I frowned, a little frustrated myself. "Sure." I didn't want to see his temper flare again.

"Would you rather die from dysentery or a zombie attack?" he asked, aiming the remote at the DVD player.

"Do I have to pick one?"

"You do on the *WARegon Trail*!" he said, his voice gleeful again. He looked at me, losing a mighty struggle to hold back his grin; it was like sunshine wrestling through forest foliage. "Death is the only rescue coming for these people."

six

When I got up to leave around dinnertime, Silas insisted on driving me home.

"It's not even dark out!" I said, but he followed me out of the den and down the hall, where Laurel was coming out of her bedroom. Another day, another pair of pajamas. Her eyes had a wild and lost look to them, as if she'd just woken up from a nightmare and hadn't gotten her bearings yet.

I lifted my hand in a feeble greeting, even though she was creeping me out again. She stared at me for a second, then looked at her brother when he said softly, "You feeling better?" Laurel didn't respond—not in *any* way. Not a nod or a word or anything. She just walked down the hall toward the bathroom. "I'll be back in a few minutes," he called after her as we headed down the stairs.

Out in the driveway, I said, "I'm really fine riding home by myself. You can, you know, go and . . . check on your sister."

But he was lifting my bike into the bed of the pickup truck parked outside. I recognized it as Arty Mayhew's old beater that usually sat in a shed beside their house, south of town. "It's fine," he said.

I didn't know if he meant taking me home or Laurel's condition.

Before I could ask, Silas turned up an oldies station and bellowed "Eleanor Rigby" along with the Beatles for the few minutes it took to drive from his house to mine. The windows were down, so everyone we passed could hear, and Silas moved his head in a strange, staccato bob that matched the music. I realized I'd gotten into the vehicle with a lunatic.

When he pulled into my driveway and parked, Silas finally glanced over at me. "What?" he asked, probably because of the look on my face.

"You're insane," I said.

"Maybe." He grinned, then his voice dropped into a more serious register, and with a poker face, he whispered, "All the lonely people, West. Where the hell do they all *come* from?"

I didn't want to smile—tried not to smile—but I couldn't stop myself.

Silas pointed at my mouth. "Aha!" he shouted. "Caught you."

I grabbed his finger, not sure exactly what I was going to

do with it, when a voice behind me said my name through the passenger's-side window. It startled me, and I gasped, dropped Silas's finger, and put my hand over my heart.

"Just me," said Elliot from beside the pickup. I noticed the Thomas family minivan for the first time. "Didn't mean to scare you. Did you forget I was coming over?"

I had, actually, but didn't say so. Instead, I threw off my seat belt and hurried out of the pickup, throwing my arms around Elliot as if I hadn't seen him for a year, squeezing him tight around the waist. He laughed. "Nice to see you too," he said. His dark hair was buzzed short for the summer, and his face and neck were already tan. He'd come straight from the farm—sweaty, smelling like hay and dust. I kind of liked it.

Silas was getting out of the cab and coming around the back of the pickup.

"Hey," Elliot said, still with me dangling off him. His voice was cold and unfriendly and embarrassed me a little.

"Hey," Silas said. "Silas Hart." He reached to shake Elliot's hand, but Elliot just stared at his hand. Silas pointed an awkward finger at him and muttered, "Right."

"This is Elliot, my boyfriend," I said to Silas.

"Awesome," Silas said, unimpressed.

Silas and Elliot both went for my bike at the same moment, but Silas got to it first. He looked a little smug as he set it down in front of me. "There you go," he said to me. "Nice to meet you, man," he said to Elliot. "See you tomorrow, West."

Then he was back in the truck, pulling out of my driveway with the music obnoxiously loud. I put my bike away in the garage, then turned around to see my boyfriend, still with his brow furrowed.

"Hey," I said, and held out my hand.

He took it, and I led him over to our front steps, where we both sat. Elliot pulled my hand into his lap and began to knead it absentmindedly. His hands were rough and calloused but so gentle. This action was older than our relationship; he'd done so ever since we were in the ninth grade and my hands hurt from taking notes. We weren't even dating then, but his hands had always been so strong and tender, and he would massage my palm, fingers, and wrists to relax me. Now it was just his conditioned response, done without thought.

"He's frickin' *tall*," Elliot said.

"Silas? Yeah."

"Does he play basketball?"

"I don't know. He runs."

Elliot muttered a disapproving *hmph*.

"*You* run," I reminded him.

"Sort of. What's his problem anyway?"

"Nothing. Why do you say that?"

"He was flirting with you in the truck."

I smiled. "You're always imagining things," I told him, then kissed him on the cheek. "Remember the time you thought Tony from Enger Mills liked me and you got all jealous when really Tru was the one he liked?"

"Tony Caprizi," Elliot said. "I still think he liked you."

"Not a week later, he was feeling up Trudy in his car!"

Elliot laughed a little, calming down. His thumbs started making wider, softer circles on my wrist.

"Tell me about your day," I said.

"We're baling hay."

"Already?"

"Warm spring," he said. "Today and tomorrow, Mickey and me are stuck in the hayloft with some kids, and it *sucks*. Suffocating as hell and Mickey forgot his gloves today, so the twine was murdering his hands. The elevator drops the bales about fifteen feet, and we all took turns getting a running start and trying to catch the bale midair."

"That's so dangerous!"

"Yeah, Dad would kill us if he knew. Toby tripped doing it, and a bale fell right on top of his head. He went down like he'd been hit by a sniper, and he just laid there. Mickey's all, 'Holy shit, he broke his neck!' and we were freaking out, and bales kept dropping on Toby. Then a couple of us grabbed his legs and dragged him out of there like a scene in some war movie."

My eyes were wide in shock. "Was he okay?"

"Yeah," Elliot said, laughing a little. "It was scary, though, so we stopped playing it for today."

"Good."

"I'm sure we'll do it again tomorrow."

I rolled my eyes as Elliot laughed. I leaned into his side so I could feel his laughter in my own ribs. "I have bad news," he said suddenly.

I jerked away. *"What?"* I demanded.

Elliot laughed again. "Calm down," he said. "I was just teasing. Here's my bad news." He rolled up his T-shirt sleeve, revealing swollen muscles with the beginnings of a horrendous farmer's tan.

We both laughed.

"What about you? Is he still a pain in the ass?" Elliot jerked his head in the direction Silas had left. I traced his tan lines, and even though his arms were sore, I knew he liked it. "What were you doing with him anyway? Detailing?"

He sounded a little hopeful, and I hated to admit, "No. We watched some stupid TV show he likes."

Elliot was about to say something more when my mom appeared on the other side of the screen door and said, "West? Dinner's ready. Elliot, you can stay if you want."

"Thanks, Mrs. Beck," Elliot said, grinning at her. "I'm late for lifting though."

"You just got here," I whined as Mom left. "Everyone is always leaving."

"I was already here for a while, waiting for you. Your mom and I had a thorough conversation about my siblings—and the DII recruiters who've been calling." Elliot rolled his eyes a little—all my parents *ever* talked to him about were those two things: family and football. "Then Libby emerged." He shuddered. Elliot, my big, strong running-back boyfriend, was scared of my sister because she was "skittish like a cat."

"Oh," I said. "I'm s—"

But he kissed me on my lips, surprising me, and I closed my eyes and kissed him back. Then he left the steps, leaving me there missing him, missing his lips—and, oddly, missing Trudy even, missing normalcy. He walked backward toward his parents' minivan and said, "Don't forget about me while you're spending time with that kid."

"Silas," I called back. "He can be kind of a prick actually. You don't have to—"

"Don't say 'prick'!" came Mom's voice through the screen door.

seven

It didn't take long to confirm that Silas was absolutely crazy.

One morning he showed up at my house wearing an honest-to-goodness windbreaker suit straight out of the nineties: purple, mint green, and what is best described as neon salmon. I curbed a grin while Silas gathered our detailing supplies from my garage. "What?" he deadpanned. "What are you staring at?"

"Your windbreaker is just so . . ."

"Fetching?" he interjected. "Voguish? Swanky?"

"Hot," I said, playing along. "The nineties neon just exudes sex appeal."

"Well, I thought so myself."

And after the sun was high in the sky and the pavement was heating up, he took off the wind suit, revealing shorts and a *New Moon* T-shirt beneath, Edward Cullen's pale face dramatically printed across the front. "Vader's competition," he said, shrugged, and started vacuuming the floors of the Corolla left in our care.

He also talked about the strangest things: "Can you ever really prove anything? How?" or "I read about this composer who said his abstract music went 'to the brink'—that beyond it lay complete chaos. What would that look like? Complete chaos?" or "You know how in Shakespeare Romeo says, 'Call me but love, and I'll be new baptized'? He's talking about his *name*, but baptism's bigger than that; it has to be. It's about identity, and wonder, and favor, you know?" or "A group of moles is called a labor; a group of toads is called a knot. Who comes up with this stuff? It's a bouquet of pheasants, a murder of crows, a charm of finches, a lamentation of swans. *A lamentation of swans*, West!"

One morning I was late coming downstairs, and Shea got to Silas first. The two of them sat drinking orange juice on the front steps and discussing Shea's question of whether fish have boobs. "I think," Silas said, sounding like a scholar, "they do not, since they're not mammals. But mermaids do, since they're half fish, half mammal."

"Mermaids aren't real though," Shea said, the tiniest bit of hope in his voice that Silas would prove him wrong.

"Who told you that?" said Silas sternly.

"You think they're real?" Shea asked.

"I can't be sure," Silas said, "but I *might* have seen one when I used to live in Florida. Probably best not to jump to any conclusions either way."

Behind me, Libby giggled. Silas glanced at us over his shoulder through the screen door and grinned. "Libby," he said, "what do you say? Mermaids, real or not?"

"I don't want to jump to conclusions either way," my shy sister said, then turned bright red.

"Smart girl," said Silas.

That afternoon, Silas and I sat in the backseat of a dusty Saturn, trading off the handheld vacuum as we talked—or rather, shouted—over its noise. I ran the hand vac over the back of the driver's seat while Silas said, "I used to think I was the only one with a crush on Emily Dickinson until a couple years ago."

"You have a crush on Emily Dickinson?"

"Durr."

"Did you just 'durr' me? Is that like a 'duh'?"

He nodded as I handed him the Dirt Devil. "But then I read this book that says it's a rite of passage for any thinking American man. And *then* I read a poem called 'Taking Off Emily Dickinson's Clothes.'"

Just the title made me blush; I averted my eyes to focus on the vacuum's trajectory.

Silas, unruffled, sighed unhappily.

"What's wrong?" I asked, frowning, chancing a glance at him.

"I finally made it into the backseat with a girl," Silas cracked, looking hard at the Dirt Devil. "This is not all I was hoping it would be."

I slugged him in the arm, and his wry smile gave way to laughter.

"Want to come over after this, watch some *WARegon*?" he asked.

"I guess," I said, but suddenly he turned the vacuum off and answered his phone, which apparently had been vibrating. It had to be Beth, since Silas scrambled out of the car and wandered over toward the church parking lot, where he'd be out of earshot.

I closed the car doors and finished the job, looking from time to time at Silas, whose brow was furrowed as he listened. When he spoke, his face looked diplomatic and impartial. One time he glanced over at the car and noticed me watching; he gave me a big, goofy smile—and then turned his back.

His call ended as I finished vacuuming. We started to work on the car's exterior, and I probed, "Everything okay?"

"Yeah, totally. Why?"

"Who was that—Beth?"

He nodded.

"Does she call a lot?"

"More often than Elliot, that's for sure."

"Elliot is *working*." I paused, then accused, "Why do you have to do that?"

"Do what?" he asked as he stretched over the roof of the car with a soapy sponge.

"Be such an ass about things. I was just asking an innocent question."

He squinted at me from the other side of the car, the corner of his mouth curling up. "Were you?" he asked.

"Yes," I hissed back. "Of course." Well, *maybe*.

"What do you two even have in common?" Silas asked as he continued to wash the car. "The big football jock and . . . oh hell, you're not a cheerleader, are you?" He glanced at me with curious wariness.

"Yes," I lied.

"I don't believe you. I just feel like—hey, where are you going?"

I lobbed my sponge back into the bucket, climbed my front steps. "Finish it yourself."

"I thought you were coming over for *WARegon*!" he complained.

With the door halfway open, I turned around and gave him a blistering glare. "Put the supplies away before you leave."

Later that night, when I was almost asleep, I got a text from Silas, the first he'd sent since getting my cell number that week: Sorry.

I wrote back: It's fine.

He texted: Sleep well. Then, a minute later: Are you really a cheerleader?

I let out a laugh and wrote back: Not on your life.

eight

I hated the dreary gray carpet of the church, the musty smell of old hymnals, and the social hour before the service, when old ladies crowded around my dad as if he were a rock star. I tried to dodge the chattering congregants on the way into the sanctuary, but it was nearly impossible.

"West!" said Mrs. Callahan, flagging me down. "In case I don't get a chance to speak with him today, please pass along our thanks to your dad. He bailed us out on our mortgage last month. Not even from the benevolent fund—just wrote us a check! Such a good man."

"Yes, of course, Mrs. Callahan. He was happy to do it," I replied.

Mr. Tennant, who lived alone with his troublemaker son, whispered to me conspiratorially, "I'm sure you've heard that

Jacob got picked up for shoplifting last week. But Pastor Beck knew just what to say to him. I don't know what we would have done without your dad. You're one lucky girl!"

"I really am," I agreed with a painted-on smile. "Thanks for coming today." My standard response.

I steered clear of James and Rhiannon Raymond, who'd once had the impudence to tell me that my dad saved their marriage. Rhiannon had gotten teary-eyed, and I'd desperately wanted to cover my ears and say, "Don't tell me. I don't want to know." I gave the couple a wide berth as I made it to the front row, where I sat between my mom and Libby, letting out a huge breath as if I'd just survived running the gauntlet.

Beside me, Libby was giggling when someone in the row behind us kept sneakily tapping her shoulder. I glanced over my shoulder to see who it was.

"Hey," said Silas Hart to me, finally getting caught by my sister. He winked at her.

"You came!" I said, a little surprised.

"I said I would."

I looked down his row. His parents sat beside him; beyond them, his grandparents.

"Where's your sister?" I asked, lowering my voice as the service music started.

"At the house."

Mom turned to me and Libs, put a finger to her lips, and gave us a look we knew well: *Eyes forward. Set a good example.* I turned to the front where the worship leaders were crowding behind the pulpit.

No Laurel. Maybe Lillian Mayhew—"Oma Lil"—had no power over her. Or maybe Laurel was, as I'd guessed, too sick to leave the house. I imagined her in Heaton Ridge, sitting on the wicker couch, staring straight ahead with those hollow eyes that had glanced off me like a rock skipping across the water.

Behind me, Silas sang with conviction:

"It is well with my soul

It is well, it is well with my soul."

He wasn't loud, drew no attention to himself, but I heard every note as if he were singing into my ear. His voice was a paradox—at once angry and brave, sorrowing and confident—and yet, the song spread over him like a blanket and rushed forth like an anthem.

Laurel's absence was like a secret that followed Silas, like dice that he jostled in his hand but never tossed onto the table. But Green Lake was a town of two thousand. I knew as well as anyone that you can't hold big secrets in such a small hand.

Agoraphobia, I thought at first—that anxiety disorder that keeps its victims chained to a safe, controlled space. But no. I felt pretty confident the move from Fairbanks to Green Lake was for Laurel (and not for Mrs. Hart's job, whatever Silas said); if Laurel had agoraphobia, she'd have wanted to stay put. Or maybe she's just really shy—but then I remembered how she had introduced herself to Dad, held out a confident hand to shake his, how her eyes had met mine with ferocity.

Oh my gosh: Was she *crazy*? Like, legitimately, certifiably insane?

Or maybe it was something *really* different—like an allergy to sunlight. It was possible: there were two girls in Enger Mills, a couple towns away, who had this. I always forgot what it was called, but the school had to put this special film over all the windows in the building, and they had to wear helmets and gloves outside.

Such speculations even prompted a dream: a strange one where I followed Laurel around the high school halls (in my bathing suit, no less), wondering about the large brass key she carried in her hands. The halls were not filled with water, but I did the front crawl nevertheless, and that detail made me laugh out loud when I woke up and remembered it.

I visited Mark Whitby at the mini-mart that week while he was working, and he—correctly—assumed I was checking up on him. Whit was the loose cannon of our group—the biggest sweetheart, but also the most unpredictable. As Elliot and I had guessed, he'd been partying over at Simon Sloane's back forty.

"But you almost got a minor there last fall!" I complained. "I wish you wouldn't drink like—"

Whit gave me a look, his dirty-blond hair falling into his eyes, daring me to finish my sentence *like your dad*.

"—like a fish," I revised lamely. Whit's dad was a very tricky subject, best left for conversations not happening in the candy aisle of the mini-mart.

Whit gave me a big grin, all teeth, then took my face in his hands, kissed my forehead with a loud *muah!* "I've got everything under control," he said, which made me worry more.

That same day, I took my family's car to Enger Mills and picked up a toasted sub sandwich to surprise Elliot while he worked, but when I got to the Thomas farm, he was nowhere to be found, even with Caleb *and* Greg *and* Mrs. Thomas all helping me look. I called him and texted him for half an hour before giving up, going home, and eating the cold sandwich alone in the church bell tower.

I tried calling Trudy, but—as usual—it went straight to voice mail. But a minute later, she sent a text: Can't talk now, but miss you! I'm coming home for the 4th of July!

This news buoyed me after a rough afternoon and filled me with such a generous spirit that when Silas called soon after and asked me to come over, I said yes.

Silas's parents were very welcoming; Mr. and Mrs. Hart invited me to call them Glen and Teresa, which was nice but a little too chummy—I'd known Elliot's parents my whole life but would never call them by their first names. Silas's parents were an attractive couple, both with dark hair like his, and they were rarely home during the day, as Glen was doing research for an astronomy article and Teresa was already advising graduate students at her new job at the university. They told me to keep Silas in line and to make myself at home in their house, to help myself to whatever was in the fridge, to let myself in whenever the front door was unlocked. "Which it usually will be," Teresa said, smiling. "I know how this town works."

I let myself into their house several times that week, heading up the stairs to Silas's room and rapping on his door as annoyingly as I could. But he always opened it grinning, as if our day included wild adventures instead of detailing cars, talking about books, and watching *WARegon Trail*. Our plans never included Laurel; our conversations rarely.

On Friday, I let myself into their house as I'd been doing and started up the stairs, declaring loudly, "If that creepy little-girl zombie in the white bonnet shows up again, I swear I'll—"

But my words and my feet both stopped short as I was hit by a wall of sound: wailing coming from upstairs, loud and feral. My heart thudded hard against my chest, but I was struck immobile by the sound of wild despair. *Laurel?*

Questions unspooled in my mind. Is this a real-life horror movie? Is someone in trouble? Are the Harts witches? Is this how a banshee sounds before somebody dies? What the *hell* is wrong?

But I landed on only one answer: I don't want to know.

I started to retreat back down the stairs, eager to escape without notice. Despite how badly I had wanted to know the

Hart family's secrets, in this moment my insides were begging to be kept in the dark.

Then—quite suddenly—Laurel was at the top of the staircase, her face spotty and wet from tears, her cry spiraling upward into alarming pitches. Silas was behind her, clutching her elbow and shouting, "Laurel! *Listen!*" They both looked at me for a second—a second that felt like a slow-motion minute—then she wrestled her arm away from him and disappeared back down the hallway.

Silas looked at me, frowning hard, and I swallowed in fear of having seen something I shouldn't have. "I—I'm sorry. I—" But my tongue felt too thick for my mouth, so I just turned around and bolted for the front door, my hand gripping the smooth banister.

"West," Silas said, angry or annoyed, I couldn't tell. When I reached for the doorknob, he called louder. *"West!"* And then he was right behind me, a strong hand on my shoulder, turning me roughly to face him. But when I looked at him, he didn't look mad at all—just regretful. "I can explain," he insisted, leading me out the door to the porch.

He sat me down on the swing that hung from the rafters, standing in front of me as if I was about to be in trouble. Laurel's banshee cries still ricocheted off the walls of my skull, but I finally found my voice. "What is going *on*?" I panted. "Did—did something—are your parents okay?"

Silas's mouth tightened into a bow, but he nodded. "Yes,

they're fine. Everyone's fine. Everyone's fine except for Laurel." He breathed out a long sigh that made him seem older than seventeen.

"I'm sorry you had to hear that," Silas said, nodding toward the house. "It still gets under *my* skin. . . . I know it's not . . ." I nodded a little, as if prodding him toward his promised explanation. "Look, Laurel has a . . . well, I guess it's like a depersonalization disorder. This . . . this . . . it's called solipsism syndrome. It's not really that easy to explain."

"Solip-*what*?" I asked, not understanding him.

"Solipsism syndrome." He sat down beside me on the swing, then looked out across his yard while he scratched the back of his head, leaving his hair there standing up. "I didn't really want anyone to know," he said, almost to himself. Then he laughed without humor. "Two weeks. We didn't even make it two weeks."

He looked so grief-stricken that I almost wanted to lean over and put my hand on top of his. "I'm sorry," I said to him, even as I blushed a little at the thought of touching him.

Silas shrugged. "It's not your fault." He struggled to find words.

"You don't have to tell me," I said quietly.

He shook his head. "No. No, it's okay. Laurel . . . she got it into her head that she's living in a dream." When Silas saw my look of incredulity, he explained, "She's only sure that *she* exists—but not that anyone else does. It's a mental state. A detachment from reality. Basically, it either makes you lonely and depressed or an asshole. Some days are worse than others. Today is worse." He smiled weakly.

It was the very last thing I would have expected him to say. Even now, as I sat blinking on the porch swing, I wondered if I had heard him right. "So . . . wait—*what*? She just woke up one day and decided reality wasn't real, or . . . how did that *happen*? Is this okay that I'm asking?"

"Yeah, it's fine. I don't know. I honestly don't. It's been like this for a few years. But Laurel has always been this way—where she gets hold of an idea and then throttles it. Or it throttles her. She and whatever idea put the screws to one another. I think it started with philosophy books and some cracked movies."

My mind clung insistently to the word "philosophy." I tried to remember something I'd heard on *August Arms* about René Descartes, but I came up blank.

"And the polar twilight," he added. "That even messed with *my* head a little."

"So is that why you guys moved?"

Silas nodded again. "We had to get her out of Alaska."

"But—I mean, we're seventeen. Doesn't everyone have these weird thoughts at our age? I know I have—well, maybe not *that* one, but . . . other things."

He was quiet for a little bit and seemed to be formulating an answer. "It's—it's not the same," he said. "Yeah, I think everyone thinks up some crazy shit from time to time, but—I don't know to explain it—it's not like that with Laurel. It consumes her. She lets it drive her crazy. It's like these ideas have eaten away part of—part of who she is. They dominate her."

Silas looked so sad that I thought he might cry, and I had no idea what I'd do if he did.

And then just as quickly, he shrugged and pulled himself together. "Now you know. Life with the Harts. We should have a reality show. Or *non*reality, I guess," he said. Silas looked at me out of the corner of his eye, then cracked a tiny grin, permission to laugh.

But I saw right through it. It was such a contrast from the normal beaming smile I was becoming accustomed to, and I wondered how such joy and heartbreak could live inside the same person.

"You realize what this means, don't you?" he asked.

"What?" I asked—or rather, leveled at him, suddenly alarmed.

"We have to be friends now, Westlin Beck."

"Oh, *do* we?" I asked, but my voice was feeble. Silas looked so broken.

"Yup," he said. "Afraid so. You know my secret . . . well, one of them."

"One of them?" I raised an eyebrow. "You don't have any other siblings, do you?"

"I'm for real, West." He shoved my shoulder with his own. "Let's be good to each other."

"Friendship doesn't work like that, Silas. You don't just *decide* to be friends."

"I just did."

"Well, I didn't."

He looked me in the eye. "My girlfriend is in Alaska, and my sister is messed up. Your boyfriend lives on a tractor, and your best friend ditched you for summer camp."

"Hey!" His choice of words stung. "She—"

"Let's be good to each other," he repeated, and his eyes were so sad and serious and intense.

"Starting when?" I said, trying to mask the panic in my voice.

"Starting now."

nine

What I really wanted was to talk to Dad about Laurel's condition. In the days following Silas's revelation, I even wandered over to my dad's office in the church to chat, but I looked through his office window and saw he had people inside. So I went up to the bell tower for a while to read—but when I came back downstairs an hour later, there was a *different* set of people in his office. And another person waiting outside his door.

Forget it, I thought, then called Silas and biked over to his house.

I had this thrill of nervousness, returning to Heaton Ridge so soon after Laurel's banshee cries had rocked my world, but knowing the Hart family's secret felt like my reinforcement.

And when I arrived, the only sound I heard was some unbelievably loud music blasting from Silas's bedroom stereo. I tiptoed past the first door in the hallway, which I was pretty sure was Laurel's, and knocked on Silas's door.

"Come in!" he called, and I entered, seeing him fussing over something on his bed. "I found some awesome garage sales," he said, proudly presenting his discoveries to me before turning down the volume on his old CD player.

"So *this* is why you need a summer job," I said as I surveyed his finds, which were laid out across his unmade bed like cheap museum displays: a dollar-sign ice-cube tray, a medium-sized box of ancient eight-tracks, a pair of lightsaber chopsticks, and a "D-Bag Poet" Magnetic Poetry set. I held up the magnet collection. "Really?" I asked.

"It's missing 'dayam,'" he said, trying not to crack a smile, "so I won't be able to write a poem about you, sorry."

I burst out laughing but tried to stifle it. On his nightstand, his cell phone vibrated. I picked it up, glancing at the screen. "Beth," I said, handing it over. He pushed a button to ignore the call, then slipped it into his back pocket.

Hmm.

"What are you going to do with a box of eight-tracks?"

He shrugged. "Dunno, but aren't they great?" I noticed his shirt for the first time then—it featured a unicorn rearing before an American flag. "Pearl of great price," he said, looking down at it with tenderness.

The thrift-store scent of used goods mixed with the smell of his room: boy, sweat, and sandalwood, all rich and milky and fresh-cut cedar. "You . . . are so . . ."

"Enchanting? Delectable? Ambrosial?"

"Weird."

He grinned at me.

"I saved the best for last," he insisted, and I realized that he was hiding something behind his back.

"Don't tell me," I said. "Macaroni art of Steve Buscemi?"

"I *wish*!" he teased. "But no." Silas revealed a carrot-colored plastic transistor radio. It was a little larger than his hand—an awkward size, like an old Walkman on steroids.

"What do you want that for?" I asked.

"Because it's awesome. *Durr*," he said. "And because we're going to use it to listen to that radio show of yours. Yes?"

Just a small token—but it felt like he'd just promised to build me a house or buy me an island. For the first time this summer, I felt like someone had *heard* me.

I couldn't find my voice for a second, but pressed my lips together and nodded. "I'd like that," I said softly.

That evening, Silas and I returned to his house to listen to *August Arms*. Mr. and Mrs. Hart were in the kitchen—and they were arguing. From the front door, I couldn't hear much of what was said, but I had little doubt it was about Laurel. "Well, just don't let her!" Glen insisted. "Just don't—*let*—her."

"I'd like to see you try, Glen. And instead you're planning—"

"Hi," Silas shouted awkwardly, announcing our arrival. "We're going up to the roof!"

Teresa came out of the kitchen and into the hallway. "Westlin! Hello! How are you? How's your family?" Big smile, no trace of conflict. My parents could turn it on just as quickly. How many times had Dad been yelling at us kids and then answered the phone in his best pastoral voice as if he were a totally different person?

"Everyone's good, thanks, Teresa."

Glen stood in the doorway to the kitchen. "Busy day today? Silas says you're teaching him to be a detailing machine."

"I'm learning lots from him too." I looked at Silas and muttered, "A lamentation of *swans*." Silas grinned. His parents looked unperturbed. I guess when you had one child who was a trivia factory and another who lived on that blurred line between reality and reverie, you had to be choosy about which questions to ask.

The roof was even better than the rumors I'd heard. The famous fire pit was the stunning centerpiece, a huge slate-colored stone ring that matched the giant planters around the edges of the patio, most of them holding plants with lemon-scented petals and waxy leaves. Set up in the corner of the roof was some large apparatus with a protective covering over it—probably Mr. Hart's telescope.

The patio faced east toward Green Lake, and the sun had nearly set behind us, turning the lake dark and steely. The moon was just starting to hint at its place in the sky. I settled myself into a patio chair near the fire pit, and Silas handed me the little orange radio. "See if you can figure this out while I start the fire." It was made out of thick plastic—like my old Fisher-Price toys—with a clear face and dial for the stations. Even with the patio lights, it was still hard to see the dial, so I tinkered with it until I found the right station and then turned the volume up. Meanwhile, Silas had made a tepee of firewood and lit the kindling beneath it.

Tonight's show had just one feature story, this time about Heaven's Gate, a cult that had committed mass suicide in 1997 in expectation of reaching an alien spacecraft in the tail of the Hale-Bopp comet. Sullivan Knox detailed the death scene: bodies of men and women dressed in black, purple shrouds covering their faces, and brand-new Nikes on their feet. The fire warmed the soles of my feet, Sullivan's voice was comfortably familiar, and Silas furrowed his brows in the most adorable, thoughtful way as he scratched something in his notebook.

"What did you think?" I asked Silas when the show was winding down. "Interesting, right?" I was surprised by how badly I wanted him to love it as much as I did.

He nodded, impressed, and put his Moleskine in his back pocket. "Is every night like tonight?"

"Some nights they do three shorter stories instead."

"Cool." Silas poked at the fire with a stick, his long shadow stretching out behind him till it joined the darkness of the night.

"Can you imagine being convinced of something like that?" I asked, leaning back in my seat and staring up at the stars. "That the earth was going to be recycled and your one shot at survival was to evacuate by eating some tainted applesauce and boarding a UFO to another level of existence?" I shook my head in disbelief. "It's like sci-fi."

"Yeah," said Silas, still moving embers around in the pit, his face orange in the glow from the fire. "I think something would have to be off in you in the first place to be able to make that jump. I mean, Laurel . . . she gets convinced of some weird stuff, but I don't think it was just the books she read that did it. She's really sick to start with." He paused, and in his silence I heard the dog-day cicadas singing. Then he asked, "But how do you unlock someone's mind?"

And when he looked up at me, I swear he was hoping for me to have the magic answer. "I—I don't know," I managed.

"Does anyone? It's like a code only God can crack."

Those words sat in my stomach, this image of God as a detective, as a sleuth or a computer hacker, one with the best of intentions. God dressed in black with glasses and a goatee, typing in confident keystrokes as he solved the puzzle of Laurel Hart.

* * *

Silas phoned me later that week, a business call: his dad had met one of their neighbors and mentioned our detailing business, and the neighbor wondered if we could see to one of his cars in the morning. "Just come to my house tomorrow," Silas said, "and we'll go over together. Not sure which house yet—I'll check with my dad."

In the morning, I drove over to Silas's house, our supply bin in tow. I let myself in, announced "I'm here!" up the stairs, then—hearing the sound of the bathroom shower and fan from upstairs—sat down at the bottom of the steps to wait.

A voice came down the hall. "West?"

"Yeah?" I asked, hesitantly.

"I'm in the sunroom. Come wait with me."

Laurel.

My pulse quickened. I didn't want to—not without Silas. I glanced toward the top of the stairs, hoping that he would suddenly appear and save me. But the noise from the bathroom droned on, and I knew I was trapped. Suck it up, you baby, I told myself. I thought you were curious.

I walked down the hallway to the sunroom, where I'd first seen Laurel. Since the sunroom faced west, early-morning, sleepy-eyed sunshine was only starting to fill the space. Laurel sat on the same white couch she had before, wearing jeans and a peach-colored tank top and reading a novel, which she bookmarked and set beside her when I stepped into the room.

"Sorry about the last time you saw me—I was a wreck that

day," she said, immediately acknowledging the elephant in the room. "Come and chat?" She gestured to the chair beside her couch. Laurel was pale, and her posture was perfect. I would not have been at all surprised to have walked into the sunroom to find her in the lotus position, fingers making the okay symbol of the *chin mudra* I'd learned in our yoga unit last year. The white couch was her peculiar throne.

I stepped awkwardly into the sunroom and sat down in one of the wicker chairs near her. She was so gorgeous, her beauty was like spurs; I felt stunned, but Laurel's mouth—at least today—was the same as Silas's: friendly, encouraging, smiling with a hint of humor, and there was no trace of the banshee. So I took a deep breath and began to relax. She's just a girl, I told myself, willed myself to believe.

"So, you've been hanging out with my brother a lot lately, I hear," said Laurel, smiling softly.

"Yeah. Yes," I agreed. "Silas, he's . . ." I searched for the right word.

In true Hart fashion, Laurel had a handful. "Remarkable? Brilliant? Prodigious? Charming?"

"All of the above," I said with a little laugh.

"Attractive?" she asked, with a sly smile.

"Oh, I have a boyfriend," I said.

"Doesn't mean you're blind."

"Ha!" I was confused but kind of pleased: this Laurel seemed so far removed from every idea I'd had of her so far. It was astonishing to think that this beautiful teenager with the knowing grin was the same person as the wailing devastation.

"What has Silas told you about me?" she asked.

"He, ah, he told me about—what's it called?—solipsism syndrome or whatever," I admitted, as though it were shameful that I knew, shameful we'd discussed it. I reached for something to soften the blow. "He said you were depressed. You seem fine right now," I pointed out, wondering if this was too forward but taking my cue from her candor.

But Laurel only said, "I have good days and bad days."

"And today is a good day?"

"I think so," she said. "When I got out of bed this morning, I tripped over Silas's guitar case that he left in my room, and I fell and hit my knee pretty hard." I noticed for the first time that she had an ice pack—or no, it was a Ziploc bag of dollar-sign ice cubes—on her right knee. "Pain—when it's a shock—is always good for me."

I looked at her and raised my eyebrows.

Laurel shrugged. "When you trip, half asleep, over your brother's stupid guitar case in the dark and smack your kneecap—you stop wondering whether the guitar case is real. So, a shock in the morning actually starts the day off better for me—although my knee hurts like hell." She laughed, a little bitterly.

"But," I started, then stopped. I had no way of knowing what would or would not upset her. I felt sure that I couldn't take on banshee-Laurel on my own.

"But what?" she asked. She looked so . . . *normal* then, like any of my friends who simply hadn't heard whatever I'd said.

"But surprising things happen in dreams all the time," I said, tentatively.

"Yeah, but they're not surprising *in the dream*. It all feels normal."

It was true, I realized. It had not shocked me in my dream to find I was wearing my bikini and "swimming" through the Green Lake High School hallway—I had recognized its strangeness only after I'd woken up. A shiver of panic ran up my spine. "Then what can help?" I blurted out. "I mean, is that okay for me to ask?"

"Sure, I don't care," she said, then thought about it, her perfect mouth gathering to the side like you see in cartoons. "Socializing, although I don't always like to do it. The more complex the person, the better. Makes me feel less sure that I could have invented them. Holy Communion, of course."

I waited for her explanation. She was reminding me of Silas right now, talking like no other teenager I'd ever met except for him.

"A God who *dies*?" she asked emphatically, one brow raised in a brilliant arch. "A God who dies and then lives again? I don't think I could invent that either. It's like a declaration. Always a good reminder for me, you know?" Like her brother, she seemed to think of communion as an interaction, as dialogue.

"You want to hang out with me and Silas later on?" I asked, a little surprised even as the invitation left my lips. Then doubly surprised to realize I assumed Silas and I would indeed be hanging out later on.

She didn't say anything for a while, but then she nodded. "Sure. We can use the telescope tonight. Dad said you can still see Saturn pretty well this month, even though April and May were better for it. And Mom and Dad will be glad I'm—"

"Laur?" I heard Silas's voice echo down the hall. "Have you seen my guitar?" He stepped into the sunroom, wearing shorts and no shirt, hair still wet and curling a little. "Oh, hey, West. Didn't know you were here yet." He didn't seem to be embarrassed that he was shirtless, so I tried not to be either—although I felt my cheeks flare up. Laurel noticed and smirked. She was right—I wasn't blind, and Silas was hot.

"You left your guitar in my room," Laurel said, and nodded toward her knee. "Found it this morning." Her voice was laced with normal teenage cynicism.

"Whoops!" he said, making a face to go along with it. "Sorry. You all right?"

She nodded, and—like some strange gang symbol—put two fingers over her heart. It happened so quickly I wasn't sure if it had been intentional or not. "West wants us all to hang out later on," Laurel said. "That cool with you?"

"Sure," he said. I couldn't quit staring at Silas, his long torso and jutting hip bones. His shoulders were marked with muscle, and the little shadow on his interior biceps made me swallow hard. Silas walked to the side of the sunroom, where there was a basket of unfolded laundry I hadn't noticed before. He took a red T-shirt off the top and pulled it on over his head. "West Valley Cross Country" ran across his chest and the back read, "Follow the Wolfpack."

And then he put two fingers over his heart, just as quickly, just as naturally as Laurel had, before turning to me and asking, "Ready to go?"

I nodded as Laurel smiled, more teen than mystery for the moment.

ten

When we stepped outside, Silas looked in both directions. "That must be it," he said, nodding toward the black car to our left. "Dad said Mr. Jensen would leave the car in the driveway. Said it was a black one. A Forte or something." We looked to the right—an empty driveway.

I frowned suspiciously at the car to our left but held my tongue until we approached and I saw the trident emblem on the grill. "Do you know what kind of car this is?" I demanded.

Silas shrugged. "A nice one?" He walked around the back and read the chrome letters. "Maserati?"

"This is a Maserati Quattroporte. A Quattro*porte*, not a Forte," I told my partner.

"Cool," he said.

"Do you realize that this car is worth over a hundred *thousand* dollars?"

Silas's eyes widened. "Of course I don't know that! I'm a writer."

"What's that supposed to mean?"

He rolled his eyes. "Look, are you being serious right now?"

"Yes. Silas, we can*not* detail this car. What if we screw up?"

"I will not use a vinyl product on leather seats," he said in awe as he leaned forward and looked through the windows.

"And you can bet your *ass* that these are leather," I said, checking out the interior. "It doesn't even *need* detailing. It's perfect inside."

Silas shrugged. "Maybe they just want us to wash it or something? Just a regular old car wash?"

"It's locked," I said, still looking in. "The car is locked."

"Did they forget?" Silas asked. Then he said, "If it's locked, are we going to set the car alarm off? This *has* to have an alarm."

I held my breath, then reached out my hand as if I were about to touch an electric fence.

Nothing.

"The alarm must be off or something. What should we do?"

"If this guy wants to pay us to wash his rich-ass car, then we should just do it," insisted Silas. "Is our stuff quality enough?"

"I think so," I said. "I have a sheepskin wash mitt that I've never used. That'll work. And we have microfiber towels. . . ." But I was still hesitant. "What if we scratch something? What if . . . what if it takes off the wax or the paint or something?"

Silas looked at me like I was an idiot. "It's not going to do that. Come on, West. We did this with like four cars last week and you weren't worried then."

"It's just . . . scary to be responsible for something so valuable, you know?"

He nodded very slightly. "Trust me. I know."

So we went to work. I washed; he dried right behind me before the sun could leave spots. When we finished, we cleaned up our supplies and sat on Silas's front porch, relieved. "Nice work, partner," he said, knocking knuckles with me just as a black Kia Forte pulled into the driveway of the house to our right.

A redheaded kid got out of the driver's seat. I recognized him even though he went to a private school in St. Cloud. His name was Jason, and he'd interviewed Trudy's dad, Sgt. Kirkwood, for some career exploration project last semester. "Hi, sorry!" he said. "West, right? Are you two the ones cleaning our car today?"

We stared at him.

"Sorry if you've been waiting around," he continued. "I had to run to the mini-mart, and it took longer than I thought. Pocket was running the till, and you know how much he talks. You have to be frickin' Houdini to escape him. Anyway, it's all yours now."

The door to the house on our left opened, and a man in a

business suit stepped outside and moved toward the Maserati. "What can I say?" the man said to the woman in the doorway. "I'm a terrible brother. You love me anyway. Hey, listen, I'll come around more often, all right?" He glanced down at the cement. "Why's your driveway wet?" he asked her.

Silas and I didn't wait for an answer or offer one. He let out a tiny cough as we hurried from the Harts' porch over to Jason and took the Forte keys from him. "Got it, thanks," I said. "We'll get right to work on that." When the Maserati rolled out and Jason had gone indoors, Silas and I started laughing, two lunatic Atlases who had each just dropped a world and let it roll into the street.

The inside of the Forte was filthy and took four hours to detail; afterward, Silas and I took my family's car to St. Cloud, where we bought a second sheepskin mitt (since the first had rather impressed us), then went to McDonald's for Big Macs and ice cream, which we ate on a bench outdoors, enjoying the evening weather and the sound of the June bugs kamikaze-ing into the lit-up drive-through menu.

"Mmm," said Silas, finishing his burger. "Damn, do I miss chain restaurants. I mean, Fairbanks isn't *big*, but it's a frickin' metropolis compared to Green Lake."

"Green Lake's not that bad," I argued.

He raised an eyebrow. "You said yourself there was nothing to do there."

It was that classic double standard that forbade others from disrespecting the same family/home/town that you insulted freely. I have cousins who live in St. Paul, where their high school is twice as big as our whole town, and even though Trudy and I rag on Green Lake all we want, when Monty and Mae say, "Oh my *gosh*, it is so boring here," my face gets hot, and I'm ready to defend small-town life with everything I have.

"I mean, you *did*, didn't you?" he pressed. He could tell I was annoyed and bumped my elbow so that my ice cream cone hit my nose.

"Knock it off!" I said, wiping ice cream off my nose, but he gave me one of those brilliant smiles of his—the kind that knocked me upside the head—and I had to smile back.

"I will admit," he said, "having things to do isn't as important as having people to do things with. Glad we're being good to each other." Then he winked.

My face grew warm, and I blinked shyly at my cone. "Me too," I muttered, wondering again if he was trying to flirt, if he did this with all the girls. "Someone has to keep you in line," I said, then mimicked our conversation from earlier in the day: "'Do you know what kind of car this is?' 'A nice one? *Maserati?*'"

Silas laughed. "Well, how was I supposed to know?!"

I smiled. "When I said how it was scary to be responsible for something valuable . . . you were thinking of Laurel, weren't you?"

He pressed his lips together, crinkled his nose up in this adorable way, then nodded. "Call me Captain Obvious."

"But you know you're not really responsible for her, don't you?"

He was quiet for a while, stirring the ice cream around his dish. "I guess," he finally said.

I was sorry I'd destroyed the mood with my change of topic and didn't push it further. "Haven't been here since spring," I said, looking up at the golden arches. "Back before Tru decided to be adventurous."

"Do you miss her?"

"A lot," I said. "But especially Friday nights. I've spent almost every Friday night at her house for the last three years."

"No kidding?"

I was relieved that the normalcy had returned to his voice. "We'd go to Elliot's football game or to a dance or drive around with friends, and then afterward we'd go back to her house and crawl into bed and whisper till three a.m."

"About?"

"Secrets," I said in as coy a voice as I dared, which made Silas grin.

It was always in those moments—those early-morning revelations—that I felt closest to Trudy. Somehow in the dark, when we couldn't see each other's reactions, we felt freest to share secrets. As daughters of respected Green Lake men, we understood responsibility and expectations and regretted the way our decisions were tied up with our parents' reputations. She'd tell me how much she hated that her dad was a cop, how she worried about him all the time, and I'd fret over my own obscurity. We'd talk about boys and insecurities; she hated her eyebrows, I hated feeling so plain. We would shed all our problems that way, every week, just like a heavy fur coat. From time to time, one of us would hear the telltale noises of stifled weeping, and we would reach out, hold hands, and fall asleep that way.

"Speaking of secrets," he said, "I know something you don't know."

"Oh yeah?" I asked, my heart racing. I *hated* that it was racing. Why was it racing?

He pointed to a particularly bright golden star. "That's Saturn."

"Really?" I asked, slightly disappointed, but still intrigued. "How do you know?"

"My dad is Glen Hart," he responded, as if that were reason enough. "And over there—see that cluster of stars, the bright ones? That's Pleiades. The story goes, Orion pursued the Seven Sisters, so Zeus turned them into swans—or maybe doves—and they flew up into the sky and became stars."

"Swans *or* doves?"

"I've heard both."

I looked at the constellation. "So, you're telling me I am essentially looking at a lamentation, right?"

"Ha! I guess so. Have you used a telescope before?"

"Trudy had one of those little FirstScope things from Scholastic when we were in third grade."

A tiny smile toyed on Silas's lips. "Yeeeeeah," he said. "Let's go back to my house and use the big-kid scope. I think it will surprise you."

Silas's grandparents were over at his house when we returned to Heaton Ridge. "Silas," Arty Mayhew shouted from the kitchen, "that you? Come help us out."

I followed Silas into the kitchen, where his grandparents, mom, and sister were all sitting around the island, snacking on some fruit. "Hi, Papa. Hi, Oma," Silas greeted his grandparents, then kissed Lillian on the cheek. She and Teresa and Silas all looked alike—dark eyes, clever mouths—but Laurel looked like her grandpa.

"Silas," said Oma Lil, "you need a haircut. You look like a vagrant. Teresa, you let them stay out this late?"

"It's summer, Mom," said Mrs. Hart.

Silas gave his grandma an exaggerated pout. "Papa's was longer. I've seen pictures."

"Don't even get me started on him," Oma Lil said.

"Vagrants," his grandpa said to Silas, eyes twinkling. "You and me, kid."

Silas laughed. "Where's Dad?" he asked.

"Up on the roof," said Teresa. "Setting up the telescope for you."

"Perfect," Silas said, grabbing some grapes from the island and popping a few into his mouth. He held out the bowl to me. "Want some?" I shook my head.

"Silas, help us out," Papa Arty said again. "Laurel's looking for a toy she says she used to play with at our house when she was little. Describe it to him, Sweet Pea."

"It was a doll," said Laurel, slightly flushed. "A ballerina in a red dress with silver toe shoes."

Silas shook his head. "You played with *dolls*?"

"That's what I said," Teresa said to her son. To Laurel, she added, "You wouldn't touch a Barbie with a ten-foot pole. It was always books."

"There were some books—" Oma Lil started.

"—no," interrupted Laurel. Lillian looked offended. "It was a doll. I remember it because of the red and silver, when every other ballerina I'd ever seen wore pink. There were little lace gloves too—fingerless ones. I just—I just need to find it."

"Maybe it's in the attic somewhere," Papa Arty said. "You can come over and look if you want, Sweet Pea."

"Okay."

"Bring a shovel," he added. Lillian rolled her eyes.

"What do you want a doll for?" Silas asked Laurel.

"I just—it would be nice to find it," she said, evading his question. "Let's go to the roof."

Silas bolted up the stairs, grabbing his guitar case, which sat just outside his sister's bedroom door. Laurel and I followed at a normal pace, stopping at the den for her to get a blanket.

"How was your day?" she asked.

"It was . . . interesting," I said, walking onto the roof with her. I still had all this nervous excitement from being around her, as if she were a land mine I had to tiptoe around. "Yours?"

She shrugged, tucking a large tweed throw blanket beneath her arm. "I'm not doing so well right now." We had just stepped outside, so I couldn't tell if it was the cool evening air or Laurel's words that gave me a chill. It felt strange to have Laurel be so honest with me; we'd had our first and only real conversation that same morning, but apparently she had decided I was someone she could trust.

Or—as I thought harder about her issues—maybe she didn't even think I really existed, in which case, keeping secrets was just silly. There was no reason not to introduce one "imaginary" friend to an "imaginary" issue. It would be like letting your thoughts play hide-and-seek together.

Silas was already starting a fire, one foot on the ring of the fire pit as he poked kindling under some logs. Laurel wrapped the blanket she'd brought around herself and sat down in one of the patio chairs. Their dad stood at the telescope—which was the size of a small cannon—finding the right bearings to view Saturn. "Sure looks pretty tonight!" he said. "Who wants to look?"

Silas added another log to the fire and nodded at me. "West?"

Glen showed me how to look through the eyepiece, and I tried to remember the last time my dad had spent any of his free time with me and my siblings. I honestly couldn't recall. I'd hardly even seen him this summer, outside of Sundays. "It's in the upper-right corner. See it?" he asked. "It's just tiny." With Mr. Hart standing near, I missed my dad so much that I almost wanted to go home and be with my own family.

Dad probably isn't even home, I told myself and leaned forward to the eyepiece.

Even with this state-of-the-art telescope, Saturn was the size of a pencil eraser with one tiny ring decorating its golden body. Unexpected excitement welled up in me like devotion, like impetuosity. For a moment, I thought I might start to cry.

"Oh my gosh!" I called out. "I can even see its ring!"

"There are actually rings A through G, plus the Phoebe Ring, the Pallene Ring—" started Mr. Hart, but Silas said, "Dad, we know, we know," from over by the fire.

"How far away?" I breathed, still unable to tear myself away from the eyepiece.

"About seven hundred and fifty million miles. It's ten times the size of Earth."

I stared, wondering at something so otherworldly. I hadn't known it would hit me like this. It's like a baptism, I thought, remembering what Silas had said about it: identity, wonder, favor. All three were working me over. "Laurel, come look," I said, my voice breathless.

She seemed for a second as if she were going to argue, but instead she stood up, the blanket around her shoulders, and walked over to us and looked into the eyepiece.

"Glen!" I heard Teresa yell up the stairwell. "My mom and dad are leaving! Come say bye!"

He left, and it was the three of us.

Laurel walked back to the fire pit, the bottom of her blanket dragging behind her like a royal robe. I followed and sat between her and Silas, who had finished poking at the logs and was strumming lightly on his guitar. When he noticed my goose bumps, he took off his sweatshirt and offered it to me.

"I'm okay," I said.

"You're freezing."

"It's fine, really."

"Just take it, West." His voice was kind, soft, powerful.

I pulled it on over my head. It smelled like sandalwood and the bonfire, and it was huge on me and very warm. "Thanks," I muttered, getting that lightheaded feeling again.

"So?" I prompted, talking louder than necessary as I tried to clear my head from my Saturn high and rediscover my place in the universe. "What are you thinking about?" I probably sounded dorky, but I let it go.

My question was for Laurel, but Silas answered. "I think of Genesis," he said, strumming a sweet sequence of chords. "How a tight little compact sentence summarizes all this—'In the beginning, God created the heavens and the earth.' God chose that as his opening line? I like the New Testament line better: 'In the beginning was the Word.' Now, *that's* what I'd have led with."

If Dad talked about the Bible *that* way, maybe I'd pay more attention in church.

Laurel said, "I think about death."

Silas and I both looked at Laurel, but she stared only at the flickering orange flame. "I'm seventeen. Seems like I only blinked and here I am. I'm speeding like a rocket toward death. I'm spiraling toward the end of now and the start of infinity. It's a countdown. But to *what*? Can't gift wrap eternity."

Who *were* these people?

"What if I made up God?" Laurel whispered.

Silas shifted in discomfort, frustrated. "Laurel, *no*."

"What if I did?" she persisted. "What if I invented the whole idea?" A tear formed at the corner of her left eye. "Just like I made up that stupid ballerina doll." She bit the inside of her cheek.

"What does the doll even matter?" Silas pressed her.

Laurel exhaled—a rough, ragged breath—and said, "It's a sort of test, I guess. It would be a touchstone."

"A touchstone?" I asked.

"An anchor," she said. "To what's real. It would help me . . . to *know*." She pressed her lips hard together. "What if I dreamed it all? What if I'm dreaming right now—of you two and the stars and this night? What if—"

But Silas did the very last thing I would have expected him to do. His strumming changed; then he interrupted his sister and started to sing an old hymn.

The song was like an answer and an argument in one.

Laurel swallowed hard, and that tear finally fell. "You know it, don't you, West?" Silas asked quietly after the first verse, his eyes looking serious, black pools of tar with tiny fires in them. I did. I swallowed and timidly joined him with the chorus.

I'm not sure I'd have joined in except for the mix of everything: Saturn bearing down on us where we sat exposed to the whole universe; the clean, warm scent of sandalwood; and the crisper smell of those lemony blossoms soaking into my skin.

And his *eyes*.

A flush crept up my neck, and it made me feel guilty. And silly. *Elliot. Beth.*

Laurel watched the flames as we sang, and when we were done, everything seemed terribly quiet, as if there were a hole in the night the shape of our voices. Laurel whispered, "Maybe I should just get some rest."

"Hey," said Silas, and put two fingers over his heart. Laurel smiled softly as she left, the train of her blanket following her all the way to the door. I was alone with her brother, a minstrel whose songs sounded like sanity, like gravity.

eleven

I spent the last full week of June with the Hart twins, who were a combined repository of curious ideas and history. Silas had four cross-country meet records at his old high school. Laurel had spent the previous semester at home, taking classes online. They had memorized all these old *Saturday Night Live* skits that they would quote out of nowhere—Silas kicking things off, but Laurel always with the response. Silas knew his sister's Facebook password and stealthily began adding interests to her profile such as "rash ointments" and "LARPing." When Laurel found out, she changed his voice mail to say that he was busy rehearsing for his Mr. Princess pageant.

It was anyone's guess as to what mood Laurel would be in when she woke up—she had a permanent seat on an emotional roller coaster—and I held my breath every time I entered their house, nervous I'd break into another of her calamitous weeping sessions. I couldn't see any logic behind what made a day "good" or "bad," but Silas assured me it was there.

Some days, Laurel seemed perfectly fine, and I marveled that I had ever been afraid of her. One afternoon the three of us made a blanket fort in their den. Using the ceiling fan as the pinnacle of our tent, we secured the ends of the blankets and sheets to the coffee table and entertainment center using two pagoda bookends and a few paperweights. Inside our fort, we sat on the den floor and watched old home videos—Silas as a toddler, covered in mud; Laurel on Santa's lap, screaming in terror; the two of them in junior high, braces on both, Silas with chubby cheeks, Laurel with a boyish bowl cut. "Ugh, turn it off!" said Laurel, laughing. "I was such an ugly duckling."

Silas reached for the remote, turned off the video, and then we lay on our backs, staring up at the roof of our homemade castle, me in the middle, wondering how exactly friendships got to this point. A few weeks ago, I could have never imagined being here with these two.

"Pick a major for West, Laurel," instructed Silas. "Go."

I groaned good-naturedly. They'd started playing this game a few days earlier.

"*Harry Potter* studies," said Laurel, propping herself up on one elbow, facing me and her brother. "For sure. Or you could be very culturally savvy and choose a language—for instance, why not pig Latin?"

"I personally think that she would be a prime candidate for a banjo performance program," said Silas. "With a minor in spoons." He moved his head to a phantom bluegrass beat.

"And then would you come to my concerts?" I asked.

"Of course we would!" said Laurel, pretending to be offended I had to ask. "We would be your groupies, West."

The game could have easily gone either way. The question of my major seemed to stand in for the larger uncertainty of what I'd do with my life, of the person I was and wanted to be, and I'd always hated thinking about my blurry outline. Yet this bizarre process comforted me—as if we were making fun of the whole enterprise—and somehow Silas knew it. He was turning out to be frightfully good at discerning my reactions, and sometimes it made me feel a little shy.

It was like I'd known him and Laurel for years and years instead of just weeks. How could we fall into such an easy routine before there had barely been time to *create* one?

Silas ran every morning before the sun began to smolder. He carried his iPod with him and used the time to memorize poetry as he circled the lake. And while he and I detailed cars or ate lunch, we'd swap stories in an endless, fascinating conversation. Mine I learned from *August Arms*; I had no idea where his came from.

Afternoons, Silas and I would watch *WARegon Trail* or—more often—read in their den. Laurel joined us about half the time—the other half, I'd hear her crying or listening to music as I walked past her bedroom door.

In the evenings, we'd listen to *August Arms* on their roof, while the summer nights wrapped their arms around us. It would be late by the time I'd head home, but I'd still make sure to email Tru and give Elliot a call before I fell asleep.

My summer had been boiled down to the bones, and those bones were the Hart twins.

"Some Johns Hopkins astronomers determined the color of the universe is this off-white they call 'cosmic latte,'" I told Elliot over the phone one night, "and Silas thinks it makes sense on a universal scale because if the rest of the universe is clean and untouched but then you add in Earth—and it's so messed up but also small and insignificant in the cosmic scheme—then the darkness of Earth pollutes the rest of the universe's purity. Just a smidge, you know? Cosmic latte. What do you think?"

Elliot yawned audibly. "I think you haven't quit talking about that kid since I answered my phone."

"Silas," I said. "His name is Silas."

"Silas, whatever," Elliot said, sounding so tired. "He's not God, you know, West."

"I know that," I snapped. "I never said that."

"You spend every frickin' day with this kid, and then when I finally have a few minutes to talk to you, you upload his conversations to me. I want to hear about *you*." Maybe it was the tone of his voice—it was tired, not hostile—that calmed me down. This was Elliot, after all.

"Sorry," I said. "Really."

"It's okay. I'm just exhausted. We've got a few new calves, and one of them isn't doing so hot. Wasn't drinking from the mom, so I've been bottle-feeding her, but today her eyes went all milky white and blue and cloudy. Blind. Super weak. Dad wanted me to take the body away after chores, but I've heard before where this happened and the calf only had a fever and recovered fine later, so I'm just keeping my eye on her and hoping for the best."

"That's so sad!"

"Yeah, and she's a sweetie too. I named her Stevie."

"As in Wonder?"

"Yeah."

I chuckled lightly.

"So tell me about you," he asked again.

But it was hard to describe my day without including the Harts, so I said, "It was good. Detailed cars. Listened to the radio." My summer sounded limp when I described it this way; all the good parts—all the interesting and worthwhile parts—included my new friends. "When can I see you?"

"Drive-in this Saturday night? *Please* say we can fog up the windows."

I laughed. "We haven't done that for a while, huh?"

"A man has needs, Westlin Beck," he said in an exaggerated Cro-Magnon voice.

"We can fog up the windows," I promised.

"Good," he said in his regular voice. "I miss you."

"I miss you, too."

He was quiet for a few seconds, and I thought we were going to hang up, but then he said, "I don't like you spending so much time with that kid."

"He's my detailing partner, Elliot," I said, as if I was talking to a child. "And my friend. Do you not trust me or something? He has a girlfriend."

"*You* have a *boyfriend*," he said with emphasis.

"I know that!"

"Well, then why wasn't that the first thing you said?"

"It was!"

"No, it wasn't. You said, 'Don't you trust me? *He* has a *girlfriend*,' like that's the one thing stopping you—"

"—stopping me from what, Elliot?"

He sort of grumbled an unintelligible response.

"From what, Elliot?" I challenged him. It was dark in my bedroom except for the glow of my cell phone, and I didn't know why I was pushing him like this except that we were both exhausted.

"Look, why are we fighting?" he asked, vocalizing my own thoughts. "We never fight, you and me. We talk through things."

"Well, you're not *around* to talk through things," I complained, still upset, though aware that I was whining while he talked actual sense.

"I'm sorry," he said, calm and sincere. Elliot. My loyal

friend through the years. "I shouldn't have agreed to work for Dad this summer, not our last summer before senior year. I got so damn worked up over buying a car—you know what Mom and Dad are like with that stupid van, treat it like it's the Ark of the Covenant or some damn Bentley. I should have put us first."

"You're fine," I said, softening at his words. "*I'm* sorry. I miss you—I miss *everyone*—and it makes me moody and annoying."

"Naw. You're great."

I'd clearly been spending too much time with Silas, since the moment he said "great," I thought of a million better words. Stop it, I told myself—or Silas.

"I'm glad you know about cars," I said instead. "You know what a Maserati is, right?"

"Huh?"

"Nothing. Good night. Don't be mad."

"I'm not mad. See you Saturday."

"See you."

Feeling better after my conversation with Elliot and a good night's sleep, I joined the Harts on Friday afternoon to read in their den. Silas lay on the floor, holding a book in his extended arm, making little envious groans every few minutes and finally declaring, "I wish this book were water, so I could take a *bath* in it. I want my toes pruny from it." On the couch, I was making my way through Silas's entire Billy Collins collection, having returned Gordon's book to him the week before. Beside me,

Laurel was shouldering through an existential crisis so that she could finish hers.

"It just all seems unfair—do you know what I'm saying?" she asked. "Like, free will or not, humanity was set up for failure."

"Laurel, finish the book," Silas said, his voice unenthused, not looking away from the page he was on. "We're trying to read."

"It's just—well, if we don't have a choice, then we were made to screw up. But if we do have free will, then it's like we're *allowed* to make bad decisions." Her voice was leaning into the frantic stages it traveled to so quickly. I wanted to remind her to breathe, remind her that nothing had changed from before she'd read the book till now.

"Laurel," Silas said, now sounding annoyed. "Five minutes, okay? I'm almost done with my chapter."

She chewed on the inside of her cheek and nodded. But only a moment later, she plodded on. "It *scrambles me up*, you know? I just—I feel just sick. I feel like—how could God set us up like that? How—"

"Laurel," Silas growled. "Calm. *Down*. If you don't want to read the book, then don't read the book."

"It's not that," she said. "Do you see what I'm saying? It feels like the ground opened up. Didn't it feel like that to you when you read it?"

Silas set his book aside, then closed his eyes there where he lay on the floor. He was gathering his patience, so I stayed quiet. He exhaled slowly then said, "I don't know, Laur. I liked the book. It made me think. If you don't want books to make you think, there are plenty out there."

"West?" she asked, suddenly turning to me, and I felt caught in the middle of an argument I didn't want to be part of.

"Uh, what?" I asked.

"Your dad's the pastor. Have you ever thought about—"

"I try not to think about anything my dad says from the pulpit," I joked, offering a weak grin.

Silas looked at me hard. Laurel stood up quickly and exited the room, making small, sad noises as she left.

I looked at Silas. "Should we . . . help her?"

"If you have a plan, I'd damn sure love to hear it." His voice was hard, all sharp edges.

Silas's old CD player that we'd been using for background music was skipping in the corner, hissing out a repetitive *ffftt . . . ffftt . . . ffftt* in the otherwise-silent room. Silas stared at me for another few moments, then reached out and gave the player a little cuff. The music resumed its playing.

"Let's go swimming," he said.

twelve

Silas drove Papa Arty's pickup, which had seen its best days in the early nineties. We stopped by my house for my swimsuit, and then by the mini-mart for sunscreen since Silas swore he'd turn red as a stoplight without it. Whit's car was in the parking lot, so I said, "Just stay in the car, okay? I'll run in and get it."

"Why?"

"Never mind. Be right back."

"But *I'm* the one who wants it."

"It's okay. Just stay."

Inside, Pocket Swanson was at the till, talking the ear off a woman whose child grabbed at the items on the counter. Whit was stocking beef jerky. "Hey, do you have sunscreen?" I asked his back.

"Hello to you, too," he teased.

I grinned. "Hey. Miss you."

"Ditto. Sunscreen's back here," he said, leading me into a different aisle. He lowered his voice. "Don't tell Pocket I said so, but you really should get it at the Red Owl. You'll pay with your firstborn here. Going swimming or something?"

"You betcha," said . . . *Silas*, who had ignored my request to stay in the truck and now approached us in the aisle. "That's what you say in Minnesota, right?" He held out a hand to Whit. "Hey, man, I'm Silas Hart."

"Mark Whitby," said Whit, a bit bewildered. "And you're . . . ?"

"A friend of West's."

Whit raised an eyebrow.

I rolled my eyes. "He's my detailing partner," I explained. "We need to go."

"You just move here?" Whit asked, ignoring me.

Silas nodded. "From Alaska."

"Awesome," said Whit. "Then you won't be a wuss when January hits. Do you sled?"

"If you've got an extra snowmobile."

"I could find one."

What was happening here?

"Do you know what classes you're taking this fall?" Whit asked.

"AP World History, Senior Lit, I don't remember what else. All that was left for electives was Agriculture."

Whit snorted. "Don't worry—you'll get shoulder-length gloves before you have your way with the cow."

Silas's eyes widened.

"Okay," I said. "Time to go." I pinched a corner of Silas's T-shirt and dragged him to the register, Whit laughing in our wake.

"Nice to meet you, Silas. Let's hang out," he said.

"Oh, we will," answered Silas.

The Green Lake beachfront is small, just a fifty-yard strip of sand with a tiny parking lot behind it and a picnic area and playground a little off to the south. I made sure we claimed a spot on the outskirts of the beach, as far as possible from the tall wooden lifeguard stand where Abby Kuiper, who was in my class at school, blew her whistle at kids in bright swimsuits. The sand burned beneath our feet, and the lake smelled strongly of fish and algae and the white clover that grew along the shoreline. I busied myself spreading out two giant beach towels while I chastised Silas. "I don't know why you couldn't just stay in the pickup like I said. Whit is Elliot's best friend. And now he's going to tell Elliot that I was hanging out with you, that we were going *swimming*—"

Beside me, Silas pulled off his T-shirt—which starkly read "Unreliable Narrator"—without a thought.

"—and . . . and . . ." Like the morning he'd walked shirtless into the sunroom, I was flustered. Only this time there was no

Laurel as a buffer. "And I don't want to give people the wrong idea about you and me because we're only business partners . . . just business partners and friends and Green Lake is so small and we wouldn't want people here to think something was going on with us, right?"

Silas grinned at my rambling. "Right," he said.

"Right. Okay."

His chest and stomach—and arms, for that matter—had the perfect amount of muscle: not bulky and overbearing, but toned and fit. He had abs *for days*. He squinted at me in the sun. "Your turn."

"My turn? What? Oh." My cheeks flared. "Give me a second." I continued to spread out our towels—which were already perfectly spread out. Get it together, I admonished myself, then stood up. Silas stared at me, expectantly. "Well, turn around," I said. "This isn't a freakin' striptease."

He pulled his lips together, still squinting, as if considering what I'd just said. Then, without a word, he turned around.

I peeled off my shorts and T-shirt. "Okay, let's swim."

Silas turned to face me. His eyes raked over my body. "I like your suit," he said with a shit-eating grin on his face.

"Thanks," I said awkwardly, crossing my arms over my chest. It was just boy shorts and a halter top, but, compared to the T-shirts I wore while we detailed cars, I was practically naked. I glanced around the beach but felt his eyes on me. "So, are we gonna swim or what?"

"Swim," said Silas. "But first . . ." He held up the bottle of sunscreen.

"SPF fifty?" I said. "What are you, a vampire?"

"I am rather fond of my epidermis. And yours. Turn around."

"I'll be fine," I said.

"Turn."

I obeyed and pulled my hair off my shoulders.

"*This* is fun," Silas said, tugging lightly at my halter top's knot.

"Don't pull on that!" I said, panicked. "That keeps—"

"Oh, I know what it does, West."

When I turned around, he raised his eyebrows and flashed an angelic grin. "What?" he asked, voice dripping with innocence. I punched him in the arm. He laughed, boyish and playful.

"Watch yourself," I warned him, but I couldn't help but grin at the way he was giggling.

He held up his hands in surrender. "Fine, fine! I'll work around it."

So he did. His hands felt *ginormous* on my shoulders and back. "You're so tense," he said, pressing his fingers into the knots in my neck. It felt amazing, and I gave an involuntary and embarrassing little moan. I squeezed my eyes shut in embarrassment. "But *why* are you so tense?" he whispered teasingly in my ear, his breath on my neck.

"Okay, all done," I said, moving away from him. "Your turn. You're gonna need to sit down or I won't be able to reach."

He obliged, and I got on my knees behind him, squeezing some sunscreen into my hands and rubbing them together. It smelled like coconut oil, sweet and exotic.

I hesitated.

"Everything okay?" he asked, craning his head to see me.

"Yeah, of course. Why?"

"You tell me."

"Everything's fine," I barked. "Now turn around."

"Always so bossy," he said, still grinning.

I took a deep breath and touched him, moving my hands softly over his shoulders and back, feeling the warm skin and lean muscle beneath my greasy palms. The ridge of his spine. His lower back. Silas was lightly tanned and a tiny bit burned near his neck, his skin so much fairer than Elliot's. Where Elliot's shoulders were thick and corded, Silas's were lithe and angled with his sharp shoulder blades. Silas had three freckles on his right shoulder to match the one on his cheek.

If I were his girlfriend, I would press my lips to that little constellation, I thought for a moment, then berated myself: Why are you even *thinking* that?!

Silas suddenly jerked when I touched his side. "Ticklish?" I asked.

He turned around, smiling. "A little."

I reached for his side again, but he said, "Oh no you don't!"

and then stood and picked me up, *over his shoulder* like a fireman's lift, and carried me laughing and screaming into the lake and tossed me in.

I popped up out of the water, feeling my wet hair plastered across my face. "You're so dead, Hart!" I shouted, throwing my arms around his neck and trying to pull him down into the water. But he was so much stronger than me that he didn't budge—only put his hands around my waist, pulled me against his bare chest, and took me under once again, this time with him.

We both came up laughing. I held out my hands to ward him off. He interlinked his fingers with mine as we struggled against each other. "I give up!" I said. "I give up. But one day, when I grow up to be a six-foot-three freak of nature like you, you're going down."

"Freak of nature, huh?" he goaded me, still with that same giant smile, still with our palms together.

"You heard me," I taunted.

"Your knot's coming untied," he said, and I gasped and reached behind my head . . . where my halter ties were still in their tight knot.

"You wish, Hart."

"You *wish* I wish, Beck."

We moved into deeper water and faced one another as we treaded the rolling waves.

"What are you doing tomorrow?" Silas asked.

"Don't know. What'd you have in mind?"

"This. Again. Or have a bonfire. Or go on a walk. Or make cookies."

"Hmmm . . . oatmeal chocolate chip?"

"Durr."

I laughed. "Okay." Then—"No, no, not okay," I backtracked.

Silas—whose grin had just gone from Cheshire cat to nonexistent—asked, "Why not?"

"I have a date. With Elliot."

"Oh."

"He's picking me up at six thirty for the drive-in movie triple-header in Enger Mills. We . . . we've had it planned for a little while now." I let out a small, disappointed breath, then checked myself: Isn't that exactly what I wanted—to spend time with my boyfriend this summer? My priorities had gone haywire.

"Another night," I told Silas.

"Another night," he agreed.

Elliot brought flowers the following evening—a beautiful bouquet of violets—and when he lifted me off my feet in a giant hug, the orange transistor radio fell out of my sweatshirt pocket. Silas was its unofficial warden, but somehow I'd ended up with it.

"What *is* that?" Elliot asked.

"An old radio," I said, picking it up, then joked, "It's how I've been dating Sullivan Knox this summer."

"You should bring it over to my house and listen with me this week."

"While you complain?" I teased.

"I won't."

"Right," I said sarcastically. "Wait here, okay? I'm just going to put this"—I held up the radio—"inside and get these"—the violets—"in some water."

As I stepped back onto the porch, Mark Whitby pulled up and parked in the church lot next to my house. "Hey, you two!" he said, walking over to us with his arms full: a set of giant speakers and a paper bag I suspected held liquor. "We're taking the van, right? Might as well all pack in."

Elliot looked at me. "Did you . . . invite Whit?" he asked quietly.

I let out a tiny laugh at the suggestion. "On our date? No."

The two boys greeted each other warmly in my driveway. "Whit, what are you doing here, man?" Elliot asked.

"Bailing on Sloane's party. Brought a little party with me though," he added, nodding toward the things in his hands.

Elliot and I looked at each other again, baffled.

"Bailing on Sloane's party . . . ," I repeated.

"You should be grateful!" Whit said to me, moving over to the minivan. "I know you hate it when I go out there." He opened the side door of the van and stashed the liquor beneath a seat and the speakers behind it.

Just then, another car pulled up and parked beside Whit's, our school friends Bridget and Marcy honking and waving from inside. The girls made their way over to where we stood, dragging lawn chairs behind them.

"Wait, what's going on?" Elliot asked. "What's everyone doing here?"

"Silas stopped by the mini-mart last night and told me this was the plan," Whit said.

"Silas?" I choked out.

As if on cue, Silas pulled his grandpa's pickup into my driveway. In true Silas fashion, he rolled down his window and flashed the most disarming smile. Laurel leaned over him and waved.

"Hey," Silas said to me.

"Hey," I whispered back, glad to see him but so confused. Beside me, Whit was gawking—presumably at Laurel.

Marcy coughed.

"Guys, this is Silas and Laurel." Pointing to each, I listed, "Whit, Bridget, Marcy . . . and Elliot." Elliot put his arm around my waist.

"Great to finally meet everyone. Ready to roll?" Silas asked.

"Wait, wait, wait," Elliot said. "Hold on just a minute." His face was flushed. He rarely lost his temper, but—only because I knew him so well—I could tell he was about to come unglued.

I put a hand on his arm and turned my back on the others.

"It's okay," I said to Elliot so no one else could hear.

He looked hard at me, his eyebrows pulled together. "*Okay?* That little shit—"

"Everyone's already here. And we haven't all hung out yet this summer. And it'll keep Whit away from Simon's place, at least for tonight." It was only the last statement that seemed to sway Elliot.

He closed his eyes, let out a frustrated breath, then said to the group, "Okay. Everyone pile into the van. Hart, you can drive yourself. Know where Enger Mills is?"

"I'm sure I can find it," said Silas coolly.

"Why doesn't West just come with us?" piped Laurel from beside him. "Then we won't get lost."

Everyone paused and looked at Elliot, whose jaw was set and nostrils flared.

"Fine," he said, his voice flat and dangerous. Everyone—including me—started moving toward the vehicles, but Elliot grabbed my arm, pulled me to him, and kissed me long and hard on the mouth. "We'll see you there," he said, then tossed one last scowl at Silas—who looked a little stunned—before getting into the minivan.

I climbed into the pickup cab between Silas and his sister. He put the truck into gear and we headed out, following the minivan. "He's a sloppy kisser," Silas remarked.

"I happen to like his kissing *just fine*, thank-you-very-much," I said, feeling my face flare.

"'Just fine' isn't how you should be kissed," he said matter-of-factly.

"*You* think you know how I should be kissed?" I challenged.

Silas shrugged and adjusted the shifter. "Sure."

"I think Elliot's hot, West," said Laurel.

"And *pissed*," I added. "Silas, you know tonight was supposed to be a date."

"It was?" Silas asked.

"I told you that yesterday."

"I must have misunderstood," he said. "Do you forgive me?" He flashed me a penitent pout. I rolled my eyes and looked away, no idea whether to be angry or not. I'd been looking forward to time with Elliot. Then again, I'd still get to be with him—only not alone.

I felt the tiniest pinprick of relief. Then guilt.

Laurel asked, "Who's the blond? With the longish surfer hair?"

"His name is Mark Whitby, but everyone calls him Whit," I said.

"Whit," she repeated thoughtfully, as if she were christening him.

After a pause, I continued the introductions. "Marcy—the one with dark hair?—she's always liked Elliot, so she's not exactly my biggest fan. Bridget, the redhead, is Marcy's best friend. Trudy and I hang out a lot with them during the school year, but there's a pretty distinct divide, two and two, to be honest."

"Nice friends," Silas commented sarcastically.

"Well, what about you?" I asked. "You never talk about anyone from Alaska."

I realized too late that I didn't really *want* him to talk about anyone from Alaska.

"You want to know about Beth? Is that what you're asking?" he said, looking straight at me. "What do you want to know?" He darted a stern look at his sister, then began. "Beth is *gorgeous*," he said with emphasis. "Her mom is Yupik, and her dad's a Swede, so she has this dark skin and almond-shaped eyes, only they're blue. And she's this unbelievable math whiz. I swear she is going to prove the Riemann hypothesis before she's even a college graduate."

"The what?" I asked.

"And she wears really short skirts," Silas added, ignoring my question.

"Well, what about you?" I asked Laurel. "Have someone on the line back in Juneau?" It bothered me to hear Silas talk about Beth, though I knew it shouldn't.

"Fairbanks," corrected Silas. I knew it was Fairbanks; I had said Juneau to punish him.

I kept my back to him and looked at Laurel. "Nah," she said.

"Nah?" Silas asked with incredulity. "She only had like a

thousand guys hanging on her every word." He grinned at her over my head.

Laurel rolled her eyes. "Like you can talk." The knot in my stomach tightened. "No one," Laurel said. "I'm way too strange."

"Quit saying that," I chided. "Besides, you seem fine tonight."

She shrugged and looked out the window. "We'll see how long it lasts."

thirteen

The drive-in screen was in the middle of a field. We arrived early for the triple-header, and the three boys in our group tossed a football around with a couple of guys from Enger Mills, our sworn enemies on the football field but our teammates on the consolidated track team. Everyone was watching Silas and Laurel, these two beautiful and exotic specimens who had shaken up our same-old-same-old world like a snow globe.

"*Please* be friendly," I'd whispered to Elliot as he'd taken the football out of the van. "He's my friend and business partner. I'd like you two to get along."

"He hijacked our date!" Elliot said back. "And what does that stupid-ass shirt mean anyway?"

I glanced at Silas's chest, which declared, "HOLDEN CAULFIELD THINKS YOU'RE A PHONY." I sighed.

"Never mind. Be nice."

My heart raced. I didn't know how to manage the tension between Elliot and Silas.

Elliot eyed Silas with suspicion and tossed these impossible-to-catch long bombs that Silas somehow still managed to catch because he was so fast. It was irritating Elliot. He was bigger than Silas—thicker, more muscular—but Silas was taller.

For his part, Whit—hat on backward, his dirty blond hair curling out from underneath his cap—was torn between football with the guys and an obvious curiosity in Laurel.

"Hey!" she finally shouted at Whit, and he jogged over toward us, looking enthused. "I wanted to say hi," she said, "so . . . hi, I guess. Did you know the name Mark means 'warlike'?"

My gosh, she's flirting, I realized in horror.

Whit, buzzed from whatever was in the paper bag, staunchly shouted, *"Ihr seid verfluchte Hunde!"* from that scene in *Gladiator.*

"Oh dear Lord," muttered Marcy.

Silas had wandered close enough to hear the whole exchange and stopped to whisper to me, "Yeahhhh, she doesn't get out much," to which I replied, "We try not to let Whit either."

We chuckled till Elliot barked, "Hart, heads up!" Silas whipped around and caught the football before it clocked him.

"Nice," he muttered.

I gave him a tiny smile and a tinier shrug.

While the sun fell lower and lower in the sky, the smell of buttered popcorn drifted over from the concession stand, mixing with the dry scent of dust and alfalfa in the rows of vehicles. Whit knew how to wire the giant speakers he'd brought so that the sound came through them, and we could all sit outside in the warm June air during the movies instead of huddling inside two vehicles. In addition to the lawn chairs, we'd taken out the seat from Elliot's minivan to create a makeshift couch.

"Well, hey there, you," Elliot said softly, sitting beside me on the "couch." "Together at last."

And then—to my surprise—Silas came and sat down, *awkward as all get-out*, between me and Elliot. "That okay?" he asked Elliot, in a voice that obviously didn't care about the answer. Then—*I could not believe this boy*—put an arm around me *and one around Elliot.*

"Uh," grunted Elliot, shifting to the left to accommodate Silas, "I'd kind of like to sit by my *girlfriend*."

"Oh, right," said Silas. "Silly me." Then he *picked me up* and set me down between them, first dragging me slowly over his lap.

"Why are you doing this?" I hissed at Silas.

"Doing what?" he whispered back. "Just switching seats with you." It was so nearly identical to what he'd said during our first detailing that for a second I felt angry at him. But no—this was Silas, my *friend*, and we were going to be good to each other this summer.

Elliot picked up my hand and began kneading it out of habit. "Where you guys from again?" he asked Silas, trying hard to be peaceable.

Silas was looking at Elliot's hand massaging mine and didn't answer.

I answered for him. "They moved from Alaska," I said, then—trying to find some common ground—added, "Silas is a runner." Elliot was a record holder in our school for football and track. "The Filipino Palomino" is what the *Green Lake Times* called him.

"Yeah, what's your mile?" he asked Silas.

For the first time since I'd met him, Silas looked a little shy. "Oh, I do distance . . ."

But I knew and shared his average, and Elliot raised his eyebrows, impressed—but a second later, he frowned. "You play ball at all?"

"Not really," said Silas. "I mostly just run."

"Shoot," said Elliot apologetically, his Minnesota *o*'s stretching a mile long, "people here care more about football. Oh well."

"Shoot," repeated Silas.

"Behave," I growled under my breath, not sure which boy it was directed to.

The movie lineup was a couple of years old. To my left, Elliot held my hand; he was finally relaxed and enjoying the movie. To my right was another story.

Silas leaned back into the van seat, long legs stretched before him, rocking his head on his neck to loosen his muscles. He leaned forward, eyes wide, and I could almost hear his mind humming.

Things always seem more important in the dark, more significant, more profound: he pushed his knee next to mine, and when I moved it away, Silas cracked his back, twisting a little in his seat, ending up half an inch nearer to me, and pressed his knee to mine again.

Was this all just to piss off Elliot? Why?

In any case, it wasn't working, because Elliot didn't even notice how close Silas was sitting to me, our bodies touching at the foot, knee, hip, and shoulder. Silas proffered the tiniest lift of the side of his lips, this sweet little grin of victory without turning his head at all.

What in the world?

Elliot held my hand, thoughtlessly making circles with his thumb. Marcy's eye wandered from the screen to Elliot every ten minutes while Bridget twirled her fingers in her long red hair, making tiny tendrils without noticing. Beside Laurel, Whit was leaning over to whisper something that made her laugh as he nodded toward the movie.

Then Whit left his seat, momentarily disappearing into the side door of the minivan, and reemerged with a bottle that he passed around the group, the smell of black licorice preceding it. I took a healthy gulp, and it burned on its way down like swallowing cough syrup.

What would Dad say if he knew? I asked myself. But Dad doesn't know—and he won't. There's church in the morning. He won't even ask about tonight.

When I passed the bottle to Silas, he waved it off, and my thoughts changed direction. Forget what Dad would think—what does Silas think?

And why did I care so much?

I couldn't even tell you what movies were playing. Something with weapons. Then something with kissing. My head was a mess, what with Elliot holding my hand on one side and Silas pressing into me on the other. I felt exhausted and—almost literally—pulled in two directions.

Which was ridiculous.

You are here with Elliot, I reminded myself. Your *boyfriend*.

It was already one in the morning when the final movie started. On the screen, a young farmhand visited a country carnival and boarded a rickety old roller coaster. Ominous music swelled in the background, so it wasn't a surprise when the coaster flew off the tracks . . . but right before it crashed, the boy woke up, no longer a farmhand but a famous actor, living in Hollywood.

"Shit," muttered Silas and glanced at his sister. I did too.

She stared hard at the screen, eyes wide, and *seemed* okay enough—except I knew her brain was working overtime with *what ifs*.

"What should we do?" I whispered to Silas.

"I don't know."

"What's wrong?" Elliot asked on my other side.

"Nothing," both Silas and I lied.

The boy in the movie was learning the ropes of life on the set of his daytime drama from his pretty costar. The two of them went to kiss and then he woke up again, this time as the oldest of seven children in an abusive home.

Laurel's face didn't betray her thoughts, but I imagined they were manic. I was worried—for her and for myself—that she might have a reaction—or worse, a breakdown, in front of my friends and in this crowd. She'd been triggered by far less before.

On the screen, the raging, drunken father hit the boy, who woke once again. Another new reality.

"Laurel," Silas said softly. She looked over at him. "Let's go." She nodded and got to her feet so readily I knew I'd been right about what was going on behind her calm exterior.

"You're leaving now?" Whit asked. "In the middle of the movie? You should stay." He tugged at Laurel's hand, and for a second, she appeared to doubt her decision.

"It's late," Silas said with authority. "Coming, West?"

I hesitated.

"We need a navigator," Silas said.

Elliot threw an arm around my shoulder. "Dude, use your phone."

"No reception," Silas said, holding up his phone as evidence.

I looked at Laurel. She had that same wild, lost look in her eyes that I'd seen before on her worst days.

I looked at Silas. "Please," he said softly.

I stood to my feet.

"What the hell? West? Draw them a fucking map." I hated the tone of Elliot's voice—jealous, possessive, incensed.

Elliot and Silas both stared at me.

"Shut the hell up," someone growled from another nearby group. "We're trying to watch the movie!"

I bent toward Elliot, kissed him hard on the lips, then apologized quickly, "I'm sorry, I'm sorry, I'm sorry. I'll call you." He stared after me as I climbed, along with the Harts, into Papa Arty's pickup: Silas in the driver's seat, me beside him, and Laurel by the window. Elliot blinked when Silas turned the pickup's lights on.

We drove the dirt path through the movie area and onto a back road between two fields where the corn stalks were climbing out of the earth. We were a few miles outside Enger Mills, and the night felt thick and black.

"Elliot's going to be so pissed at me," I muttered.

"Sorry," Silas mumbled back.

I didn't say anything to him, just leaned over Laurel and rolled the window down to let the night air work like a salve. "Laurel, you okay?"

"No." Her voice was small, even in the tiny space of the cab. It slipped out the window and was left behind in the road.

"It's just a movie," I said to her. "Just a stupid movie."

She laid her head on my shoulder and closed her eyes.

"Laur, don't let this get to you," Silas said, staring straight ahead, hands tight on the steering wheel. "It's just science-fiction shit."

But she was shaking.

"Do you have something you can take to calm you down?" I asked.

"My beta blocker's at home," she said.

"Perfect," quipped Silas under his breath.

"Shhh, okay. That's okay," I said, and took her hand. She squeezed it hard, and I let her. The three of us drove in silence, and after a while, Laurel stopped shaking and her grip relaxed. Her head felt heavy on my shoulder. "She's asleep," I whispered to Silas.

He let out a giant breath.

"I was surprised when you spoke up tonight," I confided. "I thought maybe you'd just tell her you were leaving through some twin power."

Silas snorted. "That's ridiculous," he said matter-of-factly.

"What?!" I said, trying hard not to wake Laurel. "You hear stories like that all the time. Once on *August Arms*, there was a story about twin girls—one was kidnapped and left to freeze to death in a cabin on a mountain, but the other twin knew just where to lead the authorities to find her sister, even though she had never been on the mountain and had never seen the cabin before. They climbed into the detective's car together and she would—calm as anything—say 'left' or 'right' until they found her sister."

"That's just creepy," he said. At this early hour of the morning, the road belonged to us alone. The moon was big and yellow and very low; up ahead of us, it seemed to be biting into the horizon, perhaps peeking into the windows of the Harts' sunroom in Heaton Ridge. I located Saturn on my own.

"The same night," I continued, "they told a story about these fraternal twins—the boy was playing baseball in the yard with some friends, and the girl was inside the house. The boy got hit in the face by a line drive but somehow wasn't hurt, but the girl ran out into the yard, blood dripping from her nose. You've never had anything like that?"

"Coincidence," Silas said. "The closest thing we ever had to that was . . . well, okay. So, we grew up in Cape Canaveral, and we played pickup ball with other kids from our neighborhood, and Laurel and I always knew where the other one was on the court."

I smiled. "I always forget you grew up in Florida."

"Yeah, my parents were NASA hotshots. That's where they met—they both had internships at Kennedy Space Center."

"So badass!"

"Yeah," Silas admitted. "When we played basketball, we

would do this dumb thing."

"Tell me."

He laughed a little, and Elliot and the movie started to feel far away.

"We'd put a two over our hearts." He demonstrated, holding out two fingers and placing them on his chest. "It started because of our basketball team name: Hart2Hart. Laurel picked it." He grinned without taking his eyes off the road. "I don't know. It was like a little secret code for a million things. *I love you. You're my twin. I've got your back.* It's sissy, right?"

"No," I said. "I think it's sweet."

"We still do it."

"I know." Silas glanced at me, and I smiled. "What was it like growing up with Laurel?"

"It was fine."

"The human thesaurus just described something as *'fine'*?"

"It was *curious*," he amended. "Our childhood was buried in books. Mom and Dad let us stay up as late as we wanted so long as we were reading. In elementary school, we read our Shel Silverstein books so much that we could recite every poem. We both liked the same stuff—books with magic and disguises and kid geniuses and idiot parents. Then the gulf started to widen in fifth, maybe sixth, grade. By junior high, I was reading the classics and mountains of whichever poets my favorite teacher put in my hands, but Laurel started reading sci-fi."

I loved the way he talked about books—I could tell that,

just like Gordon, Silas found them "good company."

"Laurel read this philosophy book in eighth grade—somewhere around there—and afterward, she looked at me in that creepy way of hers and asked, 'What if there is no God?'"

The brakes of the old pickup made obscene grinding noises at an intersection, and we both grimaced a little and glanced at Laurel, but she didn't wake up.

"And then sophomore year," he continued, "she started to cry a lot. I mean, all the time. I didn't know what to do or how to help her. Then, the *next* year, she quit eating. I mean, she'd eat when Mom and Dad forced her. It wasn't really anorexia—like with a lot of dancers—it was more like just losing interest in food. So her stomach got really messed up—all the anxiety and her weird eating habits—so she missed a lot of school and did the rest of junior year, at home, online."

We were entering Green Lake city limits now, driving in from the south. Silas slowed down as we drove through town, which was as quiet and still as a ghost town, the only din of noise and energy coming from the Mean Green Pub.

He drove past my house and toward his own. "You missed my street."

"I want to drop Laurel off first."

When we got to Heaton Ridge, it took a bit of rousing to wake Laurel, and she looked really confused when we did, but Silas convinced her to go inside and head straight to bed. "Got it?" he asked. "No Googling the movie."

She used the garage code and went indoors, then Silas backed out of his driveway to take me home. "She'll be okay, right?" I asked.

"I hope so, West. She's on meds, and she has a new therapist here, but nothing seems to help. You can't reason with her; solipsism always wins. She just thinks you're an illusion, a projection of her own mind. So the good days I swallow like grace on a spoon."

It was a lovely image. I wanted so much to say something useful.

Instead I said: "I'm staying with my cousins in the Cities this week."

"That's right; I think you mentioned that. Monty and Mae?" He turned down Cedar, and in the distance, Whit's and Marcy's cars still sat in the church lot. I wondered what they thought of Silas and Laurel and of my sudden exit with them.

"Yup. I'll be back for the Fourth. Trudy will be here, remember? I'll introduce you!"

He smiled. "Deal."

We pulled into my driveway. My parents had left the porch light on for me, and it glowed like a halo just above the front steps. It was nearly two a.m., nothing awake on Cedar Street but the cicadas.

"So, Elliot doesn't like me," Silas said, suddenly changing topics as I unbuckled my seat belt, realizing for the first time that I had stayed in the middle seat, right beside Silas. His familiar sandalwood smell—peppery and musky like scented lumber—mixed with the scent of freshly mown grass coming in through the open window. I thought of his knee pressing into mine tonight.

"Well, *durr*," I said.

"What's that supposed to mean?"

"You acted like a crazy person tonight—were you *trying* to rile him up? Why get him pissed off over nothing?"

"Nothing?"

"Nothing," I repeated emphatically. "*I* am dating *Elliot*"—I pointed to myself—"and *you*"—I poked his chest—"are dating *Beth*. Remember, your *gorgeous* little girlfriend in the short skirts?"

He looked thoughtfully at the spot where I had poked him. "Yeah," he said.

"Yeah?" I said with incredulity. "You drive me crazy sometimes, you know that?"

"You know you're beautiful, don't you, West?"

It almost knocked the wind out of me. *"Me?"*

"Durr," he said awkwardly to his steering wheel.

I grinned at his uncustomary discomfort. I went to open the passenger door but paused and turned back to him. "You drive me crazy."

"You said that already." He was grinning like a total goon. "Hey!" he said as if just remembering something. He reached beneath his seat and pulled out a small container. "Here."

"What is it?"

"Cookies. Oatmeal chocolate chip. Maybe now you can find it in your heart to forgive me for crashing your date."

"Maybe," I said. "Depends on how good they are."

"Oh, they're good."

We looked at each other then while the pickup engine purred. "You drive me crazy," I said again, quieter this time.

"You might have mentioned that before," he said softly.

After a long pause, I said, "I have to go." I opened the door and stepped out of the pickup. "Good night, Silas," I said, closing the door behind me.

But through the open window he called after me, "'Just fine' isn't how you should be kissed, West." His smile had returned full force.

"Good *night*," I said again, without turning around.

I didn't want him to see that my face matched his.

fourteen

The nine a.m. church service came much too early the morning after the drive-in. I had missed a couple of late-night calls from Elliot, but I knew he'd be sleeping now.

In the front row, I sat between my siblings, mouthing the words to "Amazing Grace." The Hart family was conspicuously absent from the row behind us, setting off an alarm in my stomach. Even the Mayhews were gone.

Dad's message was about God's faithfulness, but I couldn't help calling it into question as my mind focused on what must be happening at the old Griggs house that morning. I slipped away after the service and called Silas as I walked across the parking lot toward our house.

"Hey, where were you this morning?" I asked.

"Laurel's freaking out."

"Great," I said dryly.

"She was asleep when I got home, but when I woke up this morning, I found her in the den on her laptop. She'd been on the computer for *four straight hours*, looking up hypnotism and prayer healers and studying forums that discussed the movie. And searching on eBay for that doll with the red dress too. She looked like a total zombie."

"That doesn't sound good."

"No. And bastards on the movie forums were discussing this quantum mechanics *bullshit* that's got her wondering if the universe is always splitting and there are all these different realities." He paused, really upset. "Then she started crying—like, really crying. Bent-over-on-the-floor crying. Mom came in and tried to help. I was standing over them, watching it all go down like I was looking into a hamster cage. I am just so sick of this shit. West—" I heard something in the background, as if one of his parents had just poked their head into his room. "I've gotta go," he said. "I'll call you later, okay?"

"Okay," I said, wishing I were at his house, if not for Laurel then at least for Silas.

I sat on the steps alone, expecting my family to be home soon. I wondered about the methods Laurel had researched in the early-morning hours. Hypnotism. Would something like that really work? I didn't know anything about it. It sounded kinda hokey to me, but what if it could honestly make Laurel forget about ideas that were preying on her? Then again, even if it did make her forget, it would be up to the rest of us to keep her from ever rediscovering, wouldn't it? Silas and I couldn't even protect her from a drive-in movie last night; there was no way we could keep her safe. The answer was to somehow unlock Laurel's mind.

It all seemed so impossible.

I pictured her on the floor of their den, huddled over as if she had stomach cramps while her mother tried to calm her down and her brother stared at the whole scene in frozen horror. The return of the banshee. I felt terrible for Silas; I could go the rest of my life without hearing those screams again.

"Whatcha doing, kiddo?" Mom asked as she and my siblings climbed the front steps.

"Just thinking," I said. "Is Dad on his way?" I wondered how much Glen and Teresa had told him about Laurel's condition.

"Oh, he's off again, heading over to the hospital with the Talcotts. Miriam Talcott—you know, Tony and Janie's grandma?—isn't expected to make it much longer, and Dan and Monica asked your dad to come to the hospital and be with the family."

If Mrs. Talcott died today, we virtually wouldn't see Dad for the next week or so—first, there'd be the "last rites" or whatever it was that he did alongside deathbeds; then, comforting the family; then, planning and executing the funeral; and after that, a head-splitting migraine that would leave him cooped up in my parents' bedroom for twenty-four hours. After all that, he'd be behind on planning his sermon, so he'd practically live in the office all of Saturday just to get ready for Sunday morning. "This blows," I said, and then, "I know, I know. Don't say 'blows.'"

"Your dad's a good man," Mom said, parroting the rest of the town. "Come inside, all right? Lunch is in the Crock-Pot."

"Five minutes," I promised.

It was a month into summer and I'd hardly seen my dad.

Was it my fault? Sure, I'd been busy—but I thought of all the times I had sought him out, stopped by his office, asked Mom where he was or when he'd come home, and I realized that, no, *he* was the busy one.

It hadn't been this way when I was younger. When Libby was a baby, and before Shea was born, my dad used to come into my bedroom every night, read to me, and listen to me say my prayers, which usually amounted to saying "God bless" everyone I knew even a tiny bit.

There was this one book I especially loved because of its tiny pictures, and Dad read it using different voices. *Wink & Wallace Do the Waltz*—about a girl named Wink, who was hosting a dance, and about her father Sir Wallace, who had to fight through forest and fence and fire and flood to get to the party to dance with his daughter.

Mom thought it would give me nightmares, reading about disastrous obstructions before bed, but it never did—I loved the way Sir Wallace was so brave and so persistent to get to his daughter. When Dad started calling me Wink, I was quietly thrilled. It always made me think *my* dad would do anything to get to *me*. A couple of times he even let me get out of bed and stand on his feet, and together we'd "waltz" around the room till Mom would whisper up the stairs, "Kerry! It's *way* past her bedtime!"

So I'd snuggle under the covers, and he'd rub my back while he told me stories. Stories about his childhood and the trouble that he and his best friend Tommy D would get in to, about the animals that Grandpa Paul had on the farm where Dad grew up, about how he'd met Mom, about their first dates. He stayed until I fell asleep.

And even after Shea was born, we still reserved Saturday nights for our family. We'd play Mouse Trap or Cootie or watch a movie, make pizza or stovetop popcorn. I loved those nights, when the five of us were cozy in our little parsonage and we got Dad all to ourselves.

It occurred to me now as I sat outside my house that I couldn't even remember the last time Dad was in my room—those nights when he'd read me stories and rub my back felt like another lifetime. Was it Dad's fault? Was it mine, for whining about family nights and being a typical moody teenager? Was it really anyone's fault?

My heart was a heavy, wet sponge in my chest, one I needed my dad to wring out.

My dad: busy, absent, distracted—a good man.

⋆ ⋆ ⋆

Elliot called that afternoon. "Shit," I muttered when I saw his number show up. I'd forgotten to call him back.

"Hi," I said, almost flinching at what I knew was going to be an uncomfortable conversation. Then, hearing how abrasive my voice was, I overcompensated with a cheery "How's your day?"

"Hey," said Elliot, his voice flat. "Can we talk, West?"

"Of course," I said. "About?"

"You *know* what. That asshole hijacked our date, and then you *left with him*! I felt like an idiot sitting through that movie."

"I'm sorry," I said.

"Are you?" He didn't sound angry—only hurt—and that made me feel worse.

"Yes."

Elliot was quiet for a while, then said, "This sucks. This summer, I mean. It just fucking sucks. I feel like . . . like everyone was busy, so you found new friends."

What could I say? It was mostly true. "Did you want me to sit inside and read all summer? Spend every day at the beach listening to Marcy and Bridget gossip?"

"Yes," he said honestly. "I guess I did." After a moment, he said, "I hate being the jackass. It's who people expect me to be. Like being able to catch a football means I'm allowed to treat people like shit—"

"You're not a jackass."

"—and I hate that. So I'm not going to tell you to stop

hanging out with him, because I don't want to be *that guy*, you know? But I just want you to know I felt like shit when you left last night."

I breathed in deeply and let it all out in a noisy exhalation. "Okay."

"Okay?" he asked, and I couldn't tell if he was clarifying what I'd said or if he was stunned by my noncommittal response.

"I'm sorry," I amended. "Look, I can't really explain it, but something was wrong with Laurel last night, and I wanted to make sure she'd be okay."

Elliot was quiet for moment. "Really?"

"Yes."

He didn't press for any details, for which I was grateful.

"I really like the Harts," I continued, "and I want you to like them too. Let's get the whole group together again. The Fourth of July. Trudy will be home; the camp staff gets it off. We can watch fireworks from the roof of the old Griggs place. I know Mr. and Mrs. Hart won't mind. What do you think?"

"I'd rather it would be just me and you," he said.

"On their roof?" I teased.

"Anywhere," he said, and it was supposed to sound like a joke, and it was so far from a joke, and we both knew it, so Elliot rushed to say, "That sounds good. Fourth of July. I'm in. If that's what you want."

"That's what I want," I said.

★ ★ ★

That evening, I was reading and trying to avoid Libby and Shea as they raced around the house, when Silas called. "I have to get out of here," he said. "Can I come over?"

"My siblings are the most annoying creatures on this earth," I said doubtfully, hearing a high-pitched squeal from one of them and then something being knocked over. Dad had brought home these stupid paper dolls for Libby, somehow failing to realize that, at twelve, she was way too old for them, and she and Shea had been chasing each other around with them all night.

"Honestly, I can't imagine that any sibling is more frustrating than my own right now." His voice sounded so tired—as if it were dragging suitcases of defeat. I wondered at which point over the last few weeks I had learned the nuances of his voice. The sheer exhaustion I heard made me wish that I could save him.

"Ugh, family," I said. "Listen, come pick me up. We'll go somewhere else."

"Okay, bring the radio."

"I will."

"Leaving now."

I assumed that he'd text me from the driveway, but fewer than five minutes later, he was knocking on my bedroom door as he pushed it open.

"You can't be in here," I told him right away, half because my room was its usual messy hovel, half because those really were the rules.

"Your parents sent me up," he said.

"They—they *did*?" I asked.

He nodded.

"Weird. Okay. Let's go."

"Your room smells like you," he said.

"Dirty pillow and dusty shelves?"

He laughed. "No," he said. "Like black cherries and book pages. And molasses."

"Molasses?"

"Brown sugar, maybe." He closed his eyes, breathed in deeply, and confirmed, "Yup, brown sugar."

Just outside my open door, Libby tore after Shea with a paper doll in each hand, past my room and down the stairs. We followed them down.

"Going out!" I shouted from where I stood by the front door.

Mom was lost in her scrapbooking and said absently, "All right, have fun!" Dad was reading the newspaper, home for once.

Shea suddenly braked, and Libby slammed into him. "Are you the new Elliot?" he asked Silas.

Libby's eyes were as wide as I imagined my own were. Mom and Dad looked up.

"Because that'd be okay, if you are," Shea added.

I was tongue-tied, but Silas didn't miss a beat. "Sure am." He picked my brother up under the armpits, tossed him into the air, then tucked Shea under his arm like a human-sized football. He ran across the living room with a stiff arm like the Heisman pose and shouted, "Touchdown!" in the "end zone." Then he looked at Libby. "Should I spike the ball?"

She nodded, grinning, but Shea was screaming in delight, "Noooooo!"

Silas pretended to spike Shea into the ground and then, from behind Shea, held up each of my brother's hands in a victory celebration.

Libby and Shea were laughing; my mom was laughing too. My dad looked pleased—and maybe a little confused.

"We've gotta go," I said before Shea—or my dad—could ask any more questions. Silas waved to my family as we left.

We drove to the Green Lake beach, even though it was closed after sundown. Silas parked in the empty lot, and we got out of the car and walked to the lifeguard stand, me scrambling to keep up with Silas's long strides. In spite of the tiny intermission with my family, I hadn't forgotten the reason we were at the beach: things were bad at the old Griggs house. His frustration made him *fast*.

He climbed up first and then helped me, before pulling his sweatshirt hood over his head and leaning back. The wooden stand, painted white, was like a caricature of a chair, the seat so huge that even Silas's long legs barely hung over the end. "Your brother and sister are fun," he said, then admitted, "It's like the freaking apocalypse at my house. My grandparents have been there all day, and Mom's on edge. And Dad—well, it's not good."

I sat beside him, knees pulled up to my chest. A light from the parking lot shone on us, and Silas groaned to see it was a cop car's headlights. "It's okay," I said to Silas, waving to the police officer. "Sgt. Kirkwood is Trudy's dad. He'd let me get away with anything short of murder." The squad car drove away silently.

"I am *not* used to this small-town thing yet," Silas murmured. "Is it time for your show?"

"You don't want to talk?"

"We will. I don't want you to miss your show. Besides, I feel about a thousand times better already just being away from home and with you." In the dark, and with his hood up, I couldn't see his face, but a thrill went through me. I felt powerful, like some sort of human talisman. I wanted to push his hood back, cup his face in my hands so that he had to look me in the eyes, and tell him, *I will stay as long as you need.*

Instead, I pulled the radio from my pocket and we listened to *August Arms*. Tonight's stories were about the search for another dimension, theories on the JFK assassination, and a hypothetical roller coaster designed to kill its passengers. The show's host explained how a PhD candidate at a London art school created an art concept for a coaster with seven consecutive loops that inflict an intense gravitational force on the passengers that starved the brain of oxygen.

Silas turned the radio off. "That makes me sick," he said, leaning back again. "Hypothetical shit. Why do people spend so much time thinking about ridiculous things?"

"I don't know. Sorry."

"It's okay. It's not the show. I just—" We sat in the dark, quiet for a while, and then Silas said, "My dad got an offer from UA–Fairbanks to go back to teach an eight-week summer session, and he told them before that he wasn't sure, but now . . . well, I guess he's gonna do it. He tried to pass it off as some great opportunity, but I can tell he just wants to get away. Especially after today."

"That's terrible!" I said, shocked. "He's *leaving*?"

"I mean, it's been on the table all summer—actually, since before we left. We already had the tickets even. The timing just"—he sighed—"really, really sucks. Now, when Laurel's so messed up. And it's just . . . unceremonious."

It was a weird choice of words, but seeing as he was the human thesaurus, I let it go.

"And ignoble. And risky. And *necessary*."

I narrowed my eyes at him, confused. "Um, are we still talking about your dad leaving?"

Silas put his hands to his face and rubbed at his eyes as if he was exhausted—or gearing up for war. Green Lake was smooth as black ice in front of us. All the way across the lake we noticed Silas's neighbors in Heaton Ridge, or rather, their yard lights, which were perfectly reflected in the dark, still waters. Silas exhaled deeply, pressed his lips together, then looked at me and said, "So, what do you want, Westlin Beck?"

"From you?" I asked.

He laughed. "From life. From the universe. Everyone has

some deep-seated desire, don't they? What's yours?"

"Oh." Silas's question made my blurry outline appear like a strange fog. "I guess I want to go to college and get a good job. Get married someday."

"Do you?" he asked.

This time I laughed. "Uh, yes. Was that answer not good enough for you, Mr. Hart?"

He shrugged. "I just don't think that's it, that's all. I mean, sure, you might want those things—a lot of people do—but I don't think they're your real passion."

My mind raced, looking for a place to land—a passion, a real passion. "I don't know," I conceded. "I have no goals. My life is so—unremarkable."

He looked at me suddenly, frowning hard. "Okay, *false*," he said.

"No, it's true," I said. "I have no solid outlines." I hoped he would know what I meant, because I wasn't sure I could describe it to him. "I'm undefined."

"I can define you," he said. "Or start to, at least."

"Oh, you can, can you?" I teased. "Well, let's hear it, Hart."

He pulled his hood off now and treated me to that grin of his—the one that made me want to take flight, the one that felt like a storm cell was raging in my chest, thunder and lightning and hurricane-strength winds and all.

The one that left me so, so confused.

I needed Trudy to come sort me out. Something. Someone.

"Let's see. Westlin Beck," he said, "you're hilarious, and you like quirky, vintage humor, and you're so brilliant it's actually intimidating. You're jealous that every person in Green Lake gets your dad's attention before you do."

"Is it that—"

"Shh, don't interrupt. You'd do anything for a friend, and you're fascinated by words because there's nothing you love more than a good story—though I think we disagree on what makes a story *great*, a capital-*S* Story, you know? I'm still untangling it all, to be honest, but knots intrigue me. I mean, you're this incredible contradiction, but you're not *undefined*."

How did he—? An incredible contradiction? Flustered, I asked, "And what do you want?"

He didn't hesitate: "I want Laurel to be happy. I want to *not care* if Laurel's happy."

"But she's not," I whispered.

"And I do," he added, as the sky came close to hear us breathe.

fifteen

Elliot called when I was already in bed that night. "Do you think I'm a contradiction?" I asked him. "An *incredible* contradiction," Silas had said. "Knots intrigue me."

"What do you mean?" he asked.

"Like, that I'm complicated."

"I guess so."

"Is that something you like about me?" I prompted. I smelled my pillow, then some strands of my hair—did I really smell like black cherries and book pages? Maybe. The brown sugar smell was from my soap.

"I like everything about you," he said.

"You're sweet," I said, yawning.

"Did someone say you're complicated?"

"Not exactly."

"Was it Hart?"

I was quiet. I knew that bringing up Silas would only make Elliot mad. "No," I lied. "It was Libby." I rolled my eyes at my stupid choice: yeah, my twelve-year-old sister would totally be using words like "contradiction."

"I stopped by your place tonight."

"I was hanging out with Laurel." *Dammit.* I hated that I couldn't stop lying.

"Oh." He sounded relieved. "Your brother said you went somewhere with Silas."

"Well, yeah," I backpedaled. "He drove me there. To hang out with Laurel."

"Oh—I guess that's good. Is she okay? I know you said something was wrong at the movie. And she was all quiet and skittish."

"Like Libby?"

He laughed. "Yeah. Hey, Lori and Laney have been begging to have Libby over—you should come too. They miss you."

"I miss them too."

"West, what do you like about *me*?"

The sudden switch back to our previous topic jarred me. In Elliot's voice, there was so much insecurity that it broke my heart. "All our history," I said. "And that you respect me. And that you're not into high school drama. And all the thank-you notes you write to the seventh-grade girls who buy you roses on Valentine's Day."

He laughed. "My mom makes me do that."

"Good cover story, tough guy," I said. "I know better."

Elliot laughed again; I loved the sound of it, so wholesome, so familiar.

"Know what else I like?" I added.

"What's that?"

"The way you take care of Whit."

"When I can," he said, his voice bittersweet. "When he lets me."

"It's all you can do," I said, thinking yet again of Silas and how this town was full of heroes.

I was supposed to leave for my cousins' place the next day, but my aunt called in the morning, saying that she and Mae were en route from the lab to the pharmacy. Strep throat, still contagious.

With my day suddenly free, I called Silas to see if he wanted to go to the beach. He didn't answer, not all morning, so finally I just stopped over at his house. I stepped inside and shouted, "Hello?" up the stairs.

I was halfway up the flight when Teresa called from the kitchen, "West, is that you?"

"Hi! Yeah. Is Silas home?" I asked, pausing on the stairs.

She came out of the kitchen and gave me a funny little frown. "No, he's not. I thought—didn't you see him last night?"

"Well, yes, but I guess I usually see him most days."

"No, I mean, I thought he said he was going to tell you that he was going back to Alaska with his dad."

It was like a punch in the gut. "Back to Alaska?" I said, as if the three words were in another language.

"Well, shame on him," she said. "I would have thought he'd have mentioned it to you. He and Glen have had tickets for forever, but they really only made the decision yesterday. He didn't tell you?"

"No," I said, my throat feeling dry and scratchy. I clutched the stairway railing hard. "Back to Alaska?" I asked again, hoping I'd misheard her when she'd really said her son was out getting groceries.

She nodded.

I was panicking far more than was appropriate. "I should go," I said to Teresa, a little breathlessly.

"Laurel's upstairs if you want to say hi. I'm sure she'd love to see you," she said with an encouraging smile.

"I'll have to come back later." I was going to start crying in about four seconds.

As I biked back over the bridge and toward my house, I thought of the words he had used just the night before: "unceremonious," "ignoble," "risky," *"necessary."*

Angry tears of betrayal ran down both of my cheeks.

"We already had the tickets," he had said. *Tickets*, not ticket. One for his dad. One for *him*.

I thought I might throw up.

I had even asked him last night if we were still talking about his *dad*, and he had never answered.

My legs were shaking, so I got off the bike, let it crash to the ground, and sat down in the ditch. What had all that been about last night—all the "What do you want?" and "I can define you." It was bullshit—and a heartless, cowardly good-bye.

And I had thought him a hero.

I knew I shouldn't, but I pulled out my phone and texted him: Silas Hart, you are a FUCKING BASTARD.

I called Elliot. Voice mail. Trudy. Voice mail. I called Gordon, even though I *never* called Gordon.

Voice mail. *And Gordon never went anywhere.*

"I really don't care," I said aloud through a rasping voice and tears that proved otherwise. "Really," I said again and walked my bike down the main road into town.

Mark Whitby intercepted me before I got there. "You need a ride?" he asked, looking at my bike.

"I need a friend," I admitted.

We went to the beach, me and Whit, and we sat together on top of a picnic table in the shade, our feet on the same bench. The breeze coming from over the lake felt nice, but I spotted Silas's house on the other side and felt sick all over again.

"You gonna tell me what's wrong?" Whit asked, nudging my knee with his.

But it was difficult to explain my extreme reaction over a boy who was *not* my boyfriend to my boyfriend's best friend. I just said, "I'm really, really lonely."

"Did you and Elliot break up?" he asked, looking shocked.

"What? No, of course not!"

Whit's shoulders relaxed and he exhaled deeply.

"Why would you even *ask* that?" I demanded.

Whit shrugged, his classic escape maneuver.

I wondered if he was thinking of the drive-in. He said, "So tell me about Laurel," and I knew that he was.

"She's cool. She's a dancer."

"Nice."

I was irritated thinking about the Harts, Silas's betrayal still slicing through my heart. The tears threatened to start again.

"I'm sorry you're lonely," Whit said quietly.

"It's okay," I said back, even though it wasn't.

"You should come with me out to Sloane's tonight."

"Tonight?" I looked hard at Whit. "Simon's having a party on a *Monday*?"

"It's not a party, just a group of people hanging out."

"Oh. So a party, then?" I said, annoyed.

Whit frowned. "It's not a big deal. What's your problem with it anyway?"

I pretended to think. "Let's see . . . last fall . . . me, Trudy . . . following Elliot around while he called your phone till we found you *passed out in the cornfield* next to your puke? Yup, I think that's it. Trudy was about five minutes from calling her dad."

Whit pressed his lips together, stared out at the lake. "Sorry you're lonely," he said again. I lay my head on his shoulder; it was as close as Whit would come to saying, "Me too."

"Hello?" I shouted when I walked into my house after Whit had dropped me off. "Anyone home?"

"Hi," said Shea, sitting on the couch, looking small.

"Hey, kid," I said, my voice softening at the sight of him. "Where is everyone? Are you okay?"

"Mom took Libby over to see Lori and Laney. Dad's at the church; Mom told me to stay on the couch and watch cartoons till he came home to make me lunch. She said it would only be a few minutes."

"But he didn't come?"

Shea shook his head.

"Did you eat?"

He shook his head again.

"Why didn't you have cereal? Or call Mom? Or walk over to Dad's office?"

He burst into tears. "Mom said to stay on the couch!"

"Oh, *Shea*," I said. "I'm sorry, bud." I sat beside him and pulled him into a hug. His little body curled into me. I wanted to cry too. "It's okay," I said, rubbing his back. "It's okay. It's okay."

After his tears stopped, I made him a grilled-cheese sandwich and, welling up with sisterly generosity, even removed the crusts. He ate at the breakfast bar and told me about the cartoons he'd watched, already bouncing back strong, but when my dad walked into the house a half an hour later, I glared at him. "You were supposed to make Shea lunch," I accused. "He waited all afternoon for you."

Dad's face fell, and for a moment, I almost abandoned my anger for pity.

"Oh, Shea," he said. "I'm sorry. I was just headed over when Rob Taylor stopped in, and then we got talking, and then I . . . I forgot. You okay?" Shea nodded, quick to forgive as he eagerly chewed his grilled cheese. Dad ruffled Shea's hair. "Good." Then, to me, he added, "Thanks, Wink."

I nodded curtly, feeling less charitable than Shea, when my phone started to vibrate.

My blood pressure skyrocketed just seeing the name on the screen. Silas.

I took his call on the porch. "Hi," I said, my voice cold and cruel. "I hate you."

"What the hell, West?" he asked.

"Are you in Fairbanks?"

"Layover in Anchorage. West, what's *wrong*? Are you with your cousins?"

"What the hell do you think is wrong, you bastard?! You went *back to Alaska* and didn't even tell me? How am I supposed to do all our detailing alone? I thought we were supposed to be—to be *good* to each other." I bit back tears. "And I'm just so—*mad at you*."

"West."

I started to cry; his voice sounded so far away—because it was. "Who *does* that?" I half berated, half sobbed into the phone. "Who just packs up and leaves without saying goodbye? *Assholes*, that's who."

"West," he said again. He sounded amused. "I'll be back in three days."

I sniffled. "What?"

"In time for the Fourth of July. I get to meet Trudy, remember?"

"But—but your mom said you went back to Alaska with your dad," I stuttered, confused.

"I *did*," he said. "We already had the tickets, and you were *supposed* to be out of town this week, so I went along."

"You'll be back in three days?" I repeated, my heart a little lighter.

"You weren't even supposed to notice I was gone. Why aren't you in the Cities?"

"Mae got sick. Why didn't you just tell me? Last night at the beach?"

His sigh was audible through the phone. "It's complicated. I'll try to explain when I get back."

"In three days."

"In three days," he repeated.

"Okay." I felt like an imbecile about overreacting, but relief swallowed all my other emotions whole.

"Missing me already, huh?" he said, his voice smug and thick with amusement. I pictured the twisted smile on his face.

"No," I said.

"You're a shitty liar, Westlin Beck."

I was quiet, reveling.

"Hey, want to know something?" he asked.

"What?"

"I already miss you, too."

I set my face against the grin that threatened to take over my lips. "Just hurry back."

"To the girl who hates me?"

"That would be me." In a voice that didn't mean it.

"Can't wait." In a voice that did.

sixteen

I saw a little of Laurel and a lot of Elliot in the days that followed. Laurel—who had, for the time being, ceased sobbing—begged me to invite Whit to watch fireworks from their roof, and I was happy to comply. Elliot, for his part, seemed to connect my good mood to Silas's absence, and I chose not to correct him.

On Wednesday night, Elliot took me out to Ciatti's restaurant in St. Cloud, the same place we'd had our first official date back in sophomore year. Big booths and skylights and lots of bread and oil. Silas would return later that evening, so I kept my phone on me.

"I've been emailing with that coach I told you about in North Dakota," Elliot said, pushing his empty plate back. "Some recruiters are coming to watch me play this fall. We should go tour there, don't you think?"

I wrinkled my nose as I tore a piece of bread in two. "What's in North Dakota?"

He laughed. "What's in *Green Lake*?"

"Touché."

After a pause, Elliot said, *"Me."*

"Huh?"

"Me. *I'd* be in North Dakota. I mean, if I went to school there. And maybe that'd be a reason you'd like to be there too." He looked at me and pressed, "Right? I mean . . . maybe?"

"Yes. Totally," I said automatically.

Elliot looked so serious. "Tell me where you'd rather go, West, and I'll contact their athletics office and see if they're interested in me."

"No, it's not that," I said. "I don't have anywhere in mind. I just . . . you know I don't like thinking about all that. It stresses me out." I pulled my phone out of my pocket—just to see if Silas had gotten in yet. No text.

"Are you waiting for a call?" Elliot asked.

"No. Sort of." He waited for me to explain, but I couldn't. "From Trudy," I lied, and took a big drink of water.

"What if I took next week off?" Elliot asked.

I swallowed wrong and it hurt going down. "What do you mean?"

"What if I just told my dad I needed a week to have a real summer? We could road-trip out to the Dakotas and visit some colleges, see what we think."

"I don't know; I have some detailings scheduled." A road trip? With Elliot? We'd probably have to stay in hotels. And *next week*? Silas was just getting back.

"They wouldn't be that hard to reschedule though, would they? Or maybe Hart could handle them alone."

I pursed my lips. "I don't know," I repeated.

"Okay, so no road trip," he amended. "Just a week to spend at the beach and at the movies. Hell, we'll go bowling. We'll do the kind you like with all the neon—"

"Cosmic," I said, my voice quiet.

"Yeah, cosmic! And we'll drive out into the country and listen to your radio show under the stars. What do you think?"

Panic pulled at me, and I didn't know why. Here was my boyfriend, offering to do all the things I had wanted him to do this summer, and it made me feel nervous and suffocated and overwhelmed. I chose my words carefully. "That all sounds amazing—and I'm holding you to cosmic bowling, which is the *only* appropriate way to bowl—but you don't need to sacrifice a week of pay for me. I want you to get your car."

"I don't care about the car," he said.

"I do!" I teased. "If Whit drives, he'll stay to bowl and kick my ass. I know I can at least beat *you*."

"West."

I exhaled deeply. "Elliot, please don't give up a car for a few days on the beach."

"But I *miss* you," he said, reaching across the table and taking my hand.

"I miss you too," I said, squeezing it. "Look, you're the hardest worker I know. This summer might suck, but this fall . . . everything will be different. Trust me."

Later that evening, I lay in bed listening to the sound of Chuck Justice coming from Libby's room down the hall while I thought about Elliot. The handful of lies I'd told him lately made me sick. Ours had never been a relationship like that—or, before we were dating, a friendship like that. The bell tower was my one big secret; other than that, I'd always been an open book.

Until now.

Silas Hart. My friend, nothing more.

Besides, Silas had a girlfriend. My stomach turned as I realized that he had probably spent the last three days with Beth Öster—and her short skirts. I thought I might throw up.

This was ridiculous.

Trudy would be home tomorrow. Trudy would sort me out. I'd lay out my summer like a knot of tangled necklaces and let her go to work.

Knots intrigue me.

I was going to drive myself insane.

I had said one very, very true thing tonight: Elliot was the hardest worker I knew. Busting his ass on the farm, on the football field . . . making ridiculous offers to keep me happy. I didn't deserve him. I reached into my desk drawer and pulled out my "wedding ring," slid it onto my pinkie, and stared at it, letting the weight of years build a fortress around my heart.

Then I thought of Beth Öster in the pictures I'd seen of her online: beautiful, tiny, perfect. An unbelievable math whiz, according to Silas. I wondered what they'd done this week. Had they been attached at the hip after so many weeks apart? Silas would be full of stories—would I be in any of them? Had they spent the days talking? Holding hands? Kissing? *More?*

Stop it, I told myself. It doesn't matter anyway.

But it did.

I slipped into uneasy sleep until that hazy space between late night and early morning, when Silas called. "Hey." His voice was soft, tired, relieved. Close.

"Hi," I said, doing a full-body stretch like a satisfied cat.

"Did I wake you up?"

"Mmm, yup."

"Sorry."

"It's okay," I said, yawning. "You home?"

"I am."

I pulled off the ring, which was pinching my finger. "Good."

As she had promised, Trudy also came home, and we hugged like long-lost sisters. "Tell me everything," I said to her as we climbed into her family's paddleboat from their dock just before lunch. It was an ancient aluminum pontoon Sgt. Kirkwood had made before we were born. "Are the campers crazy? Do you work with any cute boys?" *Why do you never call me back?*

She laughed, put her arm through mine, and straightened her sunglasses. Her pixie hair and big eyes made her look just like a young Michelle Williams. "The campers *are* crazy . . . but also super sweet. I help with the zip line—can you believe it?—so I had to get over my fear of that pretty fast. You wouldn't believe how much we pack in to every day, West. I'm out like Sleeping Beauty every night."

"And is there a prince?"

She took a drink from a sweating water bottle. "Actually, there are *two* boys I have my eye on: Alex and Adam Germaine. They're, um, brothers."

"Trudy Kirkwood!" My jaw dropped as we pedaled the pontoon, side by side. My legs felt strong from all the biking Silas and I had been doing. "Is this summer going to have a happy ending?"

Trudy smiled at me. "I think so." She looked thoughtful and stopped pedaling for a moment. There were people grilling, swimming, and playing Frisbee at the public beach, just north of Trudy's house, and some kids playing with sparklers at the end of a nearby dock. "But what does a happy ending really look like?" She pedaled again. "Know what I mean? One person's happiness is another person's grief."

"If you date Alex, that's his joy and Adam's grief, and vice versa?" I teased.

She nudged me and laughed. "I think that *is* what I meant, yeah, but it sounds silly when you put it that way."

On the shore, Jody Perkins rode by on his lawn mower, and we waved at him, lazy with July heat. He waved back. "So what are they like?" I asked.

"Hmmm, Alex starts college this fall at Tellham and Barr University; they recruited him for their crew team. West, you should see this guy—he's really strong and so *shy*! And he's going to be a humanities major, which just strikes me as the sweetest thing. Adam is the younger one—he's our age. He's crazy. So loud and funny, the total opposite of his brother. Every time I think I've settled on liking one of them, I'll spend time with the other brother and change my mind. They invited me to spend the weekend at their house in Eau Claire. I said yes—I hope you're not mad. It means I leave again tomorrow."

"Tomorrow?!" I complained. "You just got here!"

She grimaced apologetically. "I know, I know! Some of the other CITs are going along. Ami too."

"Ami Nissweller?"

"Yeah," said Trudy. "She's way cooler than we ever thought. Really sassy and funny, even though she uses chess terms all the time and then I have no idea what she's talking about."

"Isn't that annoying?"

"Not really. She's thinking about Tellham and Barr, too,

and so Alex told us all about his campus visit, and Ami and I have been plotting and thinking if I end up dating Alex, then maybe she and I should go there too and be *roommates*. How cool is that?"

"Roommates?" I stopped pedaling.

"Yeah, you know—like in the dorms."

"I know what roommates are, Tru." I made a face at her. "I just mean—I don't know—I kinda thought *we* would end up being college roommates."

Trudy looked uncomfortable. "Oh. I mean, yeah, that would be totally cool. But you never really talk about college. And I figured you'd want to go somewhere around here. I mean, you didn't want to come with me to camp, so I thought . . ."

"I didn't want to go to adventure camp because I don't like zip lining, rock climbing, and all that other stuff you guys do there. I thought you didn't either."

She shrugged. "It's actually kinda fun." My stomach roiled with a strange sense of detachment from my best friend. "Anyway, don't worry about the roommate thing. It was just an idea to room with Ami. If you were to come to Tellham, I would totally room with you instead."

I felt a little better—even though there was no way I'd be following Trudy and her camp friends like a little puppy. Oh well, I thought. Tru would probably change her mind after she was back in Green Lake for senior year and fell out of touch with all those Camp Summit friends—and remembered that

Ami Nissweller's place was with the chess club. What was one summer compared to a lifelong friendship? We had a foundation of years stacked on years. We shared clothes and stories and this whole town.

A tiny voice inside me reminded, *But you haven't known the Harts for very long.* That's different, I argued, but it wasn't, not really.

"Your turn," she said. "I've gotten all your voice mails and texts and emails, by the way, and I'm dying to meet the new kids. What happened with Elliot?"

"What do you mean?" I asked.

"I don't know. You always sound so hopped up on this Silas guy."

This was it—my clear opportunity to talk through things with her, to have Trudy make sense of the confusion that had been stirring in me every time Silas smiled. But I was still stinging from the whole "roommates with Ami Nissweller" thing, and besides, Tru didn't even know Silas. I had to at least wait until they had met.

"Elliot and I are fine. He's just really busy, but we call each other most nights," I said. "Speaking of, why do you never call me?"

"Oh, I know," Trudy said apologetically. "It's madness at camp from dawn to dusk. And half the time I'm on night patrol."

What about the other half? I wanted to accuse.

"So, who will be there tonight?" she asked. "Elliot?"

"Yeah," I said, "and Whit. Laurel asked me to invite him."

"That's the sister?"

"Yup. She . . . she's really cool." I caught myself withholding information from Trudy, and it felt so foreign to me. "To be honest, I've spent most of the summer so far with Silas and Laurel; I've hardly seen the girls, and Whit and Elliot are so busy."

Trudy smiled a little sadly. "Green Lake is changing. So are you."

It sounded a tiny alarm in me, especially with her sad smile. I rushed to correct her. "False," I said. "Nothing has changed. Pocket Swanson won't shut up. Jody Perkins drives that lawn mower around like it's a frickin' Porsche. It's all just the same old Green Lake." I breathed in the lake air, smelling of fresh algae and water reeds.

Trudy smiled, her eyes narrowed into clever slits. "Somehow I don't believe you."

For dinner, Sgt. Kirkwood grilled, and I sat with Trudy and her parents on their deck, enjoying the weather, which would have been far too hot without the breeze coming in from the lake. "West, I see that you've been getting by splendidly without Trudy," said Sgt. Kirkwood.

I looked at him, confused, about to bite into my hot dog, which was a tiny bit burned, just the way Sgt. Kirkwood knew I liked it.

"It's always nice to have a little company for after hours in the park," he said, then winked and took a bite of his hamburger.

Trudy looked at me wide-eyed as I blushed. "Same old Green Lake, eh?" she accused with a hint of a smile.

"Silas and I were hanging out at the beach the other night," I explained. "We were just *talking*."

"Whatever you say," Sgt. Kirkwood said. He pointed at me with his burger. "If that new kid gives you any trouble, West, you just let me know. Teresa Mayhew was no perfect angel back when we were in school together. Although I don't think Lillian ever found out about any of that, or Teresa wouldn't have lived to tell the tale. But I'll handle the new kid if he gives you trouble. You just let me know," he repeated.

I laughed. "You got it." Trudy was still looking at me skeptically. "We were just talking," I repeated.

"Mmm-*hmmm*," she said.

seventeen

The weather cooled down a little later that evening. Over at the old Griggs place, Trudy was like a visiting dignitary, first hugging Whit and Elliot, then saying, "What the hell?" and hugging Silas and Laurel too. Laurel looked supremely pleased, and since Whit was enthused by the massive telescope, she escorted both Whit and Trudy over to see it. Elliot was intrigued but pretending not to be, as he, Silas, and I sat around the fire pit. I had asked him to *please* be friendly with Silas, and I could tell he was trying his hardest when he said, "So, Hart, we should run together sometime."

"Yeah, maybe," said Silas, in which I heard *Oh, hell no.*

Elliot sipped from the patriotic drink Laurel had concocted by layering cranberry juice, blue Gatorade, and Sprite. "I think you could actually keep up with me," he said, setting down his drink by his feet—and in doing so, seeing our little orange radio resting there beside the fire pit. I saw something flit across Elliot's face and he stared hard at the radio.

Silas toyed with him. "Narcissism is good fuel, am I right?"

"Uh, sure," said Elliot, dumbly agreeing.

Trudy rejoined us, and when Elliot glanced at her, I whispered, "Mocky McMockerton," in Silas's ear. *"Play nice!"*

He whispered back, "Actually it used to be Ole Mockeroli, but it got changed at Ellis Island." I loved the feel of his warm breath on my ear and neck, loved the way he had to bend low just to be at my level, loved the strange intimacy of the simple act of sharing secrets in this tiny crowd.

I burst out laughing at his Ellis Island comment. Then—as the others looked our way—I redirected their focus, asking, "Trudy, when do you have to leave tomorrow?"

"Bright and early."

"You're leaving again?" Elliot asked.

"I'm working at a camp this summer, Elliot. Hello!" she said.

"But first she has to make a pit stop in Eau Claire to woo a pair of brothers," I added.

She elbowed me. I laughed, but Elliot said, "Why is everyone so obsessed with people from out of town?"

"Who's 'everyone'?" Trudy pressed. I loved having my pushy best friend back in Green Lake, but I wanted her to just can it for once.

Elliot mumbled something incomprehensible, then stood up, saying, "I'm going to go see what Whit's doing with that girl." He walked to the other side of the roof to examine the telescope.

"'That girl' is my sister," said Silas quietly through gritted teeth in Elliot's wake.

"Oh, don't mind Elliot," Trudy told him. "He's just used to being Green Lake's hotshot."

"Well," said Silas, "he needs to relax. I'm not out to steal any stupid title from him."

"I think he's more worried you'll steal West's attention," she said bluntly. "Which you seem to have done."

"Trudy!" I admonished, completely mortified, even as Silas laughed. I felt a blaze of heat bloom across my face, and I hoped it was too dark to notice. In the near distance, the first firework exploded over Green Lake.

Elliot, Whit, and Laurel rejoined our group around the fire, and we all oohed and ahhed over the show of colorful chandeliers, raining like glitter, and bright pops of white that stamped smoke on the sky. I felt the explosions inside me, deep in my back through my chair.

Beside me, Silas took my hand—low between our chairs so no one else saw—and laced his fingers in mine. I looked at him, but he was staring at the sky, his face impervious. My mind began to race—what did this mean exactly? Were we going to discuss this? Could anybody else tell that his fingers were intertwined with mine right now? I looked around at each person, but they were all entranced by the wonder of the sky, while I was marveling at the wonder of Silas's thumb, moving an achingly slow path back and forth over mine. My heart pounded as if I'd just run a sprint.

What game was he playing?

I needed to pull my hand away. Now.

Do it now, I ordered myself. *Now*.

Now.

. . . *Now*.

Laurel's quavering voice suddenly spoke: "I don't feel well. I'm sorry." Silas dropped my hand as Laurel stood up. "I'm gonna go to bed a little early."

"The finale will be happening in just a minute," Whit said. "You don't want to see it?"

Laurel shook her head—just the tiniest bit. "I need to go to bed. Headache."

Whit stood up. "Do you need anything? Sit down; I'll get you water or . . . or something. West, do you have an Advil? Trudy?"

"I just need to go to bed," she said, a little more urgently. "Thanks for coming, everyone. Nice to meet you, Trudy. Good night, Whit." And then she disappeared through the door, Silas right behind her, following her down the stairs.

My heart galloped like a thousand racehorses. I had held Silas's hand *while my boyfriend sat on the other side of me*.

And I had not pulled away.

My high school friends looked at me. "Is she okay?" Whit asked.

I had not pulled my hand away.

Focus! I snapped at myself. *Quit thinking about yourself for one freaking minute.*

"She'll be fine," I said, heart still trilling. "She's just not feeling well." I didn't believe it was a headache for one second, especially with the way Silas had gotten up and followed her back into the house. "Look," I said, nodding in the direction of the lake, "the finale."

What did it mean that I had not pulled my hand away?

No one acknowledged the finale, even though it was impressive. A discomfort had settled over those of us on the roof like a wet fog. Dilemma à la Laurel.

"We should go," Elliot said to the rest of us. Whit looked concerned over whether he should leave without checking on Laurel first.

"She'll be fine," I reassured him. "She gets sick kinda suddenly sometimes. She just needs a little time to rest and recover." I hoped what I was saying was true. It didn't sound particularly true. My voice was shaky.

Silas's hand, holding mine.

I needed to think, needed to process.

Needed to talk to Silas.

We all went indoors, past Laurel's closed bedroom door, and down the stairs.

Out in the driveway, my mind was still flying and finding nowhere to land. I blushed as I thought of Silas's thumb making its slow, confident circles. I reached up and touched my face. My cheeks were so warm.

Elliot had held my hand a thousand times before today, a thousand times before he was even my boyfriend, and yet it had never elicited such a dizzying response.

I had ridden over with Trudy, and Elliot had with Whit, who climbed into the driver's seat of his Civic, still looking concerned and bewildered over what had happened on the roof—over what was happening inside right now. "You guys want to come over to my place?" Elliot asked from where he stood sandwiched between Whit's car and the open passenger door.

"I'm probably going to go home," said Trudy. "I have to leave so early."

"Okay," Elliot said, "then West can ride with us."

They both looked at me.

I paused for one horrible moment, and the look on Elliot's face changed before I even said, "I think I'm going to stay and make sure Laurel's okay."

Elliot stepped away from the car and leaned his head toward me. "You're choosing him," he hissed. "You're staying for *him*."

"No, I'm not," I argued. "I'm staying for Laurel."

"Whatever lets you sleep at night," he muttered.

"*Excuse* me?" I said. "Did you really just say that?"

Trudy opened her car door and climbed in, abandoning me. I didn't blame her.

"What's your radio doing over here?" Elliot asked. "The orange one?"

"It's—it's Silas's."

"You listen with him?" he accused. "Every night?"

"Not . . . not *every* night."

It was quiet for a few long seconds that felt like hours, then Elliot said in his calm, level voice, "I don't want to say something I'll regret. I'd like for you to come over tonight, seeing as we never get time together anymore and I have the night off for once. Would you please come with us?"

I couldn't look at him.

"I'm staying for Laurel," I said again, kicking at the driveway.

The car door shut—not an angry slam, just a crisp click. I didn't look up until Whit's car was nearly to the bridge.

"*Are* you staying for Laurel?" Trudy asked from behind me. I hadn't heard her get out of her car.

"Trudy!"

She didn't press me.

My heart begged her, *Please say you'll stay an extra day. I'll stay at your house tonight; we'll tell stories in the dark. Sort me out. Ink in my blurry lines*. But I didn't ask—couldn't. I was terrified she'd say no, and that would hurt even worse.

Trudy said, "Look, can I show you something? It's a secret."

I frowned, a little wounded. "Of course you can. Why would you need to ask that, Tru?"

But you didn't tell her about Silas. About *what* with Silas? *Nothing* was going on with Silas.

Then why are you still here?

"Because it's really intensely, monstrously, terrifyingly, intimately top secret and your dad's a pastor."

"That's never stopped you before."

"I know," she said. "It's just . . . okay." She nodded toward her backseat, then opened the door. I peered in next to her as she unzipped a duffel bag, dug into its depths, and—without even pulling the item out of the bag—propped it so I could see. "Just in case," she said.

"Condoms?" I asked, then hissed, "*Trudy!* You don't even know which brother you like!"

"I like them both," she said, giggling, then opened the box, fished out a couple, and said, "You never know. You might need them too." I was flabbergasted as she stuffed them into the pocket of my jeans. "Don't let your dad see!" Then she zipped up the duffel and turned back to me. "West, don't look so shocked!"

I tried to erase the emotion from my face. "I just wasn't expecting it. Have you—before?" I braced myself to hear Trudy say she wasn't a virgin, my mind already swimming with how many other secrets she'd kept from me. I didn't think she'd gone further than second base with Tony Caprizi, this guy we knew from Enger Mills who ran track with Elliot.

"No," she said, and an avalanche of relief crashed into me. "But I've never liked someone before like I like the Germaines. I just want to be ready, you know?"

I nodded yes, but really I was just thinking, *She told me her secret. She has no secrets from me.*

My turn.

"I'm not—" I began, but suddenly Trudy was serious.

"Listen, is Laurel going to be okay?" she asked.

"Oh, sure," I said automatically. As soon as the words came out of my mouth, I doubted them. "I don't know, Tru," I revised. "I hope so."

Trudy hugged me, and she did this thing where she tickled her fingers along my shoulder blades—something she'd done for years—and it felt so normal, so deeply Tru-and-West, that my fears relaxed, and I squeezed her tight until she let out a perfect Trudy laugh, and my heart hurt to say good-bye again so soon.

"Hey," I said, "you have to let me know *everything* that happens with these brothers. *Promise me* you'll find time to call—or write, even."

"I will," she said. "Everything. You too."

"Okay. Love you."

"Love you."

She got in her car, and I waved at her as she backed out of the driveway, feeling a strange sort of sorrow. The fireworks had left a slight gunpowder smell on the air, which I noticed as I turned around and reentered the Hart home, going up the stairs and knocking on Laurel's closed door, the first one in the hallway, just as I'd guessed.

"Who is it?" came Silas's voice, irritated. Such a different mood than when he'd held my hand earlier tonight.

"It's me," I said softly and waited. A moment later, the door opened, revealing Laurel lying facedown on her bed, her arms flayed out and clutching the sides, looking for all the world as if she were gripping an erratic magic carpet. It was the first I'd seen of her bedroom—dusty-lavender walls and white curtains, a bureau topped with trophies. She had a bookcase too—but neat, tidy, not the monstrosity that overtook Silas's room.

"You okay?" I asked, stepping past Silas and into the room. Silas looked out in the hallway, as if expecting to see the rest of the gang. "They left," I explained.

Laurel spoke, but into her pillow, so I couldn't make out any words.

"Come again?" I said.

This time she turned her head so that she was looking at me, although still lying down. "Gravity wasn't working right," she said. "I felt like I was going to fly off into space."

I knelt in front of her bed so that we were at eye level. "Do you feel better now?"

"I don't know," she said as her eyes filled with tears. "A little, now that I'm in my bed. On the roof . . . and watching the sky . . . I felt so light, so . . ."

"Buoyant? Weightless?" Silas plugged in. Habit.

"Yeah," she agreed. "I had to get inside and lie down. Before I was hurled into the galaxy."

Silas sat down on a silver-colored chenille blanket at the foot of her bed.

"I kept thinking of my bed," she said, still clutching her mattress, still looking at me. "The stability of the frame, the way it was immovable. I felt like I was on one of those ejector seat amusement park rides, where your legs dangle and you wait for the launch?"

I nodded, thinking that maybe I understood her for once. Untethered: isn't that how I felt half the time, as if I was fading away into obscurity? I knew it was different, but it still made my heart warm toward her. I wanted to hold her hand again, like I had in the pickup.

"My body is starting to recover its full weight now though. But I'm scared to move too much. I don't want to disturb anything," she said.

"It's getting late," I said. "Just get some sleep, Laurel. You need rest."

Silas touched two fingers to his chest, his Hart2Hart symbol. Seeing it felt like eavesdropping. "Have a sweet dream, Laur," he said, pulling the blanket over his sister.

He and I stood up to leave, and as we walked to the door, Laurel murmured, "I am."

Her words hit Silas in the back like bullets. I saw it myself, the pain on his face as if he'd been struck.

I followed Silas into the hallway. I headed for the stairs, but Silas took my wrist and redirected me back toward the den. I had this wild and crazy thought that he was going to kiss me, but as soon as he closed the door to the den, his head fell back against it, then he slid down the length of the door and sat there on the floor, looking so terribly sad. "West?" he said, miserably.

"Yeah?" I was thinking about the condoms in my pocket. *Focus*, I told myself.

He tapped my ankle with his toe. "This is going to kill me, I think. Or her, I don't know."

"Oh, Silas." I hated the pity in my voice. I wanted so desperately to ask him about earlier tonight, but I told myself, *Not everything is about you.*

"In the East, it's called 'Zhuangzi dreamed he was a butterfly.'"

"What is?"

"The dream argument. Hutton's Paradox. Laurel's world." He was silent for a time, then, "This Chinese philosopher Zhuangzi dreamed he was a butterfly, and when he woke up, he didn't know if he was Zhuangzi who had just dreamed that he was a butterfly, or if he was a butterfly who had just started dreaming it was a Chinese philosopher."

"It's fascinating," I said.

"It's *bullshit*," he said. "I hate it. I hate it—SO—MUCH." He looked up at me. "West, I would seriously love to have just one day where I didn't think about solipsism . . . or depression . . . or"—he whispered—". . . or even Laurel. Am I a monster?"

He looked so completely broken. I knew in that moment that tonight wasn't the right time to ask about what had happened between us on the roof.

I held out my hand to him and pulled him back to his feet. "No, of course not," I said, deciding then and there that I would give him a day like that, and soon.

eighteen

"Hey, kiddo," Dad said that Sunday after the fireworks, knocking lightly on my bedroom door. He poked his head into my room, where I was engrossed in a novel I'd borrowed from Silas. "I'm taking communion over to Laurel Hart, if you want to join me."

"Yeah, sure."

In the car on the way there, we were quiet, and the silence hurt.

I said, "Did you know that Mr. Hart moved back to Alaska?"

"For *eight weeks*," he said, as if correcting me. "You say it like he abandoned the family, West."

"Well, he kind of did," I insisted. "Laurel isn't doing well *at all*, and he just took off."

"From what I understand, Laurel is rarely doing well."

"That makes it okay then? For a dad to just split?"

"I didn't say that, West."

I groused in the passenger seat, not entirely sure what I was upset about. Did I want my dad to say that Mr. Hart owed it to his daughter to be near her? I stared out the window: Did I believe that was true? If I were a parent, would I give up all my hobbies and endeavors to nurse my child to health? Yes, I thought. Yes, I would. A parent's number-one duty is to be accessible, to be there.

I looked over at my dad. He was handsome, but the lines around his eyes were more pronounced and his hair was graying around his ears. I wondered when that had started. Even his eyebrows were like salt and pepper. Suddenly, this brief drive together felt like the most important thing I'd done all summer, as if it needed to have an outcome.

"Remember our old family nights?" I broached. "We haven't done that in forever—since Shea was in kindergarten probably. How about Friday night? We'll make homemade pizza and play games, okay?"

Dad glanced over at me, a little surprised. "I thought you were the one who said family nights were—and I quote—'lamer than the compulsory badminton unit in gym,'" he said.

I laughed, even though inside I was cringing. "Well, I'm not saying it now. It's been way too long since the five of us have spent time together. You're Mr. Green Lake or something."

I wanted it to sound like a compliment, but it was tinged too deeply with accusation. I put a smile on my face and tried again: "I just think it would be really fun to have a family night. Like old times."

He looked at me again, a quizzical smile on his face, as if he was trying to tell if I was kidding.

"So how about it then? Friday night?" My voice was still so blazingly cheerful. I wondered if he could hear the masked pleading in my voice.

"Friday I have a dinner meeting with the local clergy."

I huffed out an irritated breath. "Fine, never mind."

The silence threatened to swallow us whole. I leaned my head against the car window and stared ahead at the bridge to Heaton Ridge.

"I think I'm free Saturday, though," he ventured.

I grinned and turned to face him. "Really?"

"Yeah."

"I'll talk to Mom about the pizza."

We had to wait for another vehicle to exit Heaton Ridge before we could cross the bridge into it, since recent construction had brought it down to one lane. Metal poles and bright orange netting lined each side.

"You be careful when you bike out here, Wink. Tell Silas the same," he said.

"And Laurel," I added.

After a pause, my dad agreed, "Yes. And Laurel." But he was

only mollifying me—we both knew Laurel wouldn't be biking anywhere this summer.

At the Hart home, I flung the screen door open and made to walk right in, but Dad held me back. "When you're with me, you ring the doorbell," he said. I grinned wryly and pushed the button.

Teresa answered the door. "Hi, you two! Westlin, didn't I say you could just let yourself in here?"

I smirked at my dad. "Is Silas around?" I asked.

"Upstairs."

Silas's bedroom door was open, but he wasn't inside. I moved to head toward the roof to see if he was up there, but I was caught by the sight of his sloppily made bed, a copy of *Runner's World* lying there, along with his patriotic unicorn T-shirt, laid out with great care, and his open notebook.

His poetry.

I paused for only a second, listening for his footsteps, before I stepped over to the bed. Just looking felt like such an invasion of privacy; I wouldn't allow myself to actually touch it, flip the page. But I *had* to take a look, just one look.

The page it was open to read:

> *I don't exactly know what she thinks about you. It's so obvious to me that you are exactly what she needs; still, she doesn't seem to see it. I could use some direction here. Will be waiting to hear from you. Okay, later.*

Huh.

It seemed clearly about Laurel . . . didn't it? It referenced a "she" and a "you"—was it a letter? To whom? About Laurel? *You are exactly what she needs; still, she doesn't seem to see it.* Could it be a letter to a former boyfriend of Laurel's? My mind reached for an explanation. *I don't exactly know what she thinks about you.*

Footsteps in the hallway made me step away from the notebook, a little flushed as Silas came into his room.

"Knock, knock?" I said, smiling.

"Hey!" He grinned. "Was that you who rang the doorbell? What for?"

"Dad," I said, watching him as he walked to his bed, slipping the Moleskine into his back pocket before sitting down. I felt jumpy and awkward around him. In the days since the fireworks-hand-holding incident, neither of us had brought it up. I knew I should.

I kept thinking of Elliot's accusations that night, the way he had hissed, "You're choosing *him*." The hurt in his eyes. Elliot and I had been friends since kindergarten, and this was how I treated him? I felt ashamed.

But then Silas asked, "So, what's this week look like?" and his business talk snapped me into reality.

"We have detailings tomorrow and Wednesday," I said. "And keep Thursday open, okay? I have a surprise."

"Okay." He looked at me suspiciously, then suddenly

smiled and said, "I hope it's that you bought all the *NSYNC marionettes on eBay, and we're going to film a horror movie with them. Or that we're going to set up a lemonade stand in an elevator. Or that we're going to tear a hole in the time-space continuum."

"All of the above," I said, feigning defeat. "So much for the surprise."

"How did it go with Laurel?" I asked Dad on the drive home.

"She was pretty quiet," he admitted.

"Can you help her, Dad?"

I was staring out the window, and he was quiet for so long that I looked over at him.

"I can pray," he said. "I'll ask others to pray at our local clergy meeting on Friday—I won't share her name, of course, but I think it would be appropriate to ask them to pray for a sick young lady in our community." He nodded, as if making plans. "Call me crazy, but it looked like the bread and cup made all the difference in her day."

"That's the point, right?"

"Yes, West, I suppose it is."

nineteen

On Thursday, Silas showed up at my place freshly showered and in a T-shirt demanding "MORE COWBELL" in block lettering. "I call dibs on Justin Timberlake," he teased.

"Silas Hart," I said, "I have planned for you a worry-free day, a day with no discussions about solipsism syndrome, depression, or siblings." I held out my hand, palm up. "Worries, please."

Silas grinned and pretended to deposit a huge weight into my hand. I slouched under the "heft" of it, then walked to the garbage can, which was outside for collection, and pretended to drop it in. I rubbed my hands together, dusting them off. "I want to show you some of my favorite places around here. Are you up for it?"

"Anywhere," he said, and it made me think of Elliot saying the same thing so recently.

We took my family's car to City Hall and walked around the small library, really just two rooms full of books. I stuck close to his side, waging a civil war with my emotions as I thought about the week before. But it had been dark and there had been fireworks—maybe he'd gotten a little carried away and was now embarrassed and avoiding the topic.

It was a new experience to visit the library with Silas along. Every section of the library was like its own island, one Silas had explored in the past and was now showing to me—even though, in reality, it should have been the other way around, since this was his first visit here. He started in fantasy, pointing out titles and introducing me to authors—and then we moved into young-adult fiction . . . through the classics. I noticed that he did what I liked to do—run my fingers against the spines until I found one I wanted to take a closer look at.

The sound of a summer reading program came from one room over, a horde of kids and one enthusiastic adult chanting, "Chicka chicka boom boom, will there be enough room?" but the library itself was silent except for Silas, finding book after book that he'd already read, telling me lines and characters he loved, sometimes discovering we shared favorites.

"Here," he said, pulling a book of poems by E. E. Cummings off the shelf, "I'll show you something." He checked the table of contents, flipped open to the right page, marked a place with his finger, and handed it to me.

I read the line aloud: "'Nobody, not even the rain, has such small hands.'"

Silas's eyes were shining. "I still think I've never read anything better than that. The morning I first read it, I went into some kind of shock," he said. "I hadn't known anything could be so . . . delicate and flabbergasting at the same time. It's the line that made me want to write." Just like when he'd whispered to me before the fireworks, this moment felt intimate. I loved knowing this tiny but important part of his history. I wanted to know it all.

Stop it. You have a boyfriend.

"Do I ever get to read anything you've written?" I asked him.

"What? Me?"

"Yes, you, silly!" I shoved him playfully in the arm.

He blushed. "I'm just a beginner. I haven't written anything so great as all this." He gestured, indicating the shelf of poetry.

"I'd like to read it. Someday, promise?"

"Yeah, sure. Someday," he agreed, voice as soft and deep as a purr. And I didn't care about how far away "someday" was because I was guaranteed to know Silas Hart at least as long.

We checked out the poetry book with my library card, and back in my car, I put it in the glove compartment. "Next up, we're headed to Berry Acres in Shaw, just north of here."

"What's at Berry Acres?"

"What's *not*?"

Berry Acres was a family-owned farm with free hayrides, a petting zoo, and a straw bale maze. I knew that Silas, who had not grown up in a farming community like I had, would be charmed by the puppy-sized baby goats butting their little heads against his leg, by the ponies who would lick feed from his hand, the chickens pecking around his feet. We rode a wagon around the farm, the person driving the tractor pointing out the fields of apple trees and pumpkins that weren't ripe yet, the fields of raspberries and strawberries that were. The whole place smelled of trodden strawberry guts, quality hay, inoffensive manure mixed with straw, and homemade bread.

We took our time ambling through the shade of the giant bales stacked eight feet high. "They redo the maze every summer," I told him, "and in October, they make it 'haunted' and all these parents from some Shaw booster club dress up as chainsaw murderers and deranged clowns and zombie scarecrows. My dad took me there for the first time when I was ten, and I cried." Silas laughed. "Whit makes us all go every year, and I'm not kidding—I still get terrified. It's ridiculous."

Silas said, "My friend Josh back in Fairbanks would make our group of friends go to Starvation Gulch at the university every September—the students build these ginormous wooden bonfires"—he demonstrated, spreading his hands out wide—"and they burn them all at once. It's one of the oldest traditions at the school."

"Think you'll go there?" I asked as we peered down an open but dead-end lane and turned around.

"UAF?" he asked. "Doubt it. I mean, I don't know, but I think Mom and Dad are planning to stay in Minnesota for good, or at least for a long while now. Mom likes being back in Green Lake, I can tell."

"And what do you think of it?" I asked.

"I like it," he said. "It's different. It's weird that everyone already knows my mom and that people don't lock their doors or cars, but I don't hate it. The people are really nice, and I'm really glad Laurel and I got to meet you." Another dead end, and we turned around and took another direction.

"Well, I'm glad you're here too," I said awkwardly.

"And why is that?" he asked, this slight, barely there flirtation in his question.

I blushed. "You know," I said, leaning back against one of the straw bales, "for all the help with detailing."

He bit back a smile. "Right," he said. "So glad I could help."

This time I reached to shove him in the arm, but he caught my wrist, smiled down at me, and as the straw poked into my back, I thought, He's going to kiss me! And then a group of a dozen three-year-olds and their day-care leaders came around the corner, and the moment was gone.

In time, we found our way to the center of the maze, and after finding our way back out, we picked our own strawberries, a whole bucket for five dollars, sampling from the field as we picked. Before we left, we stopped at the gift shop, which smelled of donuts and sugar, to buy a loaf of homemade bread and apple butter, then we took the bread, butter, and our bucket of berries to the Green Lake beach, where we sat on the sand as we ate, watching kids splash in the water.

Outside the buoys, there were some swans on the lake, along with five tiny cygnets, little cinereous fluff balls the color of smoke with beaks that looked like pencil lead. Silas nodded toward them and said, "A lamentation of swans."

The adults were so serene with their long, graceful necks and sharp black beaks, their feathers shockingly white against the gray-green water. They looked like floating lotus blossoms.

I nodded, eating a strawberry. "Have you wondered why it's called that?" I asked.

"Yes," he said. "Actually, I've looked it up online."

"Find anything?"

"Just bits and pieces that I'm putting together myself. Nothing authoritative." I loved that he used that word. "Like, for example, you've heard the term 'swan song'?"

"Yeah, like what you sing if you get kicked off a talent show on TV?"

"Yeah. Supposedly, it has to do with the idea that the most beautiful song a swan sings is the one before it dies. I guess Socrates said something like that once upon a time, I don't know."

"Hmmm," I murmured, letting the sweetness of the

strawberry rest on my tongue.

"There's this song by Orlando Gibbons," he said, pulling it up on his phone, then reading the lyrics:

"The silver swan, who living had no note,

When death approach'd, unlock'd her silent throat;

Leaning her breast against the reedy shore,

Thus sang her first and last, and sang no more.

Farewell, all joys; O Death, come close mine eyes;

More geese than swans now live, more fools than wise.

"And Billy Collins has a poem about swans too, and he says the swans are the true geniuses because they're beautiful and brutal and know how to fly. That's Laurel, don't you think?" asked Silas. "She's the swan. She figured out how to be both beautiful and brutal."

"But not to fly," I whispered, thinking actually of how beautiful *Silas* was, how badly I wanted to touch him, to push his hair out of his eyes. "Stop it," I told him—and myself. "This is your day, and that's the second time you've brought up Laurel. Back in the car. There's someone I want you to meet."

At Legacy House, I knocked on Gordon's door, and when he opened it—dark glasses on—I said immediately, "Gordon, it's West. I have a friend with me."

His smile lit up his face. "Westie!" he said. "Come in, come in! *Pasan, jóvenes.* And whom have you brought along?"

"Gordon, this is Silas," I said, taking one of Gordon's hands and guiding it to Silas's, where they shook. "He's my new business partner. His family moved into the old Griggs house last month."

"Pleased to meet you, sir," said Silas.

Gordon smiled. "Not as pleased as I am. Come in; sit down. You two smell good, *como la playa*. Fresh water and wind. Westie, you taking care of that book of poems you borrowed?"

"Oh. It's in your barrister," I reminded him. "I brought it back a little while ago."

"Yes, yes, of course."

Silas's eyes widened at the sight of Gordon's home library as we followed Gordon into his living room. He sat in his rocker, packed his pipe, dropped the match into the jar of water, and said, "Tell me about yourself, Silas. What business are you in?" Silas looked at me questioningly, but I only smiled and nodded toward Gordon, urging him to answer.

"Well, sir, I guess I'm in the business of writing bad poetry."

Gordon was obviously delighted.

"He's just too hard on himself," I insisted. "He's a rock star."

"I am a rock star, and my Les Paul is metaphor," Silas joked.

"See, even *that* was a metaphor," I said.

"A meta-metaphor," he said.

All three of us laughed, Gordon the hardest.

Gordon chimed in, "You know, a truly bad poet wouldn't know his poems were bad."

"That's a good point, sir," said Silas, smiling. "Are you a poet yourself? Looks like you've got quite a library here."

"I'm an historian, son," he answered with a smile. "'History is still in large measure poetry to me.'"

"I like that," Silas said.

"I wish it were mine," Gordon confessed. "That's actually a quote from Jacob Burckhardt, a Swiss historian. Robert Penn Warren said, 'If poetry is the little myth we make, history is the big myth we live.'"

I thought through today's scenes: the library, Berry Acres, Legacy House. All stories.

"It's why we like *August Arms*," I surmised. "Silas has been listening too, Gordon."

"'Stories are our most august arms against the darkness,'" he quoted. "Please tell me you're a fan of Donovan Trick."

"Absolutely. Well, half fan, half bitter."

"As any true writer should be," said Gordon, satisfied. Then to me, he said, "Westie, he sounds handsome."

I blushed, but Silas laughed aloud and said, "Oh, I'm stunning. West can't keep her hands off me." That made me burst out laughing. "In fact, sir, she keeps trying to kiss me right now, even here in your living room."

My jaw dropped. *You're crazy*, I mouthed. Out loud, I said, "Gordon, you can't believe a word he says."

Silas took his cue from Gordon's hearty laughter and persisted, "Ouch! Sorry, sir, she was just nibbling on my ear and bit down a little too hard. Easy, girl."

"I am horrified, for the record," I said, laughing but

appalled. *You're in trouble later*, I mouthed very clearly to Silas, who shrugged and mouthed back, *Good*.

"Oh, young love," said Gordon, and I was too embarrassed to look at Silas to gauge his reaction, too confused to refute Gordon. "So, how's your family liking Green Lake? Is it just you and your parents, Silas?"

It came out of my mouth instinctively, protectively: "He's an only child." This time I did look at Silas—who was staring at the carpet, chewing thoughtfully on the inside of his mouth. I hadn't realized just how difficult it would be to keep Laurel out of the day's conversations. Just one day, I thought. I want just one day for Silas.

I changed the topic. "Gordon, tell us about what you're reading these days."

"Oh, I'm just finishing up *Narnia* again," he said. "At the part where the ground is taken from beneath their feet and they compare it to a black sun or dry water. That part gets me every time. It's like free fall. It's how I felt after Mavis died."

Silas ran a nervous hand through his hair.

I asked, "And what does dry water taste like?"

Gordon "looked" at me through those dark glasses, his face soft, and he said, "It's just an illusion, Westie. There is no dry water for one who loves God. No black suns either."

His words nudged at a memory in the back of my mind. "Gordon," I said, "remember the week of *August Arms* that was all about dreams?"

He looked confused, something I rarely saw on his face. As an historian, Gordon's memory was like a living, breathing thing.

"Back in January, I think?" I prompted. "There was an episode about a philosopher and some dream-argument thing."

"Ahhh," said Gordon, finally recalling. "René Descartes."

Silas looked interested.

Gordon summarized, "If dreams and reality share common features, then how do I know I'm not dreaming now?" He chuckled a little. "A massive existential topic folded into a compact statement like origami."

"I'm not much of a philosopher," I admitted, glancing at Silas and catching his eye. "I never understood why he thought it was so important to go there—you know, to take it that far."

"Well," said Gordon, now in his professorial element, "he was trying to establish doubt. Universal doubt. You know his famous statement, 'I think, therefore I am'?"

"Heard of it."

"It was all *en route* to arriving at that point, which we call the 'cogito': to doubt absolutely everything except that if you can think, then you must exist. If you strip things down and start at square one with the cogito, then your philosophy—however you rebuild it—isn't connected to tradition."

"But is that a good thing?" I asked doubtfully. "I'm not so sure."

Gordon grinned with pride. "And you say you're not a philosopher."

Gordon insisted we stay for dinner. The three of us made hamburgers and salad, and Silas ran out to the car to bring in what was left of our strawberries. It was fascinating to cook with a blind person—Gordon definitely had his own system. All his spices had Braille labels on them, and he used oven mitts when he was anywhere near the stove top. Silas and I were instructed to describe things in the iron frying pan and on the plates according to the face of a clock—"There's a burger at two o'clock, six o'clock, and ten o'clock" or the like. When Gordon got out a knife to slice a tomato, Silas offered to help, but Gordon grinned and said, "Watch me," then sliced it perfectly.

"You learn tricks," he said. "It's actually easier for me to cook alone than with someone, since sometimes they forget to tell me if they've opened a drawer or something." Silas, looking guilty, used his hip to push in the silverware drawer he'd left open. "I heard that," said Gordon, grinning.

Gordon had a can of whipped cream that we ate with the strawberries for dessert. "Mavis used to make homemade whipped cream," he said. "It was perfect. I've tried to make it, but if you whip for just a little too long, it starts to turn into butter. It's one of the few things I have never quite managed to conquer without my sight." Gordon smiled at us. "So where are you off to next?"

Silas looked at me. "I'm afraid that's classified information," I said.

Silas complained, "I tell ya, Gordon. The girl is crazy."

"But didn't you know?" Gordon responded. "That's the best kind."

Back in the car, Silas said, "You never told me."

"Never told you what?" I asked, waiting for him to buckle his seat belt.

"That you have your own personal Dumbledore."

We both laughed, then rolled the windows down as we drove. Silas stuck his hand out the window, letting it surf on the wind.

I didn't mention the tiny slipups I'd seen lately from Gordon: calling me the wrong name, misplacing his poetry book, forgetting an *August Arms* episode from just six months ago. I told myself it wasn't a big deal. My mom *always* called me "Shea-Libby-Westlin-whichever-one-you-are." Junior year, Trudy lost her chemistry book every other day. And Dad was so preoccupied with the church congregation that he forgot about things all the time.

I just wasn't accustomed to the confused one being *Gordon*.

Beside me, Silas shifted in his seat as he realized the trajectory of my car. "Your house? We're done?" He sounded disappointed.

"No," I answered, even as I pulled into my driveway and parked, "and no." I reached in front of him and took the book out of the glove compartment. "Come with me."

Without a word, we snuck across the parking lot and into the church. My heart was pounding as I made last-minute arguments with myself over sharing my bell-tower secret, but my feet marched straight to the unmarked door and unlocked it.

Silas was in awe the entire four-flight climb. I went first, and he followed close behind. He was so much taller than I was that our heads were level even when I was two steps above his. "No one else has a key?" he asked.

Stopping, I turned around and found myself looking right into his excited, dark eyes. "I have one, and I think maybe Joe, our maintenance guy, might have one too. But no one comes up here. Listen, you can't tell anyone I have that key, okay? I've never even taken Trudy up here."

"How about Elliot?" he asked.

"Nope."

At the top, Silas walked to the nearest open belfry window and gazed out over the town. The sun was low in the west, flirting with the idea of setting as Jody Perkins rode by on his lawn mower, waving to our neighbors.

Lights from the street below made it so we could just barely see one another inside the tower, but it was dark enough to feel dangerous, mysterious. I turned on the camping lantern in the middle of the small area, and warm amber light spread softly from it. Then, sitting backward on the ledge of the barred window, I opened the book. "Over there," I said, indicating the air mattress that lined the adjacent wall. "I'll read."

"This one," Silas requested, marking a page with his finger, then sat down and leaned his head back against the stone wall. "Please."

So I read:

"since feeling is first
who pays any attention
to the syntax of things
will never wholly kiss you;

"wholly to be a fool
while Spring is in the world

"my blood approves,
and kisses are a better fate
than wisdom
lady i swear by all flowers. Don't cry
—the best gesture of my brain is less than
your eyelids' flutter which says

"we are for each other: then
laugh, leaning back in my arms
for life's not a paragraph

"And death i think is no parenthesis"

Silence for a moment. My head felt a little foggy. What was I thinking? What was I doing—here, in the bell tower, with Silas Hart?

Then, "Thank you," he said, his voice low, husky, on the edge of breaking. He was quiet again, and I heard his breathing. "I feel spoiled."

Still in the window ledge, I said, "Nah. It was, you know, *okay* to spend the day with you." I shrugged, teasing him with over-the-top nonchalance. "I mean, you'll do."

"Oh, is that right?" he said, and he rose to his feet and joined me on my side of the tower. Silas stood smiling before me, at my eye level even though I was perched in the window, my legs dangling on either side of him. Then he put his hands, warm and soft, on the bare skin above my knees. The light from the lantern outlined his features, and his eyelashes cast tiny shadows across his cheek. "I'll do?" His voice was playful and gentle and low.

There was a frenetic bass drum inside me, in my neck, in my ears. I swallowed. "Mmm, yes, actually I think you'll do quite nicely," I rambled, thinking how small my voice sounded in the dim tower. He was so close, and he smelled like clean straw and fresh air. I had this vague idea that I should be protesting, that I should not be fanning the tiny flame in me.

But when Silas cupped my face in his hands, his thumbs along my jawline, and leaned in so close that our breath mingled, that flickering flame blazed into a full-on fire. "You're incredible, Westlin Beck. Do you know that?" he whispered, then quoted the poem, "'Kisses are a better fate than wisdom.'"

From somewhere inside me, I whispered back a challenge: "Prove it."

And then he kissed me—soft, sweet, seeking—and there was only room in my thoughts for one boy, *this* boy: Silas Hart, whose kiss was exploding my heart from a bud into a blossom with such alacrity that I marveled I could be so full without bursting. His mouth was asking questions without words, and I hoped I was answering them, even though I didn't know the answers.

Silas leaned his forehead against mine and looked into my eyes. "*That*," he whispered, "is how you should be kissed."

And I had to agree.

twenty

I drove Silas home after the bell-tower kiss, noticing as I drove that he was scribbling something on a piece of paper, after which he slid the paper into the E. E. Cummings book and asked, "Can I take this? I'll return it myself."

"Sure," I said. "What'd you just put in there?"

"Not much," he said. "Sometimes when I really like a book, I put a note to the next reader in it before it goes back on the shelf."

"Can I read it?" I asked, reaching for the book.

"No, you may not," he said, grinning and holding it out of my reach. I kept my eyes on the road while I grinned back and leaned as far as I could into his space.

He kissed my cheek, refusing to relinquish the book, and even though the kiss was tiny and quick compared to earlier that evening, it still made my stomach flip. "What are you doing on Saturday night?" he asked. "I want to hang out with you."

I gave up on the book. "That sounds great."

But no. We had family night on Saturday evening—and it had been my idea.

I tried to be present with my family—instead of thinking continuously of Silas, his face leaning toward mine in the bell tower, his breath sweet like strawberries and cream—as Mom mixed and rolled out the dough for two huge, cookie-pan-sized pizzas. Or of Elliot, my *boyfriend*, whom I hadn't seen since he'd accused me of something that was turning out to be true.

My stomach roiled, and it had nothing to do with hunger, even as we all added our toppings to various parts of the dough, extra cheese for me, a mountain of pepperoni for Shea, pineapple on Dad's and Libby's. The radio was playing Frankie Valli, and Mom and Libby replaced Dad's name for "Sherry." They howled, "Ker-er-rry, can you come out tonight?" Dad rolled his eyes, and Shea giggled, and I looked around at my happy family and thought about how long it had been since we'd done anything like this. I cared less about seeming cool after spending the summer with a goof like Silas.

Oh, Silas.

Oh, Elliot.

Oh, *Silas*.

When the pizzas were done, we sat around the table—such a rare occurrence that we'd had to clear Mom's scrapbook supplies off the table to make room for us all—and Dad, at the head of the table, held out a hand to me on his left and Libs on his right, and said grace. He prayed for the food, and for Tim and Lolly Spencer, whose first baby was due any day now, and for the Hart family to know peace and feel God's presence while Mr. Hart was gone this summer.

At the "amen," Dad squeezed my hand, and when my siblings practically dove into the pizza, he leaned over to me and said, "I asked everyone to pray at the local clergy meeting yesterday. Reverend Wright said he'd ask his elders to join him, and Father Ziebarth told me after dinner that he'd ask St. Hugh of Lincoln to intercede. Apparently, he is the patron saint of sick children." He laughed a little and added, "I've never quite understood sainthood."

I scraped some leftover glue off the table with my thumbnail. "Thanks," I said, and I hoped he knew how many other things I meant by that one word.

After dinner, we set up Sorry! on the living room floor; Shea, sprawled eagerly across the floor, partnered up with Dad for yellow, I was red, Libby blue, Mom green. We had just started to draw cards and move our pawns when the telephone rang.

My dad got up to answer the phone, even though Mom said, "Oh, Kerry, let it ring tonight."

All of us in the living room had gone completely silent as we heard Dad's voice change. "When? Just then, really? Do they know any details yet? Yeah, I can be there in half an hour." He rejoined us. "Bad news, crew," he said. "Tim and Lolly's baby was born an hour ago, but there's something wrong with the baby. That was Tim; he wants me to come up to the hospital. I'll be gone till late. Shea?"

"Yeah?" my brother asked, looking up from his space on the floor.

"It's up to you to win it for our team."

Shea smiled at him, but it was weak, disappointed.

"Wait, hold on," I said, feeling anger bubbling under my skin like an illness. "You can't just leave! We had plans."

"West, this is an emergency."

But having Dad leave family night felt like our own emergency.

"Just stay," I said. "Have Ed go instead." But he was sliding on his shoes. "You're leaving us—*again*."

Shea looked down at the board and said, "I don't want to play anymore."

"Yeah, this game is boring," said Libby, who had been excited to play only minutes earlier.

"No, you two," Mom said. "Come on, let's finish this game."

"Dad?" I asked. My siblings and I all looked at him.

He hesitated for a moment, and I honestly thought the look of our forlorn faces would be enough to make him stop, take off his shoes, call the associate pastor, and ask him to go instead. But he said, "Tim and Lolly are waiting for me. Sorry, guys." Then he left, pulling the door closed behind him. We stared after him in silence.

Shea grabbed the board and scattered the pieces. "I hate this game!" he shouted. He stormed away while Libby stared after him, wide-eyed.

"Libby, can you go check on your brother?" Mom asked. "West, help me pick up this mess."

But my anger had gone nowhere; if anything, it had flared when I saw how upset my brother was. I erupted when Mom said, "West, honey? Don't be upset; your dad's a good man."

"I don't understand you!" I hissed at her. "Of all of us, *you* should be the most upset! Dad is never here, and when he is, he has a headache. You're practically a single parent. You're his wife, not his servant, have you ever realized that?"

"Westlin Beck," she scolded, her eyes wide and flashing, "don't you dare say those things about your father."

"Say what?" I sassed back. "The truth? It's true that he's never around. It's true that he has *shitty* priorities."

"Do not use that language in this house, young lady," she said, her voice harsh and dangerous, not like her usual throwaway comments on pseudo-profanity. I noticed that she hadn't disagreed with me though; and yet, she would still defend him.

"Fine," I said. "Then I'll leave."

I started walking toward the thumb of Heaton Ridge, calling Silas on the way, realizing only after he'd picked up that I was probably supposed to have called Elliot. "Hey!" Silas said, his voice eager. "Family night over already?"

"Um, I guess you could say that, yeah," I said. "Can you pick me up?"

"Sure," he said. "I've got Papa's pickup. Your house?"

"I'm walking toward yours. You'll see me on the way."

I had almost gotten to the bridge into Heaton Ridge when I saw the familiar Mayhew pickup, the headlights briefly blinding me. The truck shook a little as Silas braked, rolled down his window, and said, "Hey, pretty lady, want a lift?"

Normally I'd have laughed, but I was still so pissed at my dad that I only managed a weak smile.

"Uh-oh, what's wrong?" he asked as I climbed into the passenger's seat. "Where to?" he asked. "The lake?"

"No. Let's go out to the wind farm in Shaw. Remember how to get to Berry Acres? It's near there."

We took skinny little back roads and then these terribly spooky paths through the cornfields until we were in the middle of the wind farm, this giant ridge outside Shaw that had about two hundred wind turbines on it. We couldn't see the monstrous turbines turning their slow cartwheels in the dark, but we could see—all around us—one red light atop each one, all blinking in synchrony. Black—then red lights for miles—then back to black.

"Totally creepy," said Silas, rolling down the windows before turning the truck off and killing the lights. "Like we're in the middle of an alien invasion."

"I kind of love it." The *whoosh-whoosh-whoosh* of a nearby turbine was pressing cool night air through the vehicle.

"Me too," he said. "C'mon." He opened his door, and I opened mine. In the bed of the truck, he spread out several blankets, and we sat on them, our backs against the cab of the truck, looking out on the wind farm. "Now are you going to tell me what's wrong?"

I told him about Dad bailing on family night to go to the hospital, about Shea messing up the board game, about the look on Libby's face, about what I'd said to my mom. And Silas just listened, his eyes fixed on me while I stared at the field.

"Dads suck," he surmised. "When mine left, I kinda felt like I had the shittier deal because yours was still here, but now I'm not so sure. Mine will come back, but your dad is here and gone at the same time."

"I think I'm gonna pierce my nose," I said, looking up at the blinking monster above us. "To piss him off."

"You should pierce your nose if you really *want* to pierce your nose," he said, the voice of reason, "but not just to piss him off."

I pursed my lips, thinking about tonight and about what I'd look like with a tiny diamond stud in my nose. "Yeah, maybe," I said. "Or get a trampy new swimsuit."

"That, *yes*," Silas said. "I'm in wholehearted agreement. Definitely. Please do."

"Pervert," I said as we both laughed.

"Is there another kind of seventeen-year-old male?" he asked.

"Gosh, I'm glad you're here this summer," I told him. "I'd be going crazy without you."

"Same," he said. "At least soon you'll have Trudy back too. But you're all I've got."

"And Laurel," I said.

"I suppose. And Laurel," he conceded.

"I hope I still have Trudy in the fall," I said. "On the Fourth, she seemed like a different person. Talking about going away for college and all about her new camp friends. It was like she'd forgotten about me. And she only stayed for like twenty-four hours. What's with that? It was our one chance to see each other till the summer is over."

"Things with Trudy will be fine," he said. "Everything will be fine. You'll see. The crux of the matter is that you two have history."

"History," I repeated softly, thinking how Elliot and I had history too—and yet I was sitting in the bed of a pickup truck with Silas tonight.

There was a long pause, silent except for the rushing air being pressed by the windmills, then Silas announced, "I love the word 'crux.' How could anyone not love that word?"

I giggled.

He continued, "The word even looks like what it is, like this important little block, this core."

"Mmm," I said in agreement. "How about 'cavalier'? Rolls right off your tongue."

"Applause," he said.

"Callous."

"Archaic."

"Valor," I said. "Doesn't it just make you want to *storm a castle*?" I pushed up my sleeve. "Look, I have goose bumps!"

"Tell Elliot it's over," he said, his voice calm, steady.

"What?" I said, my voice the opposite of his.

"Tell him it's over. It is, isn't it?"

Ahhh, so these were the answers I was giving him as I had kissed him back two nights ago; I was grateful for the upload.

"What about Beth?"

"I broke up with her last week; that's why I went back to Fairbanks."

"You broke up with Beth," I repeated, letting it sink in. My head was unspooling; my heart, an uncaged bird.

"It wasn't fun," he admitted. "And even though I had *no clue* if anything would ever happen between you and me, I knew I had to do it."

Silas smirked as he added, "I gotta admit: when you went ballistic after I left, that was a shot in the arm for what I needed to do. I kept reading that text where you called me a bastard like it was a love letter begging me to hurry home."

We both laughed, silent laughter, the kind that is more in the eyes than the throat.

"Why?" I asked.

Silas, still smiling softly, reached out and touched my face. His finger traced a line down my cheek and rested on my jaw, and it felt like fireworks going off in my head. He whispered, "I've belonged to you since the second you showed up on my doorstep."

I pulled his hand away and looked at him. "You *hated* me when we first met! You looked like I'd just stolen your birthday."

"I mean it." He had that wild, goofy grin on his face again.

"You're crazy."

"West." He took my face in his hands, and this time I let him. "It's true. I saw you, and I was yours."

"I don't—"

"The thing is, *I didn't want to be*. I knew Dad was probably headed back to Fairbanks soon, and I had a ticket too. I wanted to be with Beth and Josh and the rest of my friends. Get as far away from Green Lake as I could. Convince my parents I should stay for senior year. Shhh . . . let me talk. But I was finished when I saw you. At first, I thought maybe I could just ignore it all and push you away." He smiled, remembering. "And then you went for the bookcase, and I about lost it. Do you remember I left the room?"

"When you came back, your hair was wet."

"I went and splashed frickin' cold water on my face."

I laughed. "No way."

"Way. I had all these plans—Beth, Alaska, senior year—but you ruined them all. You destroyed my old plans and *became* my new plan."

Whoa.

I thought of the night we had listened to *August Arms* on the lifeguard stand, when he'd talked so cryptically about Alaska. *Unceremonious, ignoble, risky, necessary.* It all made sense now.

"I'm an idiot," I said, laughing under my breath as all the puzzle pieces came together.

"And I'm in love with you," he said.

"You're what?"

"In love with you. I love you."

"You *love* me?"

This time he laughed. "Yeah, is it that hard to believe?"

"Yeah, maybe." I was a blurry line; how could brilliance love a blur? I stared at our feet stretching out before us in the bed of the truck, his so much longer than mine. I tried to process what he had just said. He loved me—and I was Elliot Thomas's girlfriend. I had been friends with Elliot my whole life, had dated him for two years, and yet he and I had never said those words to each other. Silas and I were seventeen: Was that even old enough to know something like this? Was he being ridiculous? Were we both?

"You call me on my shit," he quietly explained. "You're my favorite person to drag down the rabbit hole. Sometimes when you're really into a book, you mouth the words as you read them. And you have a laugh you *only* use with me."

Bashfulness crept into his voice. "You're everything I want, West. I feel like—I feel like if I was lost, you would know where to find me." When he looked at me again, his eyes were shining with so much joy and affection and admiration that I thought his heart might reach out and pull me into him.

I suddenly thought, *I would. I* would *know where to find you*. It was like a revelation, only with no choir of heavenly angels, just the blinking red lights of the monsters in the field.

"I love you, too," I said.

Ahh, there was the Silas-grin! It broke like a giant whitecap over me, drowning me in the most perfect, incredible surf. He growled with pleasure and tackled me to the blanket-covered floor and kissed me so that I forgot about Dad and Mom and Trudy and Elliot and everything but *him*—Silas Hart, who *loved* me!—and the feel of his body pressed sweetly to mine.

twenty-one

The Spencer baby was fine, although born with sepsis, a bacterial infection, and needing a lumbar puncture and antibiotics. Dad stayed with Tim and Lolly till five in the morning, came home, showered, and walked over to the church to preach like normal. I was sure he'd spend that afternoon in bed, sleeping off a migraine.

"West!" my mom shouted up the stairs. "You're going to be late. Get a move on! I'll see you in our row in twenty minutes. And after church we'll have a talk about what time you got in last night, young lady. This is not a boardinghouse."

I made a face at the ceiling. *"This is not a boardinghouse,"* I repeated. When the front door closed, I sat up in bed, pulled back the curtain on my window, and watched Mom, Libs, and Shea walk across the parking lot toward the church building.

I got up and threw on a pair of shorts, tossed my hair into a ponytail, and brushed my teeth, pausing to take one thing out of my desk drawer before I took the car up to St. Cloud. The mall was open, and I went to this piercing place, but since I wasn't eighteen yet, they told me I needed to have a parent with me to get my nose pierced. My birthday was only a couple of weeks away, but it seemed like the fractiousness of the act would be meaningless if I waited till then. Maybe I didn't want my nose pierced after all.

The time on my phone told me it was almost the end of the service. I smiled a little as I thought about everyone asking where I was today, wondering what my parents would say. Would they throw me under the bus, say what a rude, disrespectful daughter I was last night? I doubted it. They wouldn't want anyone in the congregation to know that the Beck family wasn't perfect. I grinned a little in victory.

I shopped for a while, picked up a magazine with Chuck Justice on the cover for Libby, then found a linen romper that my dad would hate. I bought it, handing over my hard-earned detailing cash as if I were defying not only my parents but the cashier as well.

The service would be over now, and the phone calls would start coming soon.

But there was only one.

From Silas.

"Hey, where are you?" he asked.

"Not at church, that's for sure," I said.

"Want to hang out?" he asked.

"I have to make one stop first."

At the Thomas farm, it was Greg who led me through the barn, past the room that held the stainless-steel bulk tank, to a hay-lined pen where his brother was bottle-feeding a healthy-looking, energetic calf. Things had been awkward between me and Elliot since the Fourth of July; in fact, we had talked only a couple of times, and both times had been brief and distant.

I couldn't believe I was doing this.

"Greg, take over, will you?" Elliot said to his brother when he saw me, shoving the bottle at Greg's chest.

Greg started to whine, but Elliot gave him a look and he shut up quickly.

It was loud in the barn. I'd been in here before, but I'd forgotten about the noise of so many cows, so many milking machines. I'd never minded the smell.

Elliot stood, wiping his hands on his well-worn work jeans; his white T-shirt showed off his muscles, and his faded cap shaded his eyes—but not enough. His face was so sad, so disappointed; I'd have preferred his anger.

"Was that calf Stevie?" I asked, trying to take away the awkwardness. "She can see again?"

Elliot nodded.

"You were right," I babbled nervously. "That's so great,

so . . . wow. Good for you. She recovered, just like you said. That's . . ."

"Just do what you're here to do, West," he said. It wasn't mean, not even impatient. Just like someone powerful who wanted the Band-Aid torn off quickly.

"Elliot," I said, and then started to cry.

"I knew this was going to happen," he muttered. "I knew it from the second you told me about watching that shit TV show over at his rich-ass house. Knew it when you let him touch you at the drive-in."

I hadn't thought he'd noticed.

"What about our plans, West?" he demanded, finally raising his voice. "This fall, when I get my car? Getting food after games and bowling and shopping around for colleges? And—oh, *fuck—homecoming*." After a pause, he added, "You thought *I'd* be the busy one this summer, but *you're* the one who's never around."

I flinched—hadn't I said the same of my dad just the night before? How was it possible to feel hurt *and* be hurtful without making that connection?

"Was I such a shitty boyfriend? What did I do wrong?" he challenged.

"Nothing," I said, sniffling. "Elliot, you're great. You're the *best*. You're everything—"

"West, don't," he said. "Don't. You loved the idea of me—but never me."

"How can you *say* that? We've been friends our whole lives."

"Yeah, and you only realized how big the world was this summer." Elliot looked over his shoulder at some indeterminate next project. "I have to get going," he muttered.

I swallowed hard and nodded, still crying.

In my pocket, I fiddled with the cheap ring from our second-grade "wedding." It felt so dramatic and ridiculous to give it back to him, the way I'd planned. He walked away first, then I left and tossed it in a trash bin on my way out.

I was in the car leaving when Lorelei and Laney came rushing out of the house to greet me, but I—I just couldn't . . . so I wiped away my tears, plastered on a smile, and waved to them as I drove away.

My heart felt lighter and lighter the closer I got to Heaton Ridge.

At the old Griggs house, I took the stairs two at a time, burst into Silas's room, and crossed the room quickly to where he was messing with his stereo. "Wh—" he started to ask, but I cut him off with a kiss.

"What was that for?" he asked, looking a little dazed. "Not that you need a . . ."

"I broke up with Elliot," I said, and Silas literally swept me off my feet and smothered my neck with dorky, slobbery-sounding kisses that made me laugh as he carried me, newlywed-style, across the hall into the den.

"I wish you'd be a little more excited," I teased as he collapsed onto the couch with me on his lap. I put my arms around his neck, pressed my forehead to his. It felt so good to be here with him, Elliot already feeling further and further away. I kissed him again. "Distract me, okay?"

"You are in luck, Miss Beck," he said, then reached under one of the couch pillows and, with a flourish, produced a VHS tape.

He had found a documentary about an eighties boy band, New Kids on the Block, at a recent garage sale and then bought an old VCR at the same sale just so that we could watch it. We spent the next hour figuring out how to hook everything up, and once we had, he decided we needed to learn the ridiculous dance in one of the music videos. We laughed like kindergarteners while we attempted this, and even pulled Laurel into the den to help us with the choreography, which she learned easily after watching the music video only once. It was hilarious to watch her try to teach Silas, who was hopeless at dancing.

"I am so growing a rattail," said Silas, pretending to admire Jordan Knight's.

"Like hell you are," I said, and all three of us laughed: big, goofy laughs that felt like they had been sitting in our stomachs for years.

Laurel's smile was real—more authentic than anything I'd seen from her all summer. Silas took her hand and twirled her around, while I reveled in this moment enough for the three of us.

After dinner, still with hours before sunset, Silas and I headed into town and up into the bell tower. The breeze through the belfry windows carried the scent of fresh-mown grass. For once, Jody Perkins was using his mower to actually mow. I told Silas, "Laurel needs to eat. She looks like a ghost." I sat on the air mattress, back against the tower wall, and Silas lay on his back, his head in my lap, book in his hands.

"I know," he said, putting his book down momentarily. "She's worse than ever since the fireworks. Sometimes she won't even answer me when I ask a direct question. She skipped therapy last week. Mom doesn't know what to do. I overheard her fighting with Dad about it on the phone."

"I'm sorry," I said. There didn't seem to be anything else to say about it.

"I keep thinking of what Gordon said about black suns being an illusion. Remember?"

"Mmm-hmmm." The sun was coming through the belfry windows in streaks, and it was all I could do to keep myself from tracing his eyebrows, his nose, his lips with my fingers. I wondered what he would do if I did. He loves me, I reminded myself, and lightly touched his face. He closed his eyes.

"At first I thought Gordon had to be wrong," he said. "I mean, Laurel loves God and still has a black sun. But—no. I mean, even her black sun is an illusion, *sincerely* an illusion."

"She just hasn't figured that out yet," I said.

"Exactly!" Silas sat up then, surprising me. He moved so that he was sitting beside me, then settled his hand along the inside of my leg, tucking a few fingers up gently under the cuff of my shorts. No complaints from me. "You know, I want to believe—I *think* I believe—that God is in control of everything," he said.

I ran my fingers over his arm and was pleased to see the hair stand up there. I didn't know I had that kind of power over him. "Even over the bad things?" I asked. "Like death? Disease?"

"Yes."

"And catastrophe?"

"Yeah."

"Solipsism syndrome?"

The pause was brief. "I think so. Yes."

"Why?" I asked.

"It might sound dumb," he said. "I don't think I've ever said it out loud before."

"That's okay. It's just me."

Silas paused; then he took my hand in this strange way, as if he were someone so much older, about to impart the hardships of the world to me. "I'm a writer," he said.

"You don't say," I teased him.

He smiled a little and squeezed my hand. "Writers know

that the climax comes before the resolution." He was quiet for a second, then said, "Not just in fiction, either, West, but in real life too. How many times has the *worst* thing turned out to be necessary? Or even the *best*? Rescue wears masks, you know. It's why people say it's darkest before the dawn. Sometimes things take a long time to make sense. Could be years and years—or only a weekend. Or they might *never* make sense. But that doesn't mean you stop trusting that the world is being rescued."

It was a lot to take in. "I can't decide if I feel happy or sad," I finally said.

"Feel both," Silas replied. "But remember that rescue stories are the best kind. If you look around at the world, it seems pretty clear that God favors redemption over perfection."

I thought of Laurel in the den earlier this summer, frantically struggling through the same ideas that Silas now cracked open like a cool can of iced tea.

"It's not that easy," I said. "I mean, I get what you're saying—but it's uncomfortable, you know? Like, how do you gift-wrap that and give it to the kid whose *grandma* just died?" I thought of the families from church Dad had been helping this summer.

"No, you're right," Silas said. "It's not easy. At all. It's not a very *pretty* present. Some people might even think it sucks. But I think it's *true*, and solid ground doesn't suck."

Laurel. The night of the fireworks. Her bed some sort of ballast.

I had been looking at my hand in his, but now I looked into his eyes, which were sad and savage. I couldn't help but think back to his first Sunday in church.

It is well with my soul.

Maybe . . . maybe all anyone ever really needed was that solid ground, scaffolding that would hold long enough for you to really see the questions that crowded around you like fog. The solid ground wasn't the answer—not exactly—but it substituted for one.

"Rescue stories are the best kind?" I said, or maybe asked.

"It's like bedrock," he admitted.

Silas let go of my hand and reached for a deck of cards he'd brought along, shuffled them, and handed me half. It was a *WARegon Trail* set, which made me grin. "Slapjack," he instructed.

I moved to sit across from him, and we started flipping cards over. Seven, king, two, six.

"I'm going on a college visit," Silas said, "with my mom. On Tuesday." He seemed apologetic.

"Are you not excited or what?" I asked.

"No, I am," he said, unconvincingly.

"Then what?" I asked. *SLAP!* went my hand onto the deck of cards. His hand came down on mine a millisecond too late.

"Damn!" he said. "You're so fast!"

"Then what?" I pressed.

We flipped through the cards so quickly: ace, four, queen.

Silas said, "Laurel and I started kindergarten together, middle school, high school. I mean, durr, we're twins. It'll be weird to go to college without her."

Jack. Silas slammed his hand down on it, but I had completely missed it, staring at him, confused. "What do you mean, 'without her'?"

He looked at me. Those deep brown eyes, his pursed lips. "West, she's barely left her room this month. She couldn't handle college—she can barely handle life."

"But she'll get better," I insisted. "I mean, you guys left Alaska and everything." I needed him to believe that. I wasn't sure I could handle that job alone. "Right?" I said.

He was quiet for a moment. "Sure, West. Yes."

A conversation on the sidewalk below the tower distracted us, though we couldn't make out the words. The light had shifted since we'd arrived. "Wow, a college visit," I said, as if it was only now hitting me. "I'm behind the eight ball. Pick me a major, would you?"

"How about boy bands?"

"Or Thursday."

"Or Brian."

A plump laugh bubbled out of me like lava. "That doesn't make *any* sense!"

Silas's laugh was just as funny. "But a major in *Thursday* does?!"

"I'm Westlin Beck, and I'm a Brian major," I said. "Maybe

I'll major in punctuation," I said. "Not English. Just punctuation. Or maybe I wouldn't even have to go to school for it. Maybe I could just become an activist to help support underappreciated punctuation."

"Like?" he asked.

"Like the semicolon. And the ampersand."

"I don't think that's technically a punctuation mark."

"Oh, what do you know about it anyway? You're only a Brian major."

When I went home later that night, after we'd listened to *August Arms* in the bell tower by camp light, I expected to face a firing squad; in fact, I felt almost ready for it. I was actually disappointed to find that Mom and Dad were already asleep.

Fine, I thought. I'm on hiatus from church indefinitely till I get a reaction.

The house was quiet. I sat down on the couch and turned on some late-night TV.

"Mom said you're grounded," Shea said, leaning over the stairway banister. "What does that mean?"

"Hey, kiddo," I said softly. "What are you still doing up?"

"Libby's music is too loud."

I patted the seat beside me on the couch, and he came down the stairs to join me. I threw my arm around him. "Nothing," I said, answering his earlier question. "It doesn't mean anything. How was your day?"

"Okay," he said. "We had to be really quiet because Dad's head hurt again. Where were you all day?" I wondered if my parents had called around or just assumed I was at the Harts'. I didn't know which option I preferred.

"Around," I said. "Shea, wanna play a game?"

With one eye on the TV screen, he asked, "Like what?" I knew he was thinking of last night's Sorry! drama. The boxed-up game was still sitting on the floor near the couch.

"I don't know. Anything. Battleship."

He lit up. "Yeah, okay! I'll go get it."

"Libby's still up too?" I called softly after him.

"Dunno. Her music's on."

Libby was indeed still awake, and as Shea and I played several rounds of Battleship, she eventually joined us. "Got you this," I said, tossing the Chuck Justice magazine at her. She paged through it on the couch while Shea and I played on the floor.

"Do you ever think the bad guys really think they're the good guys?" he asked, a young Socrates casting a sideways glance at the TV while he annihilated my aircraft carrier.

"Maybe," I said. "Probably. What bad guys? Just bad guys in general?"

"Yeah, I guess so."

Libby and I looked at each other over Shea's head. He was clearly talking about Dad.

"Does that make them less bad, do you think?" I asked.

"I don't know," said Shea softly.

But Libby said, "It makes them worse." She left the room and returned with the paper dolls Dad had gotten her earlier that summer, along with one of Mom's scrapbooking glue sticks. Shea and I watched as Libby calmly, patiently glued pairs of the dolls together, face-to-face. She looked at us as she capped the glue stick, and her eyes were hurt and ruthless. This was her own tiny insurrection, and in a way, it made me proud.

twenty-two

Tuesday was strange, what with Silas out of town for his campus visit. I'd gotten used to spending every day together, and I found myself lonely without him. Shea and Libby were picking at each other, and technically I was grounded, so I barricaded myself in my bedroom, alternating between reading a book and an email from Trudy she'd sent in response to my teaser of "big news." Her reply hadn't said much, but it had said enough.

> Westlin. Beck.
>
> If you think I don't already know your "big news" is that you are head over heels for Silas Hart, then you have forgotten how well I know you. I could have told you that on the Fourth of July. Love you, girl. Sorry so short. Misses!

Trudy. Kirkwood.

P.S. Still at a stalemate between A & A.

P.P.S. "Stalemate"—that's what Ami always calls it! LOL, she WOULD.

Maybe Silas was right: Trudy and I would be fine because we had history.

I tried to ignore that this was one of just a small handful of emails she'd sent all summer, that it was ridiculously short and unhelpful, and that even in so few lines, she hadn't been able to resist including Ami Nissweller. I wondered if it would be worth my time to try to keep this conversation going.

My phone buzzed. It was Silas.

Laurel won't text me back. Been texting her for an hour. Can you go over to the house and make sure she's ok?

I asked my parents, even though I planned to leave the house regardless of their ruling. My parents and I were both unfamiliar with this "grounded" territory, and in the end, they agreed it was more appropriate for me to go than for them, so I took the car over to Heaton Ridge. The door was locked for once, so I used the garage security code that Silas had taught me and let myself in.

"Laurel?" I called, once inside. There was no response, so I started up the stairs. "Laurel?" Still nothing.

I said her name once again, this time outside her bedroom

door, and a sick feeling started to grow in my stomach. I pushed open her door, not sure what I'd find inside. She'd been so depressed lately—

She lay curled up in her bed atop a pearl-colored comforter, not moving. My heart was pounding like a tribal drum. "Laurel?" I whispered. "Laurel, get up!" I put my hand on her back to shake her.

She rolled over suddenly, saw me, and gasped. "West! My *gosh*! What are you doing?" she exclaimed. "You *scared* me!"

You scared me too, I thought, my pulse still hammering.

"I—I'm sorry," I said. "Silas said you weren't texting him back; we just wanted—to—to make sure you were okay."

"I was taking a nap," she said crabbily. "I don't usually text while I sleep. Do you?"

"Sorry," I said again, relieved she was fine—and that I'd escaped my house. Laurel sat up with her back against the headboard. I sat down at the foot of her bed, leaning my back against the wall. We were an intersection of legs. "Why are you taking a nap now anyway? It's almost lunchtime."

"I'm not hungry."

"You have to eat," I insisted.

For a second, she looked uncooperative, but then she shrugged. "Okay."

"Let's go down to the kitchen. I'll make us some lunch."

Laurel moved like a phantom. She sat at the kitchen island, watching but not seeming to really see me. Her hair was greasy and she wore yoga pants and a T-shirt. Below her eyes were circles a shade darker than the rest of her face.

The Hart kitchen was all white and stainless steel, except for the dark walnut butcher-block countertops and island. I was so used to the surfaces of our house being covered in Pinterest projects and coupons that the Hart kitchen felt sterile and unused. Except for a littering of Magnetic Poetry on the fridge.

douche y poem
for mah girl
u beeyotches obvi
ain't badass like
my bomb hottie
who got hella
junk in da trunk
fo sho

"Mom told him, 'I don't care how over the moon you are for Ms. "Bomb Hottie" Beck, if it's not down before your Oma Lil comes over next, there'll be hell to pay,'" Laurel said, smirking a little. I was certain I was blushing, but I took a photo with my cell phone.

After poking around in their pantry, I found a box of mac and cheese and held it up for Laurel to assess. "Sure," she said.

I put some water on to boil, then said, "Haven't seen you much lately—I mean, besides the boy-band dancing."

"Nope," she said.

I leaned on the island toward her. "We're worried about you."

This time she smiled a little bit. "Me too. I'm not okay at all, West." She had a pinched look to her face, the look that people get when they're fighting back tears.

"Isn't your therapist helping?" I asked.

She let her head roll back, staring up at the ceiling in the frustrated way Shea does when Mom tells him to clean his room. "No," she said. "It's not working. I want to try something new."

"Okay," I said. "Like what?"

"I don't know, a blue pill."

"Blue pill?" I asked. "Oh, *The Matrix*."

She nodded. I put the pasta into the boiling water and stirred it around, hot steam rising from the pot.

"There's something I've never understood," I said quietly. "How can you not know when you're sleeping and when you're awake? When I woke you up just now, I scared you and you woke up *so fast*. I mean, aren't you aware that you're awake every morning when you *wake up*?"

"Seriously?" she asked, narrowing her eyes at me. "You've never dreamed that you woke up?"

"Okay, fine," I admitted. "But every night? Over and over, the same dream? Dreams are crazy! They aren't real and . . . and . . . logical like this is, like real life is!"

Laurel only looked sad. "West," she said patiently, "when

you're dreaming, everything seems normal. Skating on grass or walking on the ceiling or playing Quidditch all *seems* normal while you're dreaming. It's when you wake up that you realize that it wasn't."

"So?"

"So, what if I wake up, and all these things I thought were normal—having a family, sleeping in a bed, drinking water—are actually bizarre?"

"Drinking water—bizarre?"

"Dreams feel normal when you're in them."

Silas had told me that it was useless to argue with solipsism, that it would always win. I hunted around for a colander to strain the macaroni; Laurel got up, opened a cupboard, and pulled one out for me, then took butter and milk from the refrigerator.

I prepared the pasta, mixing it all together as I said, "Okay, so I'll admit to you that what you fear is possible. I'll give you that. But it's *improbable*. Do I get points for that one?"

She smiled slightly as I handed her a bowl of steaming mac and cheese. "I don't care about probabilities. If something were one-in-a-million, I would wonder if the one had found me. It's the uncertainty that's torture."

Why couldn't I enter into her suffering? I spooned out a bowl for myself, looking hard at the spoon, the dish, not wanting to meet her eye. I thought back to that first day in the sunroom, when I'd seen the light go out of her eyes. *Look at her,*

I berated myself. *Would you at least look at her?*

I leaned back on the countertop, trying to seem casual, and looked across the island into those lost, sorrowful eyes. "Silas misses you," I said.

"I miss Silas every day," she said softly. "It breaks my heart to look at him and think, *You're not real. I have imagined you. When I wake up from this, I will not have a twin.*"

I swallowed hard.

"I know what you're thinking, West," Laurel continued. "And it's true. There are so many things I would love about this life . . . so many things. This incredible house. My parents and how passionate they are about their work. I love that we met you this summer, love how happy you make Silas. I love the way I feel around Whit, and I want to know him *so bad*—I mean, I want to know every little thing about him. And Silas." She pushed her spoon around in her bowl. "He's the greatest person I have ever met. If I woke up and found I had a different brother, I would hate that other brother, just for not being Silas. I would honestly rather trade in real life for this dream, if it is a dream. I am that terrible of a person, West. I would trade in my real parents and real siblings for this dream family."

She was breaking *my* heart as I realized the truth of why her condition was so debilitating. "Laurel," I said quietly but with force, "Silas is your real sibling. The only one you've got. And you're pushing him away."

"Yeah, sometimes I seem to know that," she said, "but I can't . . . can't hold on to it."

I said, "If you were dreaming, you couldn't be having a conversation like this, right?"

"Like what?"

"Like, what's it called, meta-dreaming? That doesn't happen, I don't think."

Laurel frowned at me as if I were infantile. "Of course it does," she said. "I've definitely had a dream within a dream—that's what makes it so hard to determine how many layers down I am."

"Oh."

"The family stuff isn't the worst part though," she admitted. "Sometimes I wonder if I invented God, made the whole concept up. Then everything goes haywire—I wonder if maybe we're puppets, or dolls in a dollhouse, and there's this omnipotent being who is moving us around and making us interact. What if it turns out that the ultimate reality is that a child was in charge? Or what if we're characters in a book? That would make the author a god. Or what if something evil is actually in control of the entire universe, only it has disguised itself as something good, and after we die we learn the truth that all good was actually defeated before the earth was ever made, and everything we ever took as virtuous was just evil in a mask?"

"Laurel."

"Or what if there was actually—"

"Laurel, *stop.* You can convince yourself of anything if you let yourself. You can't let yourself."

She looked at me, wide-eyed, a little stunned. "*Let?* Oh, West. I wish it were that easy. Worrying about life-as-a-dream is difficult but not impossible. Worrying about a foundation that can't hold the weight of your soul? That's agony." She swallowed hard and bit back tears. "It makes me wish I didn't exist," she whispered, and there was so much truth and devastation in the sound of it that I didn't doubt her for one second. "Sometimes I just want oblivion."

The hair on my arms stood on end.

"I'm tired," she said suddenly and got up to return to her room.

"Laurel, listen," I said, following her out of the kitchen. She looked annoyed, and I almost backed down, but she had once said that socializing was good for her, even if she didn't want to do it. "You shouldn't be alone so much."

She paused on the stairs, considering me. "Okay, then," she said. "Come with me to Papa and Oma's house."

"For what?"

"You know."

twenty-three

The Mayhews lived in an old farmhouse, like Elliot's, a little south of town. Lillian made Laurel tuck in her shirt and then launched into a lecture on why my dad ought to be preaching with the New King James translation, but Arty quietly ushered us away from her and showed us the stairs to the attic.

"There's a lot up there, Sweet Pea," he told Laurel. "But you're welcome to look. I've looked a little too—no doll, but I found some books you used to like. You should take them with you when you leave."

Laurel kissed his cheek. "That sounds great, Papa."

The attic was full of treasures: books and antique jewelry and a wooden rocking horse with yarn for its mane. Laurel found an old flapper hat made of lace and beading and put it on her head. She examined herself in a full-length mirror that was propped against one wall and, satisfied, sat down on a purple velvet sofa and pulled up a box. Determined to keep the conversation as far as possible from what we were searching for, I asked about Mark Whitby.

"He's *gorgeous*," she said, pawing through the box. "Don't you think he's gorgeous?"

"He's *Whit*," I said, a little flummoxed as I peered behind a wooden headboard. "I've known him since kindergarten."

"And you've never had a crush on him?"

I shook my head. "No. Trudy did."

"Really?"

"For like ten minutes."

Laurel laughed. "Tell me about him."

"I don't know," I said. "He's the catcher on the baseball team, and he's really funny and sorta dorky. Oh, and super sweet. Like, a lot of guys can be pricks sometimes, but he's just a total sweetheart."

"That's what I think too," she said, tucking her feet beneath her on the sofa. I wondered if she and Whit had talked outside of the drive-in and the fireworks.

Something about her voice made me almost think so.

"He's really close to his mom; they live out near Shaw with his little sister Jenna and his stepdad. Whit—his dad committed suicide when we were in eighth grade. The obituary in the town paper was really vague, but people knew. Everyone in town was talking about it for months."

"He told me that," she muttered.

I was shocked. Whit almost never talked about his dad. "When everyone was over for fireworks?" I asked dubiously.

"Of course not!" she said, appalled. "We talk on the phone sometimes."

"Oh," I said. "How did that happen?"

"He stole my phone on the Fourth and put in his number, so I called him."

"Good for you!"

Laurel looked embarrassed. "I sort of said, 'Hey, it's Laurel Hart. It was fun seeing you again. I really liked your khakis,' and he said, 'My khakis? My *pants*?' all laughing and weirded out, you know, and I just begged, 'Please don't hang up.'"

"I liked . . . your *khakis*?" I repeated, trying not to laugh.

"I panicked, okay?" she said.

"Well, he obviously didn't hang up."

"No," she said, smiling. "He didn't."

"And he told you about his dad?"

"Not in that first call."

I wondered how often they talked.

Laurel said, "He told me about his dad's drinking problem. He said there was this time when his dad was drunk at one of his baseball games and got escorted out, crying. He was so embarrassed—Whit, I mean."

I remembered similar scenes all too well—Mr. Whitby always weepy, Whit always embarrassed but too sweet to shame his dad in public. In fourth grade, our little group went to Whit's house for his birthday, and his dad was drunk and mopey, and Whit was so humiliated. Trudy and I went outside to the trampoline while Elliot hung back and talked Whit through it. I had wondered if we should be inside with him, but Trudy said he'd feel worse.

"He also told me about the car running in the garage."

"Yeah."

Laurel's voice grew soft. "Whit said the worst part was that there was no note. Not that he was the one who found the body, not that his dad had been so happy just the night before—but that there was no note."

I didn't say anything. I knew most of these details, but it had been a long time since I'd thought about them. Whit didn't talk about it much—if at all. Well, maybe he did with Elliot, but not with me. I was glad he'd told Laurel. Each of them had such deep sadness; I wondered if sadness worked like magnets.

Laurel continued, "That's the most selfish thing I can imagine ever. Suicide, I mean." She paused, thinking. "I suppose a lot of people probably think solipsism syndrome is about as bad."

I shifted uncomfortably and redirected the conversation. "Whit hit his growth spurt late. In kindergarten, Trudy and I thought of him as another one of our dolls. Even though he's tall now, he was the shortest guy in our grade till like seventh grade. Can you picture him at five foot four?"

Laurel grinned with affection. "I'd have to bend down to kiss him."

"You've kissed him?" I exclaimed.

She laughed. "Not *yet*, silly. But I plan to." She grinned wryly. "Silas has always been tall," she mused. "He was at least six feet straight out of the womb."

We continued searching the attic for nearly an hour. There was no sign of a ballerina doll in a red dress. On the drive back to her house, I kept Laurel from wondering what that meant by reading the titles of the books her grandpa had sent home with her: *The Talking Toothpaste*, *Blankets for Monsters*, *Vivien's New Friend*. She didn't remember any of them.

Back in the Harts' den, we turned on *WARegon Trail*—I was getting used to the gore by now and had even developed a tiny crush on the show's badass pioneering protagonist—but we had the volume way down so we could talk about TV shows and internet memes and the latest Chuck Justice song, "Ransom Avalanche," which I knew because Libby blasted it from her room 24/7. Laurel grabbed Silas's guitar and played her own cover of it—I didn't even know she could play—and when dinnertime rolled around, we ordered out from Mikey's, the only place in Green Lake that delivers. As always, the conversation seemed to come back to what I should study in college.

"Clowning. For sure," she said, poking a last French fry into ketchup. "Or actually, no—maybe waterfowl."

"How about puppetry?" I pretended to consider.

"Absolutely not," Silas said, suddenly appearing in the den doorway. "Friends don't let friends major in puppetry."

"Even if I am a 'bomb hottie' with 'hella junk in da trunk'?" I asked innocently.

"'Fo sho,'" he said. "You forgot 'fo sho.' Can't say I never wrote a poem for you."

He sat down between me and Laurel on the couch, throwing an arm around each. "My two favorite girls. Oh! *WARegon Trail*! My two *favorite*, FAVORITE girls." He turned the volume up.

Silas's college visit in the Twin Cities had gone great. "Their creative writing program is fantastic, West," he said to me up on his roof that evening before the *August Arms* episode.

"Yeah?"

"Yeah. Most of the English professors there have published books, and they have this really cool literary magazine run by the students. And the campus is amazing—brick buildings a hundred years old, and they're crawling with ivy. It's on a lake—well, I guess pretty much everything in Minnesota is—but anyway, it has seven miles of lakeshore and its own island with a community garden. You really should check it out too. We . . . we could . . . go together."

By the way he was stammering, I knew that he meant *we could go to college together* and not just *we could go visit the campus together.* I liked that he was thinking of me so far in the future. Then again, college really wasn't that far away—senior year was starting in a month, and I'd turn eighteen in just a few days.

Even though I'd done my best to steer clear of the college conversation, I'd always imagined living in a dorm with Trudy on the same campus as Elliot—my little Green Lake world packed up and moved to wherever Elliot could get a scholarship. And now, Elliot was out of the picture and Trudy wanted to be roommates with Ami Nissweller at Tellham & freakin' Barr. Each of them had incited panic in me this summer when they'd broached the topic.

But with Silas . . . it would be a different adventure, but a good one. No panic there.

"It was just an idea," he said in a rush. "I don't mean to tell you what to do. Forget I said anything."

"It's okay," I said. "I like that idea."

"Yeah?" he asked.

"Yeah."

"I got some info for Laurel too," he said. "They have a BFA in dance there. Mom and I asked the recruiter lots of questions, and it seems perfect for her." When Silas paused, I heard the words he didn't say: *if only she were healthy again.*

"We had a good talk while you were gone," I said.

"About what?"

I hesitated, knowing much of it would upset him. "Well, lots of things."

"West. Tell me. I want to know."

"She just has all these strange ideas about God—I can't even remember them all. Like evil being disguised as good or that we're in a puppet show. 'How many layers in' she is," I added, using finger quotes. "Freaky stuff."

Silas let out a frustrated breath. "But I didn't know she had all those crazy theories," he said. "It's more Descartes, that bastard. Is she really only seventeen? She drags those years around like they're a backpack full of bricks."

On *August Arms* that evening, Sullivan Knox trod lightly through a story of seven Rwandan schoolchildren who had visions of the Virgin Mary, in which she showed the children a river of blood, people killing each other, and decapitated corpses.

Years later, civil war broke out in Rwanda: a genocide. In one hundred days, an estimated one million people were killed—seven every *minute*—many beheaded with machetes and dumped into the Kagera River.

"It was the vision, come true," Sully said. "A river of blood, bodies without heads. Three of the Our Lady of Kibeho apparitions were later declared authentic by a local bishop."

"Do you believe it?" I asked Silas, not sure what to think.

He shrugged, the flickering bonfire casting light and shadows across his face. "Maybe. I mean, I believe in the burning bush. But God speaks softly sometimes too."

"To you?"

"Maybe."

"What does he say?"

Silas leaned backward and looked at me with narrowed eyes and a crooked grin. "I can't tell if you're making fun of me," he said. "Are you?"

Was I?

I thought of the story he was referring to—God speaking to Moses from a bush blazing with fire that did not burn it up. I'd heard such stories a hundred times in Sunday school as a child: God as a pillar of cloud, the sun standing still, the Red Sea parting like a crowd before a king. Did I believe them? I hadn't really thought about that question—what do I believe?—for so long. I'd just been limping along from Sunday to boring Sunday, doing my best to avoid encountering it all. Had I been creeping around corners to hide from Dad—or from God?

"No," I said. "I'm not making fun of you. What does he say?"

Silas was quiet for a moment, an odd, lingering moment that made me wonder if I'd been too forward in asking a question like this so flippantly. But then that moment was over, and Silas looked at me. "He says to abide."

Again, I expected a shit storm when I got home that night, since I'd been given permission to check on Laurel but had then stayed out for the rest of the day, ignoring my parents' calls as the day had gone dark. But my parents and Shea were already in bed. I knocked on Libby's bedroom door.

"Come in," she said, and turned her music down. She was on her bed, paging reverently again through the magazine I'd given her.

"Were Mom and Dad pissed that I didn't come home right away?"

She wrinkled her nose. "You're not supposed to say 'pissed.'"

I rolled my eyes. "Were they?"

"I don't think so."

"Did they mention it?"

"I guess. Mom said something to Dad, and he said, 'Well, she's almost eighteen. Can you blame her?' and Mom said, 'I suppose.'"

"Oh," I said.

"That's good, right?" Libby asked, her finger marking a page.

"Yeah," I said, oddly disappointed. "Great."

twenty-four

When I walked into Silas's house on the morning of my eighteenth birthday, he handed me a bouquet of white calla lilies, then hooked a finger under the belt of my romper and pulled me toward him. "Westlin Beck," he said, his forehead pressed against mine, "does your dad know you dressed like this today?"

No, actually, he does not.

"I like this," I said, tugging lightly on his tie.

"Picnics bring out the best in me."

But it started raining around eleven that morning, so we decided to picnic in the sunroom instead of at the lake, where Silas had planned. Around noon, the storm picked up, and the rain that had begun as a slow drizzle whipped into a frenetic downpour. It was surreal to be in the sunroom—glass walls, glass ceiling—almost like being inside a colossal car wash. It was darker than it should be at noon, and colder too—although I wasn't sure if it was from summer's tilt toward autumn or from the storm itself. Silas found some tea lights in a kitchen drawer and placed them all around the sunroom, lighting all one hundred. The storm outside thrashed the trees in the yard, but indoors, the little flames blinked like cats' eyes.

My legs looked tan against the polar bear fur on the floor, where we sat eating turkey and avocado sandwiches and cucumber salad. There were grapes and cheeses, and sparkling cider, which we drank from his parents' champagne flutes.

"To Westlin Beck, on her birthday," said Silas, toasting me. "May your year be full of delights and desserts. Oh, hey! I forgot!"

He had made chocolate-covered *bacon*.

"Sprinkled with sea salt," he said proudly.

I was flabbergasted. "You . . . are my favorite person. Ever." The sweet mixed with salty was exactly perfect. "You did all this yourself?"

"Mom helped a little before she and Laurel left this morning," he admitted.

"Where did they go?"

"Minneapolis. To meet with some doctors about alternative medicine. Laurel doesn't want to keep seeing her therapist. . . . I guess he keeps trying to find some childhood trauma as an explanation for it all—and Laurel kept saying no, no, no, no. This guy just thinks she's buried it all."

"That's awful. Of the counselor, I mean."

"Yeah. And Laurel's not stupid—she told me how therapists can unintentionally 'implant' a false memory just by suggestion—so she said she wasn't going to talk to someone who'd *insist* that her childhood had left some big scar or whatever."

"She said that?" I asked. "Wow."

"Yeah," he said. "Really kick-ass for someone so fragile." I nodded. "I just think there is something broken in her mind. I wonder if there's a tiny switch deep inside her—it would be the easiest thing to turn it on or off—but we've got to *find* it first." Silas smiled sadly at me, his eyelashes so long they made him seem almost shy for a moment.

The rain was drumming on the roof so hard, so consistently. It was its own lovely music, in a way. We talked more about college and Donovan Trick's forthcoming novel and the history class we'd share when school started in a few weeks—then we blew out the tea lights and retreated upstairs to watch *WARegon Trail.*

Trudy had sent a birthday card, which made me laugh but had a disappointing lack of news—Germaine brothers or otherwise. But sitting beside Silas in the den, I couldn't bring myself to care about it too much. This was a lazy day, and I couldn't have loved it more. No parents around to tell us we were rotting our brains, no Laurel around to remind us how broken life was. Just me, Silas, and some zombies. I rested my head against Silas's shoulder and we watched the strong fathers protect their wives and children from the undead. I lifted my head and looked at him, his eyes glued to the television set, so intense. I leaned over and kissed him quickly on the cheek, then looked away, trying to lasso my grin. A moment later, he pounced.

"Trying to be stealthy, Miss Beck?" he asked. "You must have forgotten that I am a ninja. Bow to your sensei!"

I couldn't stop laughing as I watched him remove his tie and wrap it around his forehead. The loose ends hung forward and brushed my ear as he leaned over and kissed me—it tasted like dark chocolate and apples. The screaming and gunfire from the television sounded a world away, Silas's body covering mine like the most perfect armor. I suddenly realized why he liked *WARegon Trail* so much—he liked the idea of fighting an enemy you could *see*. He gave me a beaming Silas-grin as he said, "Let that be a warning to you, missy."

"I liked that warning," I admitted, so close to him that we were still sharing breath.

And he kissed me again, and it was the clumsiest and most beautiful kiss I could imagine because neither of us could stop grinning, our smiles as big as the sun when it bursts over the horizon.

That evening, after the rain stopped and it was dark, we stole away to Green Lake to swim, though the park was closed. The wind had blown the clouds away, and the moon felt small and distant. We splashed around as quietly as we could in the chilly water until our teeth were chattering and then we waded back to shore, climbed into the lifeguard stand as we had done before, and wrapped ourselves in a giant towel, wet shoulders pressed together, staring at the moon's long reflection on the water, like an arrow pointing our direction.

"Did you read the Billy Collins poem about the planet with four moons?" Silas asked, his voice low and husky in the night air.

"Mmm, I can't remember." I leaned into him and kissed the freckles on his shoulder. He shivered.

"It's good. Really good. But it ends on this depressing note about how there would be two lovers on a beach, and even though they were feeling so close, they were actually each looking at a different moon." He pressed in closer to me.

I thought mostly of the feel of his skin against mine, but also about how—months before the Harts moved to Minnesota—*August Arms* had run a story on scientists' suspicion that a second moon had once orbited Earth but had crashed into its twin, sticking there and creating the lunar highlands on the side of the moon we never see.

Silas looked at me, his eyes fierce with joy, and I couldn't tell him about what I'd heard. He wouldn't believe it anyway, I realized. He held the Genesis account of the "two great lights"—sun and moon—in his palm like a favorite storybook.

"I want to know God the way you do," I said suddenly.

Silas nodded, sincere. "You want an august arm against the darkness," he said. He slung an arm around my shoulder and kissed the top of my head. "I wrote a poem, because of our conversation the other day. Want to hear it? It's—it's just a draft, not done. I call it 'Truest Anchor.' Or maybe 'Truest Pillar.' 'Truest Atlas?' I—" He was nervous to share and babbling.

I put a finger over his lips. "Shhh," I said. "Let's hear it."

He spoke soft and slow:

"The broken heart has
its own stark splendor.

"Everything in readiness:
curtain, heaven, hell, heel.

"War before victory.
Wounds before cure.

"Darkness destroyed
by the glory of dawn."

It sounded like a secret in the night air, floating just above the lapping gunmetal waters. "I like it," I said, my voice barely audible.

"Hmm?" he prodded, and it sounded like the tiny sound a bird makes.

"It's okay, you think?" I asked. "To value brokenness, just for the fixing?"

"Hope so," he said, "because I do."

I thought of Sunday mornings: my dad sharing from the pulpit, the congregational hymns, the tiny wafers in a silver tray we passed down the aisles each week—for once, instead of seeming boring and expected, it all seemed sort of beautiful.

Silas's faith covered him like a shield, rode on his brow like a crown.

And then, of course, there was Laurel, whose days were measured by how close she carried these absurd truths to her core: communion reminded her of what was *real*.

"'Darkness destroyed by the glory of dawn,'" I said, seeing how the words felt on my lips. They felt like a story that belonged to me.

"What should I title it?" Silas asked quietly.

"How about just 'Truest'?" I said. "And let that be it?"

Then he kissed me and I knew he understood.

twenty-five

Silas and I brought the leftover chocolate-covered bacon to Gordon's apartment the next day. Gordon sat in his rocker, nibbling on a piece, then after a pause pronounced us "geniuses of the modern world."

"Just Silas," I said. "It was his idea."

"It was for West's birthday. Eighteen years old."

A frown flashed across Gordon's face for a moment. "Eighteen?" he said, as if to himself.

Silas looked puzzled, but I took a guess at what Gordon was thinking. "Betsy's older than I am," I said softly to Gordon. "I think she's in Spain."

Abruptly he said, "She came back in May. Brought me a gift." He pointed toward one of his bookshelves, at a long decorative wooden block etched with a quote: "A country without a memory is a country of madmen." I hated the irony, since Gordon's own memory had been slipping lately.

"That's from Betsy?" I asked.

"It is," he said. "She was studying language and philosophy and quite fell in love with George Santayana. It's his quote."

A country of madmen. I hated that it made me think of Laurel.

"Gordon," I asked, "remember when we talked about Descartes?"

"I do, yes."

Good.

"Can you tell us more about the dream argument? Or, actually, how to refute it?"

Silas looked serious suddenly, staring at Gordon with wide, hopeful eyes.

"Well, that's interesting you'd ask," Gordon said, sounding fully himself again as he spoke about a long-remembered subject. "Descartes, by the end of his *Meditations*, actually refutes it himself. Remember what I told you about the cogito—'I think, therefore I am'? How you let doubt strip everything down to just that and then rebuild?"

"Yes."

"Well, he never intended for someone to *refuse* to rebuild. For someone to get stuck at the dream-argument stage was never the point, you know. To claim a person is living a dream is a heavy, heavy claim for him or her to make."

"Her," said Silas, without explanation.

"Her," Gordon repeated, so softly you could barely hear it. For a moment, he looked a little sad, and I knew that he had understood Silas's comment correctly—that this conversation was not a hypothetical one. He pressed his lips together, let out a doleful sigh, and said, "Heavy claims need a lot of support, and there's just not a lot available."

"How do you mean?" I asked.

"Are our senses sometimes deceived? Yes. But we shouldn't take that too far; they don't fail us *often*. It's like refusing to use a seat belt because *sometimes* seat belts fail."

"Yeah," said Silas, "but what if you somehow can't quit believing the seat belt will fail you? Even if you've never experienced that?"

"I don't know, Silas," said Gordon. "There are minds that hiccup sometimes—skip like an old record player. I don't know how to right that needle."

Silas frowned. "I don't know about record players, but when my CD player skips, I usually just give it a smack, and it sorts itself out."

I laughed, in spite of the conversation's heavy tone. "Yeah," I teased. "Why don't you just slap Laur—*her*—when she gets stuck?"

Silas laughed and stuck out his tongue at me.

It made me laugh too, and I steered the conversation toward lighter topics, though my gaze kept drifting to the carved quote on the shelf, wondering if *history* could ever give Laurel roots the way it did Gordon.

Afterward, Silas and I returned to my house.

"What was up with Gordon today?" Silas asked as we abandoned our bikes beside the driveway.

I shrugged. "He's getting old."

"Getting?"

"Sometimes he confuses me with his great-granddaughter," I said. "It's okay."

"Is it?" he asked.

Before I could answer, Elliot drove into my driveway and parked his parents' minivan in front of us.

"Um . . . ," said Silas. "What the . . . ?"

"What *happened*?" I asked as Elliot stepped out of the vehicle. Except for the windshield, the entire vehicle was covered in what looked like neon Post-it Notes.

"Someone pranked me," Elliot admitted, the irritation in his voice thick and gruff. "Yesterday at some point. I think it was Tom Carver and that Tennant punk. And then it rained a shit ton. I wasn't even supposed to take the van out of the *garage* while my parents were gone. They'd kill me. Oh. Happy belated birthday, West." He kissed my cheek lightly, his eyes allowing no entrance to his thoughts. Silas noticed and laced his fingers through mine, drawing me close. It was silly, and for Elliot's sake, I took a step away from Silas and toward the van.

"What happens when you . . . ," I asked, reaching out and pulling off a damp Post-it. It left a sticky residue. "Damn."

"Do you know what to do, West?" Elliot asked. "I thought maybe you'd seen this done before. Can you use Goo Gone?"

I shook my head. "Goo Gone is for household stuff. I read online somewhere that you have to use spray-on deodorant and attack each mark. It could get expensive."

"I'll pay for the materials, and I'll help!" Elliot insisted. "It has to be done before one o'clock though. That's when my parents get back."

"West," Silas said, a warning in his voice. "That's less than two hours. We can't possibly get it done in two hours."

"We'll call Whit," I said. "And Marcy and Bridget. And Laurel can help too."

"Yes, good!" said Elliot, eager.

"You two go buy the deodorant—remember, the spray-on kind—and I'll get everyone else over here to start peeling off the Post-its," I said.

The look they each gave me would have been hilarious in other circumstances—on Elliot, a look of mild shock; on Silas, skepticism. All because I had assigned them a task to do together. "Just do it," I said, rolling my eyes. "And hurry!"

After they left, I called Whit and the girls, and everyone said they'd hurry over, except for Laurel, who was hesitant. She had barely stepped outside her house the whole summer—and each time she had, it had amounted to a crisis. "You know what," I said, "you don't *have* to come."

"Whit will be there?" she asked.

I rolled my eyes again. "Yes, he's already on his way."

"All right," she resolved. "I'm coming too."

Bridget and Marcy arrived first, and together we peeled off all the Post-its. The damp ones came off easily enough, but the ones that had dried left behind bits of crusty paper, as if they'd been glued down. "I hope your idea works," Marcy said to me, "otherwise, we're not going to see Elliot until after graduation."

Whit arrived just as Elliot and Silas were returning from Red Owl with supplies, and we all got to work. When Laurel arrived, Whit looked up and smiled.

Laurel had showered and come with her long hair still damp. She had used concealer under her eyes and had put on mascara and lip gloss, and she looked about a thousand times better than she had the other day when we'd searched the Mayhew attic. "Hey," she said, and this comment was clearly directed to Whit and Whit alone.

"Hi," he said, and she walked over to him and gave him a small, awkward hug.

"How did it go at your uncle's?" she asked him. I had no idea what she was talking about. I saw Bridget and Marcy raise their eyebrows at each other.

The sun was high and bright in the sky, and we all worked silently. Elliot had obviously told the others about our breakup. We'd all been friends so long, it was like a mini divorce. Bridget and Marcy were Team Elliot, except Marcy liked Elliot, and Silas had secured his singlehood, so she alternately regarded Silas as a kitten killer or Jesus Christ. And then there was poor Whit—Whit, who had been friends with Elliot for years—but who had known me just as long; he'd be the child who had to choose which parent to live with. Plus, he seemed to like Laurel, so that complicated matters further.

After about ten uncomfortable minutes, Silas started to quietly sing "Bohemian Rhapsody," a ridiculous choice. Bridget and Marcy gave each other half-amused looks. Elliot didn't look up. Laurel started giggling.

Then Whit joined in. By the end, the two of them traded off high-pitched "Galileos," and almost everyone was singing along except Elliot, who was working hard at the crusty spots of glue with deep intensity. Eventually, though, he grunted something.

"What did you say?" I asked.

"It's not 'scare a moose.' It's 'Scaramouche.'"

"Scaramouche?" Silas repeated.

"Some clown character."

Elliot went back to work, but Silas and I grinned at each other.

We followed this up with a wholehearted attempt at the *WARegon Trail* theme song and then a mockery of Chuck Justice's latest single, after which Whit grabbed Laurel's shoulders and planted a kiss on her lips. Silas's mouth fell open, just a little.

But Laurel looked so surprised—and so pleased.

"I think I am high on Right Guard," I announced when we finally finished. The van looked so clean that Elliot decided to take it home via some back roads before returning it to the garage just to remove all suspicion. Whit, hat on backward and crooked grin on his face, asked Laurel if she wanted to go for a walk to the lake, and she agreed. Silas briefly pulled Whit aside before he and I snuck across the parking lot to the bell tower.

"So, I'll go running with him. With Elliot, I mean," Silas said to me as he followed me up the four flights. "If he ever wants to."

I turned around suddenly. *"Really?"*

He bumped into me. "Yeah, Elliot's not so bad."

I frowned.

"Okay, okay, maybe he is," Silas said, backing off. "Are you mad? You're mad."

Ignoring him, I finished climbing to the top, Silas on my heels.

"West?" he asked tentatively. "What'd I do wrong here?"

"Everything is just so easy for you," I said, annoyed. "I've been friends with Elliot my whole life, and then I destroyed our friendship—*for you*—and now you two get to be buddy-buddy? That's not fair."

"We are *far* from 'buddy-buddy.'"

"You know what I mean." I pursed my lips and looked out the nearest belfry window.

"West?"

"It's just hard to grow up in a small town. There are . . . *rules*."

"And I'm breaking them?"

"*I'm* breaking them. I *broke* them. I'm making everyone choose Team West or Team Elliot."

"And you think I'm choosing Team Elliot?" he asked, an eyebrow raised.

"Yes. No. Not—that's not—not exactly what I mean. It just gets confusing."

His hand snaked out and pulled me toward him. I let him. "Never mind then," he whispered. "I won't go running with him." He settled his hands on my waist and began to kiss my neck, softly, slowly, whispering against my skin, "I am *always* Team West." His low voice almost growled the words out like gravel.

"You'd better be," I murmured, a small grin on my face.

Silas's lips made a slow trail down my neck, and when he reached my shirt, he pushed it off my shoulder and continued his path until the fabric stopped him once again. My nerves felt raw and exposed, and I could still hear his throat grinding out my name. "Silas?" I whispered, and it was as if he knew what I wanted, because, suddenly, his lips were pressed to mine, forcing my mouth open, and we were tasting each other.

Kissing Elliot had never felt like this. With Silas, I had this relentless feeling that I would never get close enough to him, no matter how hard I tried to erase the space between us.

It was this chaos of *touch*: his hands against my shoulder blades, mine around his neck, our bodies pressed together. I slipped my hands beneath his T-shirt, sliding them up over his stomach, feeling the firm muscle there beneath his skin. And then his hands were at the waistband of my shorts, his thumbs hooked into the elastic near my hip bones.

I drew a short, sharp breath.

"Sorry," Silas said, lifting his hands up in an almost comic "don't shoot" stance.

"You're fine." I took his hands and placed them back on my hips and leaned up to kiss him again, but he turned his face to the side so that I kissed his cheek instead. I pouted, and Silas actually laughed at me.

"Tuck that lip back in," he teased. "West, we . . ." He didn't finish his sentence, but I knew the unspoken words were something like *need to slow down*.

I wanted to say, *To hell with slowing down*, but I was worried what he would think of me if I did, and wait—wasn't the guy supposed to be the one who always wanted to push things further? It had always been that way with Elliot, at least.

We retreated over to the air mattress, our usual spot where we liked to read, our backs against the cool stone wall. "What do you think about Laurel and Whit?" I asked, trying to distract us both from the lingering awkwardness left after whatever had just happened.

"I threatened to kick his ass if he messes with her," he said.

"Just now? That's what you were doing when you took him aside?"

"Yeah," he said, then laughed. "Laurel overheard."

"Oh gosh."

"I feel bad. Her face was bright red. But we're okay," he said, tapping his Hart2Hart sign over his chest. "I don't even know what's going on with them." He glanced at me suspiciously. "Do *you*?"

I shook my head. "Not really. I know they talk on the phone sometimes. I'd love to listen to their conversations. I bet they'd be so . . ."

"Strange? Clumsy? Gawky? Maladroit?"

"Yes," I said. "Maladroit. Totally maladroit." I shoved my shoulder into his. "*You're* maladroit, Hart."

Silas grinned. "Hey, I thought you liked to con people into telling you their secrets. Get crackin' on these two! Come to think of it, I'm not actually sure that you've conned *me* out of any secrets this summer."

"You told me about Laurel," I said, resting my chin on his shoulder.

"Sort of. You kinda walked into that one." Silas kicked off his shoes.

"True," I agreed, then whispered in his ear, "So tell me a secret."

"Okay." Silas pressed his lips together and was quiet for a long time.

"You don't have to," I started, but he said, "Sometimes she embarrasses me. Sometimes I'm . . . ashamed of her. When she showed up today? It's so obvious something's wrong. And that makes me ashamed of myself. I'm my sister's keeper, and I don't want to be."

And for just one moment, I wondered how Silas would choose if it was Team West versus Team *Laurel.*

I didn't want to know.

twenty-six

August arrived, and I spent the afternoon detailing a car on my own. Without Silas, it took almost twice as long. I called him three times, but there was no answer, and every time I got his voice mail I got more annoyed. He finally showed up just as I was waxing the hood.

"Hey," he said.

"Hey."

"Let me do that," he said, reaching for my rag. I surrendered it to him easily, exhausted as I was. He stretched himself over the hood, all elbow grease and stony silence.

"Well?" I asked his back.

"I was at Papa and Oma's."

"You could have called."

"I was looking for that damn ballerina doll."

"Which doesn't exist," I added, pointed and cold.

He turned around, his eyes savage, and hissed, "Don't *ever* let her hear you say that." I blinked at the severity in his voice, and he immediately softened. "Shit. West. I'm sorry. Shit. Shit, shit, *shit*." He turned away from me.

I wrapped my arms around him and pressed my face into his back, breathing him in: soap and sweat and lumber. "What is it?" I asked.

"Laurel locked the door to her room, and Mom went ballistic."

"Oh no."

"She kept pounding on the door and shouting for Laurel to open up. We both did." He squeezed his eyes shut. "Nothing. No reaction. We didn't know—"

"What did you do?"

"Got Dad's power drill from the garage and took off the door handle *and* the lock."

"And?"

"She was on her bed, staring at the ceiling. She looked over and seemed *surprised* to see us standing in the doorway. It was like she'd never heard us begging her to open the door, West! Like she'd never even heard the *drill*."

"I'm so sorry."

"And then Mom was bawling, and I was just so pissed at Laurel for doing this to us that I wanted to find that doll and rub it in her face till she *choked* on reality. I forgot about our detailing and didn't call and didn't hear my phone and you had to do everything on your own, and I *hate* that I let Laurel get in the way of everything, but I don't know how else to *be*."

He sat down then, completely spent, right on the driveway pavement with his long legs stretched out before him and his elbows resting on his knees. I joined him.

"I'm sorry," he said again. "The car looks great. Nice work."

I smiled.

"So, what's next?" I asked.

"Mom's been on the phone with Dad; they're talking about checking Laurel into a residential facility in St. Paul."

"What do you think about that?"

"I don't know," he said. "I really don't. Earlier this summer, after we first moved, there were lots of days when I thought she would be just fine and that it would all pass, but this week was terrible, West. Dad doesn't know what to do—if he should come home or whatever—but Mom said, 'Too late now.' She's pissed."

"You're sure it has nothing to do with him?" I asked awkwardly. I liked Mr. Hart.

"I'm positive. Laurel quit seeing her therapist because he kept suggesting that, remember?"

I nodded. "All summer, I've been wanting to help her," I said, "but I never really knew how."

Silas let out a giant breath. "I know, West. Same here." He looked years older than his age.

"I saw inside your notebook once," I admitted. "Earlier this summer. It was open on your bed, and I thought it was a letter, but . . . it was a prayer, wasn't it? A prayer for Laurel—about how she needed God. *You are exactly what she needs.*"

Silas looked up suddenly. His eyes were dark and intense.

"Are you mad I saw it? I'm sorry."

"Don't worry about it." There was a curious look on his face. "It was a prayer, but it wasn't for Laurel."

"Who . . . ?"

"It was for *you*."

"Me?"

"Yeah."

". . . did it work?" I asked, thinking how his poem had sunk its teeth into my heart.

Silas said softly, "You tell me."

Later that evening, when it was just me and Libby alone in the living room, I made an announcement: "I like Silas Hart."

"*Ob*viously," she said, rolling her eyes in a purely twelve-year-old way.

"Are you still sending fan mail to Chuck Justice?" I asked her.

"Every week," she said, grinning. "I slip the letters into Dad's stack of mail, and he pays for the stamps without even realizing." It made me smile.

"What do you like about him?" I asked her.

"About Dad?"

"About Chuck, you goon," but she was teasing me.

"Everything."

"Yeah, but like what?"

"He's so cool. His songs and his hair and the way he likes cinnamon ice cream."

"No one likes cinnamon ice cream."

"Chuck does. I do."

"Since when?"

"Since forever," she said.

"Well, I guess you're perfect for each other then," I mocked.

"We are," she said seriously. "There was a quiz in the magazine you gave me, and it said so. What do you like about Silas?"

"Everything," I said, copying her.

Then I squeezed her knee, where I knew she was ticklish, and we both giggled and batted at each other for a while till a pillow fell off the couch, revealing the glued-together paper dolls that had been hidden beneath it.

"Remember these?" Libby said, picking them up.

"Yep."

I turned on the TV, flipping idly through the channels while, beside me, my sister worked carefully to peel apart the paper dolls. I don't know what she had expected, but the glue had dried and hardened, and it was an ugly process—shreds of each doll torn away and left clinging to the other. Libby tossed the finished product into my lap: a paper girl, her face and chest torn off, with the boy's stomach still adhered to hers.

"Well, that didn't exactly work, did it?" I asked.

"It worked just the way I guessed," she said, her fingertips playing with the scraps.

Mrs. Hart was at her parents' home for dinner when I traipsed over to Heaton Ridge later that week to listen to the radio with Silas. As soon as I let myself in, I heard it. Hysterics from upstairs. The return of the banshee. Only this time, there was another voice shouting too.

I barreled up the stairs and into Laurel's bedroom, pressing open the door that no longer had a knob. She was in the corner of her bed, the silver chenille blanket pulled up to her neck, weeping uncontrollably while Silas screamed at her.

"What?!" he roared. "This is absolutely ridiculous. *Ridiculous!* You are driving me insane, do you understand that?" He was pulling at his hair and looked a lot like a crazy person in that moment.

He started pacing, not far, just two or three steps in one direction and then back, fast, frenzied. Then he got in her face, put his hands on her mattress, and leaned into her, so that their faces were less than a foot apart: "What the hell do you want me to say to you, Laurel? That we are just ideas in God's head and when he sneezes we'll be gone? Is that what you want to hear? That you're the only real person and that your subconscious is the most brilliant thing ever because it's imagined an entire life for you? Is that what you want? You want someone to corroborate your ideas? It's *fucked up*, Laurel! Do you hear me?" Spit collected at the corners of his mouth.

Laurel's eyes. They were scared. Wild and wretched.

"Silas, stop it," I demanded. My head was spinning with all the noise.

Now Silas shouted in my direction. "Don't yell at *me*!" He pointed an accusatory finger at his sister. "She's the one who thinks there's a giant chicken in the sky puppeteering everything. She's the one who—" Laurel looked so bereft, so completely broken in the corner, that I flew at Silas, without really thinking what I was doing. He grabbed my wrists and held them tight. I twisted but couldn't get free until he released me. He didn't say anything, but the look in his eyes goaded me, dared me to try it again; he was high on adrenaline—and melancholia, which was stronger.

I glared at him as I rubbed my right wrist, which was red from his grip. But it gave me an idea.

Without another thought, I bypassed Silas and slapped Laurel—hard—across her left cheek. There was a harsh clap and a quick, stinging rip across my palm.

"What are you doing?" Silas thundered, grabbing my shoulders and yanking me away from his sister.

But the change was almost instant. Laurel's weeping simmered even as the star appeared on her cheek. "She said shock is good for her," I explained, my shoulders still clutched by

Silas. "Like when she tripped over your guitar case."

Although Laurel's bottom lip quivered, her banshee cries ceased.

"The skipping CD player," I said. Then I jerked away from Silas. I joined Laurel on the bed, kneeling on the mattress, moving toward her. "Listen to me," I said. "This is real life. Do you need me to slap you again to prove it?" She shook her head, still looking amazed. *"And so what if it's not?"* I said. "If this is a dream, then we're going to make it the best damn dream you've ever had."

twenty-seven

So began our last weeks of summer, Laurel's pilot light relit.

She was being social and sleeping normal hours. She opened the windows all throughout the house. She even went grocery shopping, on her own and unprompted, bringing home "what sounded good": Lucky Charms, diced pineapple, cheddarwurst, and a tub of cookie dough that we ate with spoons. Laurel sat at the head of the table, laughing as Silas told jokes.

It galvanized him. He was full of plans for us—every day, a new adventure: swimming, hiking, riding every roller coaster at Valleyfair. We bought eighties prom outfits at a thrift store and convinced the photographer at a portrait studio that we *wanted* the photos to look awkward.

Mrs. Hart surprised the four of us with tickets to see *Carmina*

Burana at the Minnesota Dance Theatre.

"You clean up nice," I told Whit when I opened the Harts' front door and saw him standing on the doorstep in a tie, holding a bouquet of white forget-me-nots.

"It's the khakis," Laurel said, moving past me, taking the flowers, and kissing Whit on the nose. "These are my favorite!" she said of the flowers. Her dress was such a pale shade of pink that it seemed almost cream. The bustled hem hit right below her knee, and it looked like Aphrodite-turned-prima-ballerina had come down from Mount Olympus for the evening in her strappy copper heels.

I wore a lacy strapless dress and a pair of Laurel's boots. The heels on those suckers were at least three inches. "So this is what the weather is like up here," I said to Silas as he joined us at the front door. Teresa had made him wear a blazer, and I wanted to fall at her feet in thanks. His hair fell into his eyes, and the jacket fit perfectly in the shoulders.

When he saw me, he lit up and shook his head.

"What?" I asked.

"I just can't believe I'm so damn lucky."

I wasn't sure what to expect, but *Carmina Burana* was fascinating. From the first intense chords of "O Fortuna," my pulse was racing as if there was a subwoofer inside me making my blood throb. The lighting, the orchestra, the dancers—everything was perfect and powerful, and the best part of it all was sneaking glances at Laurel. Her foot tapped along to the music, her eyes were wild, and she leaned forward in her seat as if the stage was calling her home.

Afterward, as we'd walked through the parking ramp back to the car, she couldn't stop herself from dancing, her dress flowing around her like water as she moved. It made us all smile.

Silas drove his parents' car; I had shotgun; Laurel and Whit sat together in the backseat so close she was practically in his lap. Silas leaned over me and pulled a brochure out of the glove compartment. "What do you think about this, Laur?" he asked, handing it back to her.

It was information he'd collected on his college visit about the school's degree in dance. Laurel stared at it, chewing on the inside of her mouth the way her brother sometimes did.

"It's just an idea," Silas said. "You can toss it if you want. Here, I'll take it back."

He reached for it, but Laurel snatched it away. "Calm down, you spaz," she said. "I think it looks awesome. I'm just thinking of how out of shape I am."

"There are studios in St. Cloud," I said. "And—it's not the same thing—but next week is the Green Lake street dance."

"Street dance?" Laurel asked.

"Yeah," said Whit. "We have it every year the Friday before Labor Day. You'll love it."

Silas looked at me from the driver's seat, his dark eyes full of sparks, and started singing the familiar "one-two, one-two" rhythm of "O Fortuna," replacing the unknown foreign lyrics with "bum-bum, bum-bum," until I looked the translation up on my cell phone. "The last line of the song says, 'Fate crushes the brave,'" I shared.

"Not always," said Laurel from the backseat.

When we got back to Green Lake that same evening, the four of us retreated to the Harts' den. On the couch, Laurel rested against Whit while she used the remote.

That left me and Silas to the papasan. It was big enough for us both, but just barely. He let his long legs stretch down to the floor, and I rested my head over his heart. "What's the movie, Laur?" Silas asked, and I grinned because—with my ear to his chest—the words sounded like a sort of purr.

"*Où Te Trouver*," she said. "*Where to Find You*."

The two boys groaned.

"Settle down!" Laurel told them. "There are subtitles."

Only there weren't. Just a man with an exceptional beard speaking in rapid French to a beautiful woman. "Look at that thing," marveled Silas at the facial hair. "I'll bet that guy's beard has a beard."

"You're jealous because you can't grow any facial hair yourself," his sister taunted from the couch.

"Of course I am!" he said, rubbing his jaw. Then he tilted my chin up to look at him. "Do you think I'm less of a man, West?"

"Yup." I bit his finger.

"When God said, 'Let there be light,' that beard appeared," said Laurel, muting the film with the remote.

"You guys are so weird," Whit said, but he looked happy with Laurel leaning back into him and the glow of the TV reflecting in his eyes. One of Whit's arms reached across Laurel from shoulder to shoulder, and she was holding on to that arm as if it were a buoy. It struck me for a moment just how much sadness was sitting on that couch—but how you'd never know it tonight.

Silas said, "That beard invented the wheel, jazz music, and emoticons."

"It speaks fourteen languages well," I said, laughing, "and one badly." They all looked at me. "It keeps it humble," I explained.

"That beard's hobbies are kicking ass and taking names," Whit tried.

"That beard is a vigilante," said Silas, my human thesaurus.

"It owns property in Spain."

"It will stop global warming."

"It exists in another dimension."

"It has honorary degrees from Princeton and Yale."

"That beard breastfed the sun, moon, and stars." This was from Laurel, after which there was a moment of silence before Silas chimed, "Awkward."

We were really, really tired. But we couldn't stop laughing.

The bearded Frenchman and the beautiful woman on the screen were sharing a kiss, and Laurel sat up and tugged at Whit, saying, "Come say good night."

Whit, holding Laurel's hand, followed her obligingly but not before Silas pointed at him sternly and said, "No funny business." Whit rolled his eyes.

"Can *we* get up to funny business?" Silas said once the other two had left.

I turned my head to face him. "Hypocrite," I whispered, smiling.

"She left kinda fast, huh?" he said. "Should I check on her?"

"No," I insisted. "She's fine—and probably making out with Whit right now."

Silas pretended to gag.

"You're too protective," I said. "Take a break, Hart."

He smiled. It was crowded in the papasan, but still we didn't move to the couch. "You're right," he said, wriggling a little to get comfortable and resting his head against my shoulder. "Want to run away together?"

"Yes, please," I said. "Where to?"

"Mexico is always good. And we have Papa Arty's truck."

"I doubt the pickup would make it that far."

"It could get there. Probably not back."

"Then again, we wouldn't need to get back," I said. He looked up at me and grinned.

Silas took my hand and said, "We'll drive as far as we can and hitchhike the rest of the way. We won't stop till we get to the beach. Somewhere near ruins. We'll build a little hut roofed with thatch and get jobs at a local resort so that we can buy loads of books. And every night, we'll watch the sunset turn everything to copper and then go to our little hut and make fun of that day's tourists."

I leaned my cheek against his hair, which was curling slightly from the humidity outside. He smelled like shampoo and dryer sheets.

"I'm game," I murmured. "Or we could go north too, you know."

He yawned a little. "Mmm, true. We could go to Alaska. You'd like it there. We'll get a cabin and read aloud by the fireplace. I like that idea." His voice was starting to thicken with fatigue, and I heard Whit's car start out in the driveway. "We can pick blueberries."

I craned my head back in order to look at Silas; his eyes were closed, and in that moment, he looked like a little boy.

"Blueberries?" I said—but very quietly.

He yawned again. "There are . . . there are blueberries . . . everywhere . . . in September."

I didn't know if it was true or not, but I felt his breathing get slow and heavy, and his arm was hot against mine. I tried to picture us alone in a cabin, a fire blazing in the corner, listening as Silas read his poems. We're just kids, I reminded myself.

A few minutes later, as a reminder of that fact, Teresa

appeared in the doorway of the den wearing a robe. "Hey, you guys? It's getting late. West's parents just called—" She smiled down at her sleeping son, and I was grateful that he was cuddled up next to me so innocently, though I was terribly embarrassed that my parents had called—and probably woken up—Mrs. Hart.

"Silas," I whispered, nudging his head with my shoulder.

His eyes fluttered open.

"I've got to go."

"Mexico?" he asked groggily.

"Not tonight," I whispered.

In the final days of summer, Silas and I took Laurel to Legacy House to meet Gordon. "Delighted to meet you, Laurel. Come sit, come sit. What business are you in, young lady?"

"I'm not sure," she said, honestly, sitting on the couch beside me and twisting her fingers nervously in her lap, all while glancing around in awe at Gordon's many bookshelves. "I'm not usually sure of much," she admitted.

Gordon smiled, lit his pipe, and I knew that he knew he was talking to the elusive "her." "Occam's razor," he said, as if offering her a gift. That wonderful, homey smell of cherry pipe tobacco filled the room again.

"What's that?" asked Silas, standing near the window.

"Essentially," said Gordon, "it's a principle that says the simpler explanation is better than the complex one."

"Why's it called a razor?" I asked, plucking a peppermint

from a small bowl on the coffee table in front of us.

Gordon opened his mouth to answer me, but Laurel beat him to it: "It's a philosophical term . . . a device that lets you 'shave away' unlikely explanations."

Gordon smiled. "We have a young philosopher in the room today," he said, pleased.

Laurel smiled too, but only a little. "Philosophy was my gateway drug," she admitted. *To what?* we wondered, the question hanging in the air like Gordon's pipe smoke.

"She's also a dancer," I said to Gordon, then unwrapped my peppermint and popped it into my mouth.

"A philosopher *and* a dancer!" he exclaimed. "Nietzsche said he could only believe in a God who dances!"

"I didn't know that," she said. "But I think he *does* dance though." She waited another moment, staring off into the distance in thought, and then she said, "I'm sure he does."

Afterward, Silas and I had Holy Communion with Laurel on the beach: grape Crush and Goldfish crackers and Silas's reassurances that it was not irreverent. We spread a bedsheet over the sand. A cool breeze came over the water from the southwest so that Laurel's hair blew out behind her like a bridal veil. Silas read a poem he'd written in his notebook:

"The low moon lags beside men out late,
whose shadows stretch like secrets
down this ordinary street.

"Did you know?
There is a blood that works like bleach.

"What words work
if God cooks you breakfast,
burns his fingers on the fish?

"The collision of common and celestial
holds her like a jealous palm."

"Silas, that's really good," Laurel said as she leaned back on her elbows, looking out at the waves on the water.

"It's about you, Laur," he said. He handed me the bottle of Crush and Laurel the bag of Goldfish. The bubbles of carbonation burned my throat as I swallowed.

"I know," Laurel said, then tasted a cracker, God's body. "I am held by that jealous palm. I believe that. Right now, I believe that." She closed her eyes, perhaps in prayer, and breathed in the scent of the breeze: algae and white clover that carried over the water onto this holy space.

twenty-eight

Laurel and I crowded before the mirror in her room, assessing ourselves and each other as she did my eye makeup for the street dance, which was starting soon. "Your hair is *perfect*," I whined. "Mine doesn't do anything I want it to." Her room smelled like hair spray, and she had music from *Swan Lake* playing on her iPod dock.

"Oh, whatever!" she said, her hand absently tousling the loose curls she'd put in. "You're gorgeous, West. There. Done. Your eyes look like black holes I'm going to fall into."

"Is that a good thing?" I asked.

She shoved me in the shoulder. "You dork. Take a look."

I usually didn't wear any makeup, but Laurel had put eyeliner and mascara on me, and now my lashes looked about eight miles long and perfect. Laurel had been conservative with me—her own eyes were covered in thick, gold-glitter eye shadow that perfectly matched the highlights in her hair.

"What are you going to wear?" she asked.

"This," I said, extending my hands to show her my most basic of outfits—a pair of jeans that had been lying on my bedroom floor for the last month or so and a T-shirt.

Laurel frowned, then looked through her closet. "Here, try this instead." She handed me a dusty pink button-up that was light and sweet and pin-tucked with lace. When I put it on, she nodded her approval.

For herself, she chose a pair of the palest blue jeans and a low-cut white cami, along with this sleeveless denim top that she wore open.

"You look *incredible*."

Her cheeks flushed. "Shhh, don't. Hey," she said quietly, "so . . . when Trudy comes back, we're still going to hang out, right?"

"Durr," I said, rolling my eyes and grinning at our reflection in the mirror.

She smiled softly. "I owe you, West."

I frowned. "For what?"

"For everything, but especially these last couple of weeks. I feel like myself—really like myself—and happy, like I'm walking on a rock instead of in a moon bounce. You know what I mean?"

"Yeah," I said, even though I didn't—not exactly.

"Anyway, I just wanted to thank you before . . . before the summer is over. And while I'm still me." Suddenly her smile slackened, and she looked at me and said, "Who knows how long it will last?"

"Knock that off," I said. "You've turned a corner, Laurel."

"I hope so," she said. Then her voice changed again. "West, you hottie! Silas isn't going to be able to take his eyes off you tonight!"

There were police barricades on one end of Elm Street and, on the other, a stage set up with huge speakers hanging from the top of the framework. My family had been there before dark, but the carnival games and cakewalk were long over, and a different crowd was out. The Mean Green Pub had a station on the street full of kegs; you had to have a special stamp on your hand to show you were twenty-one, but it was ten p.m. and already dark out and no one was paying much attention to that: tons of kids were getting wasted under the trees that lined the street. I watched Laurel and Whit each pound a drink or maybe two and then stop to talk with Elliot, who sat as if enthroned on a nearby front porch with some of his football teammates, one whose house it was. I saw Elliot glance around—presumably for me—but I ducked into the crowd of people dancing on the street, pulling Silas along behind me.

A mediocre band played covers. Silas faced me in a T-shirt that (somewhat) appropriately said, "Hold Me Closer, Tony

Danza," dancing like a goof, awkward and clumsy—and somehow it was the most adorable thing ever. This tall, lanky boy, all arms and legs and *eyes*. His were electric.

Laurel and Whit had found us in the crowd and were dancing nearby, his hands resting low on her hips. Laurel looked so natural and so beautiful that I couldn't help but laugh at the wide gap between her and her twin, the gangly but gorgeous boy whose fingers were intertwined with mine. When the song slowed, I put my arms comfortably around Silas's neck and looked up at him. "Laurel seems good tonight," I said.

He nodded toward his sister; she was playing with the long hair at the base of Whit's neck and laughing at something he was saying. "She's having a blast," Silas said. "I haven't heard her laugh like that since she was thirteen."

Tiki torches lined the street, staked into people's yards. The sun had set, and the street was packed. The air felt warm and thick with humidity, and I thought I might have heard some thunder far off. I worried it might rain but soon forgot about the weather when Silas settled his hands on my hips, his fingers resting on the skin where my shirt had ridden up.

"Tell me what you're thinking," I whispered, my head feeling cloudy.

"I'm thinking that it's been an incredible summer," he said softly, then he leaned down, kissed me on the forehead, and said, "Because of you."

Then I was up on my tiptoes, pressing my lips against his,

my hands on his chest, feeling the muscle beneath the thin cotton. It was so warm in the crowd. "Let's get out of here."

We retreated to the church bell tower and climbed the staircase holding hands, giggling and stopping every few stairs to kiss. Up at the top, I turned on the camping lantern while Silas leaned into the window ledge. When I joined him, I saw that Jody Perkins had ridden his mower out to Elm Street, the purr of the motor inaudible above the more distant music.

The feel of Silas's bare arm against mine was electric, sharpening my senses into cold steel: I knew what I wanted to happen next.

Thoughts raced inside me: *Will Silas want it too? Is it wrong? We're in the frickin' church bell tower! What would Dad say if he knew?* Angrily, I shoved the last question off. Dad didn't—wouldn't—know. He never asked me about myself anymore, and he didn't know me well enough to see it on my face. Right? I looked at Silas, still gazing out the window, the breeze lifting his hair off his face. He was so beautiful. My cold steel sharpened to a point: *this was exactly what I wanted.*

But I kept thinking how he had put the brakes on recently. *What if he doesn't want me—like that?* What if I embarrass myself? Warm and a little dizzy, I took a deep breath, my back against the tower wall beside the window Silas leaned over. Awkwardly, I shoved my hands into my pockets—and there was Trudy's gift. My insides churned, a slow, deep, yawning sensation. And Silas was completely unaware.

Or maybe he wasn't. He stood up tall and looked down at me, and there was conflict in his eyes. And intensity. I wondered if my eyes had the same hungry look as his. The noise from the dance was drowned out by the sound of my pulse hammering in my neck behind my ears. My heart slammed against my chest. He was standing *so close.*

"West?" he asked softly, and his voice cracked.

Yes, *now*, I thought, then put my hands on his chest, stood on my tiptoes to kiss him, and felt his arms go around me. But his response was different than usual. This kiss was deeper, somehow more desperate—as if the end of summer was so much more than just that. Silas took the lead, pressing me against the wall with his body, his hands at my waist, fists curling in the hem of my shirt. In his shadow, I felt like a wire about to snap.

An alarm exploded inside me when his cold hands slipped under my shirt and touched my bare stomach: fear and guilt—but pleasure too. I gasped a little against his mouth but then kissed him harder, encouraging him, and felt his hands move from my hips, up and over my rib cage, to my breasts. He looked at me, and I nodded, and he started to unbutton my shirt.

"Dammit," he said when his fingers worked clumsily at a button without success. I reached for the buttons, trying to help him out. "No," he whispered. "Let me."

Silas had a look of fierce concentration on his face, and it was so adorable that I leaned forward and kissed his ear, letting my lips linger there, barely grazing his skin. "You're not making this any easier," he mumbled through a grin as he finally finished with the buttons. He peeled the shirt off my shoulders.

We kissed again, then Silas pulled his shirt up and over his head. I laid a hand on his bare chest—his heart was pounding just like mine. "Should we, like, lie down?" he asked.

It was a ridiculous question, but I was grateful to have direction. We climbed onto the mattress, and he leaned over me, breathing heavily. I slid out of my jeans as he watched; in only my underwear, my thoughts raced with insecurities. But Silas stared at my body, swallowed hard, and pressed his knee between my legs. "You're so beautiful," he whispered.

Then he placed a gentle hand over my heart so that he could feel it race, just as I'd felt his; it rose and fell quickly with my chest, and Silas's eyes moved to meet mine. They were serious, unblinking. After a few moments, he leaned in and kissed the hollow of my throat so gently that I got goose bumps. Then he locked eyes with me again and reached around and unclasped my bra, so easily that I whispered in panic, "Have you done this before?"

"No," he said, shaking his head slightly; his voice was low, quiet, making his whole body hum like a cello string.

"With Beth?"

"No, shhh," he said again, and relief rushed me, and as I lay before him, vulnerable and shaky, I noticed that he was still trembling too. Silas ran his fingers from my shoulder down to my hip, so lightly, barely touching me, as if he were afraid. I felt afraid, too: Silas, the boy who had chattered incessantly all summer long, was silent, and it felt so strange, so foreign.

"It's just me," I whispered, breathless, and he laughed a little, ducking his head in this bashful way, and I laughed too. It was so sweet, so endearing that my heart swelled like a balloon. "I love you," I said softly, reaching up to touch his face.

"I love you, too," he said, no pause, no hesitation, and the words were like a cradle. And then Silas leaned into me, one arm on either side of my head, kissing a trail from my mouth to my jaw to my throat. "Damn, you smell good," he breathed into my neck. "Like brown sugar. West, I don't have . . . I wasn't . . ."

I reached over to the pocket of my jeans and pulled out what Trudy had left for me. Silas looked from the condom wrapper back to me, and for a brief moment, I worried that he was going to stop this runaway train. His eyes searched mine, looking for . . . I didn't know what. I was looking in his for a decision.

"You sure?" he asked so quietly I barely heard him, and I could only nod; he pursed his lips, exhaling long and slow, and unbuttoned his jeans. He tried slipping out of them, but he tripped over them awkwardly and kind of *fell* back on top of me.

"Ouch," I said.

"Sorry," he muttered.

"It's okay."

We were clumsy and quiet and it hurt, but I didn't cry. I felt this strange dichotomy: pain, yes—but also joy that lapped at me like I was lying on a beach and it was rolling in with the tide. I felt small beneath his strong body, loved the weight of it crushed against mine, the feel of skin against skin, the roll of his hips, the tiny noises he made, the way he smelled salty and sweet like sweat and sandalwood. *I love you*, I thought. *I really do*.

After, Silas lay propped on one elbow, making circles on my stomach with his finger, his touch so light it gave me goose bumps. He leaned over, his breath hot on my bare skin, and kissed the invisible mark he'd drawn, his lips like this strange, delicious, searing burn.

Outside, it had started to rain—soft and almost musical, and still somehow warm. Summer's last hurrah, met with applause.

Silas and I lay facing each other, a blanket spread over us, and he whispered, "Sorry I hurt you," and I said, "I'm not," and leaned in toward him. We stayed that way, foreheads together, whispering until we were silly with exhaustion. In a way, it was good—being that tired—something to break the solemnity of the evening. It felt like we were Silas and West again, goofy and talkative, just undressed.

"Tell me what you're thinking about," I said for the second time that night.

"I don't know," he said. "You. Naked."

I laughed. "At least you're honest."

Silas grinned. "You?" he asked.

"That school starts in four days."

He groaned and ran a hand through his hair. "Mood killer," he teased. He looked into my eyes with a soft expression on his face and stroked my hair in a way that made me feel beautiful even though I was a sweaty mess. "Want to go to the home-coming dance with me?"

"Only if you promise to do the boy-band dance," I said, trying to keep a straight face.

"And ruin *any* chance of making friends?" he asked with a laugh.

"It's all a part of my wicked plot to keep you for myself," I said.

"Oh, I see how it is," he said, tucking my hair behind my ear. "You think I'm yours now, hmmm?"

"Mmm-hmmm . . . aren't you?" I asked quietly.

"Since you showed up on my doorstep," he said, and kissed me, and it felt like we were the only people awake on earth. "I'm sure Laurel took the car home," Silas said then, reaching for his cell phone and seeing that it was after two a.m. "What was your curfew tonight?"

"One thirty," I said.

"Mine was one," he admitted as he ran his fingers lightly along my arm. "We're gonna be in trouble."

"If they're asleep, they won't even notice," I said. "Besides, what will they do? Ground us for the rest of summer? School starts in *four days*."

As we both groaned and laughed again, a series of sirens sounded in the distance, and I raised my eyebrows and said, "Ooooh, someone got busted. You knew someone would with all those kegs there tonight."

Silas was frowning, his dark eyes troubled.

"What's wrong?"

"Nothing," he said; then he sat up rather suddenly, the blanket falling off of him. "I thought . . . We should probably go." The hair on his forehead was curling a little from sweat, his bare chest pale in the darkness. He stared toward one of the belfry windows, listening to the sound of the sirens fade behind the rhythm of the rain.

With one hand, I held the blanket against my chest as I sat up beside him; I leaned in close and whispered against the flesh behind his ear, "Did I not just remind you that summer is almost over, Hart?" I placed my palm against his chest.

"Well, when you put it that way . . . ," he said, grinning, and pressed his mouth to mine as we fell back against the mattress.

We woke up the next morning when the sun had half risen on a town that smelled clean and raw like damp soil and earthworms and the yellow cress that grew in the sidewalk cracks.

"Oh shit," said Silas, sitting up and reaching for his clothes. "We're going to be in trouble." He checked his phone. "Oh shit, oh shit, oh shit. I missed like fifty calls from my parents. Wake up, West! Get dressed." He stood up quickly and hopped around, trying to pull his jeans up. "Your dad is never going to let us hang out again. Ever."

"I won't let that happen," I said sleepily, snuggling into the blanket and grinning at the way his hair stood up in the back. I felt drugged with the events of the night before. My body felt sore in the most perfect way.

"You won't have a choice if your dad murders me in the next ten minutes."

I frowned from my spot on the mattress. "Just go home. I can take care of my parents."

Silas shook his head firmly and pulled on his shirt. "No way. I'm not making you face the firing squad alone."

"They probably haven't even realized I'm gone."

Now dressed, he rejoined me on the mattress and kissed my forehead. "They will if my parents called yours," he said.

We argued the entire way down the four flights, but when we walked across the wet parking lot toward my house, my dad was on the front steps, waiting, watching. My eyes went wide, and I smoothed out my shirt—Laurel's shirt. Silas reached for my hand and held on tight. My dad started to walk toward us.

"Pastor Beck," Silas said, "I know this—"

"Silas, get in the car," my dad said.

"Dad!" I said, ready to lie, a little surprised at just how ready I was. "Relax. We fell asleep."

"Pastor Beck—" Silas started again.

"Just get in the car, Silas. I'll drive you."

"Dad!"

"Look," my dad said, and his voice was strange, "there's been an accident. Get in the car, Silas. I'll tell you about it while we drive."

Silas's hand went suddenly slack, dropping mine; his face was stark white. "What?" he asked. "What hap—"

"In the car."

This time Silas obeyed. Dad said, "Go talk to Mom," then ducked into the driver's seat, Silas looking terrified. I was left in the driveway, a sense of dread gnawing at my stomach as the summer truly ended.

I kept Silas's gaze as they backed out of the driveway, then stormed into the house, shouting for my mom, my blood pounding. She was sitting at the kitchen table, staring at it but not seeing it. "Mom?" I asked, panted.

She looked up, her eyes full of sorrow. She said, "West . . ." and the strength left my legs as I knew—*knew*—it was Laurel.

twenty-nine

Instead of helping me up, my mom knelt down beside me on the floor and put her arms around me. "Shhh, West."

"What happened?" I gasped.

"Shhh," Mom said again, pressing her face into the back of my neck.

"*Tell* me," I insisted. "Is she—?"

"She's in the hospital."

She was alive. Laurel was *alive*.

"It's not good though, honey," my mom said softly. "The car—or truck, I guess it was—went through the guards and over the bridge. Around two o'clock this morning. It was—well, obviously, there was an impact. They're worried about head trauma."

"Was Whit with her?"

"No, it was just Laurel."

"Is she awake?"

"I don't know many details," she confessed.

I shrugged her off me and stood up, starting to pace. "I need to see her. I need to see Silas. I'll call Whit; he can drive."

Mom was still kneeling on the floor. "West," she said. Without looking up, she shook her head—just the tiniest bit, almost unnoticeable.

Suddenly fatigued and void of emotions, I slumped onto the couch. It was like being underwater—everything muted except my own heartbeat. I vaguely heard Shea and Libby come into the room and Mom tell them to go back upstairs.

The next few hours were strangely dreamlike. I lay on the couch with my head in my mother's lap, drifting in and out of sleep while she stroked my hair. Whenever I'd wake up, I'd have a vague feeling that it was better to be sleeping, so I'd allow—or force—myself back into an unconscious state.

Around dinnertime, when my body finally refused sleep and my stomach started growling, I sat up on the couch beside my mom.

"It's okay to cry, honey," she said. "You don't have to be strong."

"She'll be okay," I said and believed it. The words felt sturdy; it made me feel strong to say them. I could picture it now: Laurel with bruises, a few broken bones. She'd need casts and maybe PT, but who cared about that? Whit would buy forget-me-nots and bring them to her hospital room, and we'd all be giddy with relief.

I had a bowl of soup and some saltines and was feeling better on the whole when my dad came back home.

My stomach hollowed when I saw his face, worn and somber, in need of a shave.

"Kerry?" my mom said, reaching out to grip my arm.

He just shook his head.

"You're lying!" I accused, standing up and wrenching my arm away from my mom. "You're a liar."

"West. She was semilucid in the ambulance but not once she got to the hospital. She—she held on for a little while . . . till Silas got there. She died about an hour later."

"Stop it!" I shouted, putting my hands over my ears. "You're lying!"

No. This wasn't right. It couldn't be real.

"I picked up Glen from the airport this afternoon. The family is together at their house. Arty and Lillian are there, along with Teresa's sister's family. Listen, West, it's important for you to give the Harts some space right now," he said. "I'm sure you're worried about Silas and feel sad about Laurel, but you need to just let them grieve as a family. And Sgt. Kirkwood wants to talk to you."

"Me? What for? I didn't—I wasn't—"

"It's okay," Dad reassured me. "You're not in trouble. No

one's in trouble. He's just trying to get the whole story. What are you doing?"

I'd moved swiftly to grab the car keys off the breakfast bar and was now at the door. "I need to talk to Silas."

"The Harts need some space," he repeated, walking toward me.

"*You* just came from there," I accused.

"I'm their pastor," he said, setting his hand against the door.

As if that would stop me.

"I'm his *girlfriend*," I said, yanking the door open and pushing past him.

"West—"

But I was gone.

I headed for Heaton Ridge, calling Silas on my way over; he didn't answer on the first try, so I called again, and again, and finally on the fourth call, he picked up. "Are you okay?" I asked, realizing what a dumb question that was as soon as it left my mouth.

"No," he said. His voice was small.

"I'm on my way over," I offered, as if that would somehow make things better, as if I had a rescue packed away like a physical object on my person. "Be there in a few minutes."

"I'll come out to your car."

"Okay." The sound of his voice shattered me.

Just drive, I told myself, refusing to look into the ravine as I crossed the bridge. *Just drive.*

The driveway was filled with cars. I let the car idle on the street, my nerves all jangly as I waited for him to come outside, and when he did, he looked so defeated, my throat caught. He was still wearing yesterday's shirt, his hair messy, unshowered, my sweat still on his skin. It drove into my gut like a linebacker: Laurel was dead.

I turned the car off, stepped out. I hugged him, but it was one-sided, as if he was allowing it. "Do you want to go somewhere?" I said. "The lake? We can talk?"

"I really should stick around here for now," he said, his voice so flat it didn't even sound like him. "My parents, they don't want me to go anywhere."

"Let's sit on your porch," I said. My legs felt like they might give out under me.

We sat down on the swing where Silas had first described solipsism syndrome to me. Now he sat there slumped in the seat, making his long legs look even longer. "I . . . I don't know what to say," I admitted. Just twenty-four hours ago, I'd been getting ready for the street dance. Here in this house. With Laurel. An image of her eyes flashed in my mind—all that glitter, golden brown like a fawn.

"There are no skid marks," he said.

"Huh?" I asked, confused.

"Skid marks," he repeated. "There are none." Seeing I still wasn't catching on, he prodded my shoe with his toe. He whispered, "Are you gonna make me say it, West?"

There are no skid marks.

No skid marks.

And suddenly I realized what he meant. The bridge. The bridge over the river to Heaton Ridge. If it had been an accident, she'd have hit the brakes. There would be marks on the bridge. "You mean . . . you mean, you think she meant to go over?" I whispered. "Silas, *no*."

"There's no note," he said, his chin trembling despite his set jaw. "I looked before anyone else—her room, I mean. Tore through everything. First thing I did when I got home. There's a note to Whit inside a notebook, but it's more of a love letter than anything else."

"Silas, she wouldn't have. It was just a—just an accident. She'd been drinking. It was raining. The brakes on the truck weren't great. You know that."

"The paramedics said she was talking in the ambulance. Babbling. Semilucid. She kept saying she was sure. Sure about *what*—about her decision? To end things?"

"No," I said. "No. If anything, the opposite! Like on the beach—the jealous palm. She was *sure*."

His face changed again, from anger to grief. "I should have been there," he whispered, staring blankly at the porch floor. "This is my fault."

"No," I said again. "It's *not*. Don't say that."

"It is," he said, and he squeezed his eyes shut tight. "It *is*! I should have been there to drive her home. Should have looked harder for that doll. Should have pushed her more—or less—or . . . I don't know. I should have—should have been there."

The lake was visible from his front porch, between two of the neighbors' houses on the other side of the street. The swans were the only ones out there today, four of them, gliding like specters over the water, barely leaving a ripple in their wakes. It felt like a year since summer had been here, since young swimmers had played in the lake, since kids had sat sunning themselves on the beach across these waters. We'd had communion with Laurel there only days before, and it felt like a lifetime ago.

Silas started to shake beside me; I leaned in to hug him again, but he shrugged me off.

"She will never be older than seventeen," he growled. It was a dangerous sound; in his voice I heard a trace of the night he had lambasted his sister. "Nothing makes any sense," he said. "She seemed better those last few days than she had all year. Why *now*?"

I pressed my hands against my temples to press out the beginnings of a headache, but also to occupy my hands, which were desperate to touch Silas. I looked out at the lake, at the swans crowding together—a lamentation of swans—and I thought of the swan song: *the most beautiful song a swan sings is the one before it dies.*

But hadn't she said to me once that she thought suicide was the most selfish thing a person could do? Yes, she had, when we were talking about Whit's dad. She couldn't do it on purpose—could she? And yet, I remembered her reflection in her bedroom mirror, her eyes serious as sermons as she said, "While I'm still me."

Silas was thinking of the same thing: "I feel so guilty, and so pissed. If she meant for it to happen—if she did it on purpose—then I hate her." He looked at me, and his dark eyes flashed. "If she . . . I hate her, West. I hate her, but I want her here so bad."

In my mind, on repeat, was the image of Silas, twirling Laurel in their den, her grin like the equator. "I just feel desperate to know the truth—and then I want anything *but* the truth," he said. "And I want to feel this resolution. She's gone. And it's my fault." His last words were barely audible.

"Silas, it's not your fault," I repeated, as I began to understand just what losing Laurel would cost Silas.

"I can't do this right now," he said.

"Do what right now?"

"This. You and me."

Panic punctured my heart. "What? What are you saying?"

"If I had been there for Laurel, she'd still be here," he said. "Not just last night," he continued. "All summer. I let myself get distracted with you. It was a mistake." He didn't meet my eye.

It was as if Silas had slapped me. "Distracted? I'm a *distraction*?" I spat out the word, tears pricking at my eyes.

"West, stop. You're not hearing me right." His eyes were

closed and his head sagging. "I'm just saying—"

"You said it was a mistake."

"All I'm saying is that I should have been focused on my family—with Dad gone and Laurel so messed up. I didn't mean—" He looked at me a little pleadingly.

But I was stung. "You keep saying it was your fault, but if I'm the one *distracting* you"—I thought of last night, the conflict I'd seen in his eyes—"then you must think it's really *my* fault she's dead."

He didn't answer.

I climbed out of the swing and tore down the porch stairs. He scrambled down after me, and with those long legs, he caught up to me quickly in the lawn. "West, no, wait!" When I ignored him, he grabbed my shoulder and spun me around. "Listen to me. I'm fucked up right now, do you understand? *Fucked up*. I just want some space to think."

"You're *supposed* to want *me*!" I roared. I stared hard at him.

Silas was crying.

Everything warred in me: the desire to hold him, to press my lips against his temple and make him feel safe—and the compulsion to fly at him, or to call him a coward.

"You're supposed to want me," I said again. I felt overcome with my selfishness, that I could say these words at this moment, but I was wild with loss. "I gave up *everything*," I whispered. "For you. *To* you."

He lifted his hands to his face but still didn't speak.

And I thought back to June, when I had asked him what he wanted.

It had always been about Laurel. Always.

So I walked away.

Back at the parsonage, I thundered into the house and up the stairs to my bedroom like a guided missile, ignoring the questions. Dad told the family, "Just give her some space." I closed the door, pressed my back against it as I slid down to the floor. Shame made me want to keep all my secrets, but my guilt made me want to spill everything. I was hiding, but I wanted so badly to race down the stairs, climb into Dad's lap, and tell him the story of my summer and especially of last night.

Shame and sorrow and *space* pulled at me.

It was astonishing: yesterday, it was summer; yesterday, we were dancing.

I threw myself onto my bed. My fingers raked the sheets, their softness like an accusation. If what Silas said was true, then I deserved no comfort.

I was still wearing Laurel's shirt—it smelled like Silas, and the scent stuck to my throat like dust. I struggled out of it and threw it on the floor. Then, wanting to slip out of my *body*, I clawed at myself, leaving scratch marks on my arms and stomach. I thought of his finger making slow, gentle circles. . . .

NO.

The TV was on downstairs, though I couldn't make out

which show. I still half expected—half *hoped* for—footsteps, a hand on the doorknob, a face to peek through the door as it opened.

There was only silence, only space.

On my nightstand, a collection of books. His. A dance theater program. Hers. A photo of all of us, the whole group in thrift-store prom outfits, looking deliberately awkward and trying not to laugh. There is this staggering light in all our faces, at home in our eyes.

In the photo, Laurel's smile is real and true and raw. Everyone is looking at the camera, except for Silas.

He's looking at *me*, affection flashing from him like some kind of holy spark.

I pushed it over, and the frame crashed loudly to the floor.

But still no one came.

thirty

I woke up to a phone call from Trudy. "West! Holy *shit*, my dad told me what happened. Are you okay? Don't answer that. I've been waiting for you to call. What can I do? How can I help?"

I was quiet, overwhelmed. I pulled back my curtain and saw my mom and siblings cross the parking lot on their way to church. Dad had already been there for hours. They looked so small out my window, so much farther away than they really were.

"West, are you there?"

"Yeah."

"Do you want to come over?"

"Yeah, maybe." My voice didn't even sound like my voice.

"Hold on a sec, okay?" I heard her talking to someone

briefly before she said, "My dad said he's meeting Whit at the station soon and is wondering if you can come too."

"Okay."

"She said okay!" she said to her dad. "Do you want us to come pick you up?" she asked. I assumed she meant her and her dad.

"My parents are in church," I said. "I can take the car."

"Okay," Trudy said. "Then you can come over here afterward, all right?"

"All right."

Whit's car was parked on the street outside the tiny police station.

Sgt. Kirkwood poked his head out of his office when he heard the door open. "West," he said, then folded me into his arms for a giant hug. "I'm so sorry," he said. "Come in. Join me and Mark." I wondered where Trudy was. Maybe I'd misunderstood her.

"Is that okay?" I asked faintly. "For you to talk to us both at the same time?"

He smiled gently. "There's no foul play suspected, West. I just have a few questions." His voice was soft and reassuring, and it tricked me for a moment into believing everything was okay.

Until I stepped into his office and saw Whit.

He was standing beside Sgt. Kirkwood's desk, and his face

was swollen and dark around the eyes. His lips were chapped, his mouth red even outside his lip line. He wouldn't look at me.

I snapped.

I flew at him, shoving him. "What happened?" I demanded, the words scraping my throat as they came out. I gripped Whit's shoulders and shook them with a strength I never knew I had. "How did this *happen*? *How the hell did this happen?*" I repeated like an invective.

"West, sit down," Sgt. Kirkwood said softly. "Both of you, sit down."

I started to cry; Whit seemed primed for it too. He looked so thin, so broken. I threw my arms around Whit and buried my face in his chest. He put a feeble hand on my back that brought no comfort.

"Sit down," Sgt. Kirkwood repeated, and this time we listened. "Now, let's get this straight," he said, his voice low like a hum. "No one's in trouble. We just want to sort out what happened on Friday."

"Did you talk to Silas?" I asked, manic.

"I did. He told me you two left the dance early."

I wondered just how much Silas had shared.

"Let's move backward," said Sgt. Kirkwood. "You saw her last, Mark?"

Whit nodded. It was so strange to hear him called "Mark." It felt like another person was in the room with us. "We were dancing. Till late."

They were maybe the saddest words I had ever heard.

"Were you drinking?"

Whit stared at the desk separating us from Trudy's dad. He didn't speak.

"It's okay, Mark," Sgt. Kirkwood coaxed. "Let me ask it this way: Was Laurel drinking?"

Again, Whit nodded. Slowly. "Not . . . not much. Maybe two . . . two of the party cups the bar was using. Maybe only one, I don't know. I know she had a little." Suddenly he looked up at both me and Sgt. Kirkwood, his eyes serious and fierce. "I asked her if she was okay to drive home. We couldn't find West and Silas. Where the hell did you two go?"

I swallowed hard and stared at the corner of the room, where a fake plant sat covered in months of dust. "It was hot. We wanted to get away from the crowd."

"We looked all over—" Whit started, and guilt slammed into me again.

"What did she say?" Sgt. Kirkwood interrupted, and I knew he knew. "When you asked her if she was okay to drive?"

"Yes, she said yes."

"That was the last thing she said to you?"

"We—we said good night. Then she kissed me and got into the truck." Suddenly he hit himself against the forehead, over and over, growling out, "God, why didn't I just fucking drive her home? Who *does* that?"

I reached for his hands to stop him, but he pushed me away. Just like Silas in his yard, Silas on his porch. I laced my fingers tightly together.

"It's okay, Mark." Sgt. Kirkwood's voice was so gentle, so calming. I felt grateful Sgt. Kirkwood was the one asking the questions and not some officer I didn't know. I hated every single thing about this meeting except for his voice. The glare of the floor, the thrift-store smell of the old wood paneling, the taste of the air being recycled through the window AC unit, the look on Whit's face—the combination was making my stomach churn.

"I think she killed herself!" Whit erupted, and the look on his face told me I wasn't the only one having stomach problems just then. "I think she . . ."

Sgt. Kirkwood's eyebrows lifted, but only for half a second. I went stone still.

"Why's that?" Sgt. Kirkwood asked quietly. "Did she say something to you?"

"No," Whit said, then started to retch.

Sgt. Kirkwood handed over his trash bin just in time for Whit to vomit. "Set the bin outside the door, son. Go clean yourself up."

Whit climbed over my legs and left for the bathroom, wiping at his mouth.

How could any of this be real? It felt like a nightmare. I wanted to wake up. Just like Laurel.

"Did you know that Laurel had . . . problems?" I asked, my words just a breath.

He smiled sadly, nodded once, just barely.

"Did Silas say the same thing to you? Like what Whit just said?"

"No," he said, looking genuinely surprised. "Does he think the same thing?"

"I don't know," I said honestly. "He wonders."

I hated talking about Silas; it made me feel like I was back on the porch of the old Griggs house, having my heart ripped out of my chest.

"Can I go?" I asked Sgt. Kirkwood. The scent of vomit was creeping into this small space.

"Just a second," he said as Whit reemerged, eyes bloodshot and face blotchy.

"Mark, I'm aware that Laurel Hart had some issues, but I need to know why you think this might have been a suicide."

"I don't," Whit said, stone-faced now and with a new story. "I didn't mean that. She'd been drinking. It was raining."

"And the pickup is so old and hard to drive," I offered, my head a little dizzy from the suffocating smells. "The brakes were terrible."

"Yeah," Whit agreed, so much force behind the one word that I knew he was lying. Well, not lying—not exactly. Not purposely trying to lie to Sgt. Kirkwood. Whit was trying to convince himself.

"West, what about you? You'd interacted with Laurel earlier in the evening on Friday?"

I nodded, distracted. "She was—she was good. And at the dance, the happiest I'd ever seen her."

"Anything else we should know?" Sgt. Kirkwood asked.

I tried to think through the evening, looking for something—anything—suspicious. Or, hell, even *not* suspicious. *Anything* to help answer questions.

"Silas said there was a note," I piped up.

Neither Sgt. Kirkwood nor Whit looked surprised.

"It was for you," I said to Whit. "Not *that* kind of note, just—"

"I know," he said.

"Oh."

"We're holding on to it for a little while," Sgt. Kirkwood told me, "but it seemed unrelated to the accident, so chances are we can relinquish it to the family soon. We'll hope to pull together a full police report after the investigation is over. You two can go."

Whit and I stood to leave. "How long will that take?" I asked.

"A month, maybe two."

"And then we'll know what happened?" Whit asked. A flicker of something passed over his face—hope? determination? expectation?—and I knew that he, like me, needed answers. Sgt. Kirkwood looked sad. "No guarantee of that."

I wondered: If I knew it was an accident—bad brakes, bad weather—would I feel some relief, knowing I couldn't have prevented it? Would Silas give himself a reprieve—or would he still feel guilty because he knew how to handle the truck better than his sister did? I didn't know what Whit would feel, especially with the alcohol involved.

But if it was a suicide. . . . My mind teemed with possibilities.

Sgt. Kirkwood said, "Be *careful* out there, kids."

I drove directly to Trudy's house. She pounced on me the moment I walked in the door, pressing her arms around me, cooing comfort in my ear. It was exactly what I needed. "Can I stay here tonight?" I asked. "In your bed? I don't want to be alone."

"Of course!" she said. "We'll all squish together and make room."

"We'll . . . *all*?" I asked.

"Ami's here too!" Trudy said.

"Hi, West!" said Ami from the top of the stairs.

"Hi." So that was the "us" in "Do you want us to come pick you up?" from before.

"I heard about what happened," Ami said, looking genuinely sorry. "I'm so, so sorry. What can we do to help?"

Unable to stop myself, I gaped at her a little in disbelief. First, that she was using "we" to describe herself and Trudy, as if they were a team. Second, that she could be so removed from the events of the weekend and still try to insert herself into the mess. "I—nothing," I said, then added, "Thanks."

We lounged around Trudy's room, which was once a refuge for me but now felt so compromised by the presence of a stranger. Some weird song I didn't know played over and over on Trudy's laptop, the hot summer jam from Camp Summit, no doubt.

"Do you want to talk about it?" Trudy asked me.

I shook my head, thinking, *Not in front of Ami.*

So while the girls talked about counselors I didn't know and reminisced over camp memories, I sat uncomfortably on Trudy's bed, silently flipping through a stack of Trudy's mail, seeing it without really seeing it, giving my hands something to do. I was drowning in summer memories of my own and feeling lonelier than I had when I'd been alone with my grief.

While Ami rehashed a story from a camper-versus-counselor activity, I looked up and saw Trudy staring at me. When she caught my eye, she mouthed, *Are you okay?*

I stared back for a moment, then slowly shook my head. But before she could do anything about it, I stood up to go. "I just remembered something I need to do at home," I said. Trudy knew me well enough to recognize it was a lie.

Outside of the bell tower, I'd never kept secrets from her before, but just now I wondered if I would start. I felt protective of these memories. They were mine. Well, mine and his.

And I also felt selfish with the grief, which belonged to just a small knot of us in this town: me, Whit, Silas and his family.

Tru followed me out to my car. "What's going on, West?" she asked.

I looked at her. "She was my *friend*, Tru."

"I know," she said. "And I'm really sorry."

"Me too. I'll see you at school?"

"You don't want to stay here tonight?"

"I don't think I should."

Trudy looked at me for a long while. "Okay."

"I'll see you at school," I said again, then ducked into my car.

I backed out of Trudy's driveway, wiping away tears and missing her more in that moment than I did even over the summer. If I'd only gone with her to Camp Summit, then it would be me and her telling stories in her room. I would be singing along to that ridiculous song instead of suffering this crashing, hopeless loss and guilt, because I would have never met *them*.

The thought pulled at my heart as I drove the tired streets. Never met the Hart twins? Could I really wish for that?

The answer was there in a moment.

Yes.

thirty-one

When school started, there were whispers up and down the halls: *A girl died, and did you know it might have been suicide?* Since very few of us at the high school had known her, it was mostly gossip, though the administration invited local clergy to join the school counselors in offering the students support and a chance to talk. Pockets of female underclassmen sobbed and comforted each other, annoying me to no end.

"What's *she* crying for?" I lashed out in the direction of one frenetic sophomore.

Her friends glared at me, but the weeping one just spluttered, "Didn't you hear about the girl who died? Her name was Laura, and it—could—have—been—*any* of us!" She dissolved into hysterics, and I stormed away without even bothering to correct her.

Later that day, I saw those same sophomore girls through a classroom window, bawling to my *dad*, of all people. He looked so strong, so full of profound consolation, and it made me furious because all he'd offered me was *space*.

There were rumors that Laurel had been crazy, gossip that twisted the accident site into a hanging, allegations that the brother had something to do with the death. But at lunch, Elliot stood up in the cafeteria and announced, "I will *kick anyone's ass* I hear talking about it." I assumed the announcement was mostly for Whit's benefit, but Elliot's eyes found mine in the crowded lunchroom and he nodded, just once.

The whole school smelled like a department store, everyone in new outfits, and I walked the halls in a daze. Conversations sounded like blurred whispers. Whit avoided me, and Bridget and Marcy acted as if I was either going to break into pieces or else set fire to the school. And while Trudy had been at my side that morning, pressing her upper arm against mine in a show of solidarity, I hadn't seen her since. Sometimes I felt as if I needed a support beam to keep me standing. Once, I would have made the request of Trudy; once, she would have known without my asking.

Again I wondered if I should tell her about Silas and our night in the bell tower, but I was already in shreds, and silence was the simplest guard against becoming the most pathetic confetti. It made me think of the night Libby combed her fingers through the ravaged remains of those peeled-apart paper dolls and dropped them in my lap. "It worked just the way I guessed," she had said, and remembering that made me feel so foolish. Out of the mouths of babes and all that.

Elliot and I had fifth-period English together. When I entered the room, he was talking to a group of football players, but he looked up and offered me a sad smile before breaking away from the guys and crossing the room to me. "Let me know if there's anything I can do for you, okay?" he said to me. He opened up his arms, and it was *so damn easy* to fall into them.

The week was long and lonesome. Dad spent evenings over at the old Griggs house, and I spent them alone in my bedroom, wallowing in guilt and grief, trying to come to the surface long enough to learn calculus. I overheard my dad mentioning an autopsy to my mom, but when I asked for details, he said he didn't know.

"How is Silas?" I asked, trying not to sound desperate.

"You'd know better than I would," Dad replied, headed off toward his bedroom. "He doesn't say much to anyone else."

Dad didn't know. He still hadn't realized what had happened between me and Silas. I could hardly imagine the Silas my dad had just described—quiet, reclusive, broken.

"How—" I started to ask, but Dad was already gone.

I didn't even know what I was going to ask. Nothing. Everything. How does he look? Has he been eating? Does he go running? *Please, God, let him run.* It would probably be the finest choice of medicine for him right now.

Does he ever ask about me? Does he still blame us?

I knew the answers to those: no and yes.

I didn't want to go to the funeral—really, *really* didn't feel ready to face Silas—but of course I went anyway.

Libby stayed home with Shea while Mom and I walked across the parking lot to join Dad at the church. Inside, we passed my dad's empty office—and the discreet, locked door to the bell tower—then up the stairs to the lobby of the sanctuary, where I hadn't been in over a month.

The whole building felt cold; in the front of the church was the coffin, surrounded by flower arrangements—forget-me-nots in blue, pink, white. When I saw Silas in his suit, I felt my throat constrict and tears prick at my eyes.

"Coming, honey?" my mom asked, pausing at the open doors to the sanctuary.

"In a minute," I said, then retreated to the ladies' room, where I came undone.

My heart was going *too* fast. My throat felt raw. Even though tears were expected at a funeral, I wiped away all evidence of my crying with a wad of toilet paper. I willed myself to *breathe* while I waited for my face to return to its right color, staring into the tiny mirror above the sink, which reflected a second mirror on the wall behind me. Image after image after image trapped between the two, shrinking into a minute infinity. "Just a second!" I shouted when someone jiggled the doorknob. My voice sounded strange: a facsimile of the real thing.

With deep breaths, I stepped out of the bathroom and made my way back to the sanctuary. My parents were standing together near the front, but off to the side. A part of me wanted to take them each by a hand and drag them from this place; another part wanted to leave Green Lake on my own and never, ever look back.

I hung back in the lobby until Silas left the sanctuary with some cousins before I approached the coffin. The center aisle felt a thousand miles long as I made my way to the front.

Laurel's eyes were closed; her face looked plastic. She was wearing the same dress she'd worn to *Carmina Burana*.

Someone stepped up beside me. Papa Arty, his tears quiet but devastating. "Sweet Pea," he murmured, his lips barely moving. "Sweet Pea, *how*?" Then he glanced over at me, and though his gaze was soft with empathy, it felt like an indictment. I hurried away.

I had thought I'd sit beside my parents, but when I saw Whit sitting alone a few rows back, I joined him instead. He had this strange, pained look on his face as if he had bit into something rotten. It occurred to me that he'd probably worn that same charcoal-colored tie to his own father's funeral years ago. When my eyes lingered on it, I knew he interpreted my thoughts. "It's the only one I've got," Whit whispered.

People had flown in from north and from south, relatives from all over. Papa Arty and Oma Lil, along with Glen's parents, sat in the front row with Glen and Teresa and Silas. Beside me, Whit stared at the back of the pew, at his feet, at his hands—anywhere but the front.

My dad officiated. His face was perfect: grieved but consoling, sorrowful with that small strength of hope that came from his core. He looked directly at the Harts while he spoke from the podium, "Today we celebrate the *life* of Laurel Judith Hart." I wanted him to look at *me*.

There was no mention of suicide—of course—just a continual stream of platitudes about heaven, about the people Laurel had touched, about the pleasant memories of her we were left with.

Bullshit.

Instead, I thought of Laurel's sadness, of how she struggled to let people in. Thought of her wasting away right in front of us.

A few relatives spoke: Laurel's aunt—Teresa's sister—about one of Laurel's performances. A cousin shared a funny story about a time she and Laurel got caught taking mud baths. Then Silas stood up.

"My sister . . . ," he started, then stopped. His hands gripped the edges of the podium, white knuckled. "My sister was beautiful and brutal." I saw Teresa clutch at Glen's arm. Then, Silas said, "I wrote this poem for her. 'The low moon lags beside men out late. . . .'"

He struggled and strained against words that he still desperately wanted to believe. He had meant for this poem to feel safe, protective; it felt so backward here at a funeral. I stared at his lips, at the way he formed each word with intentionality, like each one was a gift for his sister—which I supposed was true, both then and now. The church was full, but this moment was between Silas and Laurel alone.

Silas's voice faltered. He pressed his lips together, and I could see him swallow hard. Bereft, he looked up, looked into the crowd. I knew it wasn't *me* he needed—just strength somehow—and though it cost me, I straightened in my seat and met his eye, nodded once. That second felt like ten minutes, and I swear I wanted to run to the front of the church and hold him, wanted to take the paper from his trembling hand and read it myself.

He looked back at the poem. "'What words work . . .'"

You're a distraction, I reminded myself bitterly. *Just a distraction.*

I was the only person in the room—except maybe for Whit, I didn't know—who understood what it meant when Silas adjusted his tie at the pulpit, his two fingers pausing for a millisecond over his heart.

Displays were set up in the lobby: photos and trophies and a looping home video of Laurel's dance recitals. On a table with the guestbook sat the small pile of picture books Arty had given her the afternoon we'd spent in the Mayhew attic. I signed my name to the guestbook, offered the pen to Whit—who refused it with a terse dismissal—and then opened *Vivien's New Friend*.

Inside, the illustrated girl from the cover held a doll—a tiny ballerina with a red dress and gloves, and small silver toe shoes.

My breath caught.

I closed the book and moved it to the bottom of the stack.

Without warning, Whit hurried toward the door. Suddenly on my own, the same panicked feeling returned. My mom was talking with Mrs. Hart. My dad was talking to Silas. Dad had a hand on Silas's shoulder, and I could almost feel the weight of it, the strength and solace of it.

I hurried out after Whit.

I was surprised to find it was still morning. The funeral had seemed to last hours and hours. Whit was making a beeline for his car. I jogged to catch up to him. "You okay?" I asked, wondering if I looked as destroyed as he did.

"I don't think so," he said, his voice quiet, hoarse.

"Are you going to the burial?"

He already had his car door open. He turned around and shook his head, just slightly. "I can't do it. I can't watch them. I have to go."

"Whit," I said, and it was a plea.

He paused but didn't look at me.

"Whit, I have no one to talk to about this," I said.

"You have Silas," he said.

"No. I don't." I didn't elaborate.

After a few more moments of silence stretched between us, he nodded his head toward his passenger door. "Get in."

Whit's mom and stepdad weren't home, so Whit went straight for the liquor cabinet, grabbed a big bottle of whiskey, and took it outside, where the two of us sat on a trampoline, trading off the bottle between us.

"Is this wrong, you think?" I asked after taking a gulp that burned my throat. "When alcohol is what probably killed her?"

"You think that was it, then?" Whit answered. "That it was a drunk-driving accident?"

"I don't know," I admitted. "Do you still think she . . ."

"I can't decide which way is worse," he said.

"Silas thinks it's my fault," I said. I hadn't meant to say it aloud.

"No, he doesn't. Why would it be your fault?" Whit responded. "That's stupid. He thinks it's *his* fault."

"It's because of me that we . . . disappeared." I paused. "How do you know he thinks it's his fault?"

"He told me," Whit said, taking another drink. "I went over to their place to get the note."

"What note?"

"The note Laurel was writing to me in a notebook." Whit

tipped the bottle up, slammed another gulp, and then pulled the note out of the pocket of his dress pants. "Here."

Dear Whit,

You've made me happier than I've been in ages. Whatever happens, I'm hoping

"Is that it? It ends in the middle of a sentence?"

He nodded. "What do you think?"

"Are you asking me if it's a suicide note?"

Whit looked grave. "I told her the worst thing my dad did was not leave a note. Was she trying to . . . spare me?"

"I don't know." I looked at the note again. "I mean, it's maybe a little weird that she didn't write, 'You *make* me happier'—present tense—but it doesn't prove anything. You'd think if she knew it was a good-bye letter, she'd have finished."

"But what does 'whatever happens' mean? And what was she hoping?"

"Oh, gosh, Whit," I said, leaning back and staring at the clouds. "Could be anything. Like, it could mean, 'Whatever happens between you and me this next year, I'm hoping we'll stay friends.'"

"Or 'Whatever happens *to me*, I'm hoping you'll forgive me and move on,' that sort of thing."

"I don't know," I whispered.

"Seems like that's all anyone ever says these days."

"I hate it. But the police report—that will have some answers, right? That'll be good."

"Yeah," he agreed, lying down beside me.

"How are you doing?" I asked. The whiskey was starting to get to me: I couldn't remember if I'd asked him this already.

Whit turned his head and looked at me like I was crazy. "I'm fucking awful," he said. "You?"

"Same."

"The night before my dad died, we played catch. Did you know that?"

I shook my head, took another drink. It was either because I was lying down or because I was tipsier than I thought that a little came spilling out the sides of my mouth. "Shit," I muttered. I felt it drip down my neck.

"We played catch," Whit continued, "and he seemed so happy. He told me about the day I was born and about when Jenna was born, and about when he and Mom got married, and I thought things were getting better. And then . . . not even twenty-four hours later, he was gone. And no note.

"Laurel," he continued, "was so happy at the dance. I should have known. I should have said something." He started to cry.

"No," I said. "Shhh, you couldn't know."

It would be so convenient to blame Whit. I *wanted* to blame him. Anything to make it someone else's fault. My tongue felt loose and ready, and I wondered if I was drunk.

"Did you—?" My words died on my lips. I had been going

to ask, *Did you love her?* but it was one answer I didn't need. Maybe didn't even want.

We lay on the trampoline, our heads together, and Whit cried. "I sh'd go," I said, my words slurring a little.

"I drove you," Whit reminded me. "I'll call someone to come get you."

"Not my parents."

"No."

I forgot everything for just a moment while Whit dialed a number on his cell phone. "Yeah, can you come get West?" I heard him say as I eased into a stupor and fell asleep.

thirty-two

“You’re an idiot, Whit,” I heard someone say what felt like only a moment later. “You got her *drunk*?”

“You don’t know anything about it,” Whit replied. “You barely even knew her.” This I took to mean Laurel. “And I didn’t force her to do anything.” This I took to mean me.

I blinked my eyes against the late-afternoon sunlight.

“You knew she’d be a lightweight,” he accused. “She hardly ever drinks.”

I sat up. My head felt a little dizzy, but mostly okay.

It was Elliot.

“Hey,” he said. “I’m your ride. Let’s go.”

I didn’t argue, but I felt stupid. I climbed down off the trampoline, then stumbled, falling onto my butt.

“Oh shit,” Elliot said, presumably still to Whit, “I’m going to have to sober her up before I take her home. She'll be dead if her parents see her like this."

"Hey, watch your words, man. Fuck you," said Whit.

Elliot helped me up off the ground, slung an arm around my waist, and helped me move toward the driveway.

"Bye, Whit," I chimed lazily.

We approached a junky white Pontiac with rust stains near the wheels. "No more minivan?" I asked, nodding toward the car.

"Finally saved up enough for this piece of shit," he said, kicking at a tire. "C'mon, let's go." He opened the passenger door for me and helped me in, taking care with my head, then walked around the car and climbed into the driver's seat.

"What about Whit?" I asked.

"He'll be fine. He's not going anywhere."

"You yelled at him."

"He yelled at me too. We do that. We'll be okay. Where to? I can't take you home yet."

"I don't care." I just wanted the wind in my face.

"Here, drink this," he said, handing me a bottle of water. "Whit's an asshole. He could have gotten in big trouble for drinking with you today."

"Really?"

"I don't know. Probably."

"I think Sgt. Kirkwood likes him."

"Sgt. Kirkwood likes everyone," Elliot said. "But the last

girl Whit drank with is dead."

Those words started to sober me up.

"Laurel," I said, looking out the window.

"What?"

"You never say her name."

"Look, are you pissed at me?" he asked.

I looked over at him, shocked. "No. Why would I be? Are you pissed at me?"

"A little," he admitted.

"That's . . . fair," I said, and he actually grinned.

Despite what I had said before, it turned out I did care where we went, because Elliot chose the public beach on Green Lake. Seeing the lifeguard stand, sentry of the empty beach, gave me this spastic attack of memories: wet shoulder to wet shoulder, feeling safe. The image felt like a paper cut on my heart, and I flinched a little, remembering. In my head, I heard Silas's voice, soft and low through his chattering teeth, reciting:

The broken heart has
its own stark splendor.

Did I believe that? *Not today.*

"Keep drinking that," Elliot said, nodding at the bottle of water. "Feeling any better?"

I gulped the water.

"How ya doing after—you know?" Elliot asked.

"I don't know," I said, unbuckling my seat belt and turning to face him. "Bad?"

"Is that a question?"

"No, I guess not. It's a statement."

"How's he doing?"

He meant Silas. "I don't know," I said. "We're not really speaking right now."

Elliot's eyebrows went up. "What happened there?"

I shrugged, not wanting to talk about it, especially not to Elliot. Hadn't he guessed something was up when Whit called *him* to come get me?

"Thanks for picking me up."

"Not a problem."

"I treated you like shit, and then you didn't even think twice before coming to get me from Whit's house."

"Ahh, that would be false," he confessed. "I thought *at least* three or four times first."

"You still did it." My eyes were stinging, but I held back any tears; loneliness blanketed me. "I never deserved you," I said. "I'm sorry."

"West—"

"You've always been there for me."

"And always will be," he said, leaning over to kiss my cheek.

But I turned toward him and kissed his mouth. I saw his eyes widen in surprise but felt him receive me as he returned the kiss. I wasted no time crawling over the center console into his lap. I straddled him, kissing him harder and harder, while the steering wheel dug into my lower back.

His arms wrapped around me, and my hands were behind his head, forcing his face to mine. Our mouths bruised against each other, tongues forcing teeth apart, devouring, greedy. We had never kissed like this before. I tasted blood, and I wasn't sure if I'd bitten his lip or he'd bitten mine.

Elliot felt my tears on his face before I felt them on my own. I heard someone making a quiet sobbing noise, and was mildly surprised to discover it was *me*.

"West," he said, pulling away.

But I kissed him again, harder. "Please," I said, embarrassed at how much it sounded like a plea.

"West. West, stop," he said, surprisingly gentle as he conceded, "It's not me you're missing right now." He looked regretful. "I wish it was." Then he wrapped his arms around me and shifted my position so that he was holding me while I cried into his shoulder. "It's okay. It's okay," he said, and I was being rocked like a baby by this huge football thug. I couldn't stop my tears. "Shhh," he said. "Is this about Laurel or about Silas?"

I couldn't bear to tell him it was Silas, so we talked about Laurel instead. It all came rushing out like a manic feed: "There were no skid marks, and some people think it was a suicide, and I don't know what to do for Whit. I didn't cry when she died, and I feel like I was supposed to, and I *didn't*. The funeral was miserable, and we skipped the burial like total cowards. I should have *been there* that night, and I . . . we . . . we *weren't* . . . and now she's gone. And what if it's all my fault?" My tears wet his T-shirt.

Elliot didn't say anything, but the silence didn't feel like judgment. Only like solace, like a place I could maybe rest a while.

"Do you believe in heaven?" I asked Elliot, my head still heavy against his shoulder.

"I don't know, West. Do you?"

I was quiet for a second, then whispered: "'Death I think is no parenthesis.'"

"Huh?"

"Elliot," I said suddenly, "I need to go to the library. Right away, before it closes. Can you take me there? Now?"

"After you get off my lap," he said.

"Oh, right, sure," I said, scrambling off.

"What's at the library?" he asked as he drove.

"I'm not sure." Please be there, I thought. Please.

After he parked outside City Hall, I told him to stay in the car, that I would only take a minute. "Please be there," I muttered over and over as I walked to the poetry section.

"Need help finding anything?" an amused Janice Boggs asked from the reference desk.

"Thanks," I said. "I already know where it is." My eyes scanned the last names of the authors, looking for the familiar lowercase letters. An irrational fear choked me as I pulled the book from the shelf.

There in the corner of the tiny Green Lake Library, I flipped through the pages until a small scrap of paper fell out and fluttered to the floor. I picked it up, read his handwriting, and my heart tore open like cheap fabric. Again.

To the next person who reads this poem,

I was about 99% in love with her before these words dripped off her lips. Now the excesses of adoration are spilling from me like blood from a wound.

Hope you are as lucky.

thirty-three

The next couple of weeks seemed to last a thousand years. After school I'd stop by the station to see Sgt. Kirkwood, hoping for some sort of news, some sort of update. "West, I'll make sure you know the police report is here just as soon as I find out, okay?" he finally told me. "Give yourself a break. Go shopping, out to eat—something to keep your mind off it. Call Trudy. I know she'd love to see you."

"Okay," I said, but I didn't call.

Instead, I spent my nights at home: calculus, my distraction; and sleep, my escape.

Silas called one night. His name on my cell phone screen incited riotous panic inside me, and just as I collected the strength to answer, it quit ringing. He didn't leave a message, and it made me wonder if the call had been an accident. I was too scared to call him back.

His absence was a hollow cavity in my chest. I kept picturing Libby with those damn paper dolls, the way they ruined each other when torn apart.

What if Silas and I had just stayed at the dance? What if I had said something to Laurel earlier that evening? Was what Silas and I did that night wrong, and were we being punished? What if Whit had driven Laurel home? If he had, would he be gone now too? What if *Silas* had been the driver? He'd be . . . he'd be . . .

I couldn't even bear the thought.

And always, always the big question: Suicide or accident? Was one preferable? Did absolution for the rest of us come with either option?

Whit and I—and Silas, if I knew him at all—awaited the results of the police report as if it would put ground back beneath our feet.

Silas.

He had once said that if he was lost, I would know where to find him.

But I didn't—I was lost too.

He joined the rest of us at Green Lake High School about three weeks after classes had started. In a school this small, I couldn't avoid him, even if I wanted to—which I didn't, not exactly. His first day felt about a million years long: every class period was like a Band-Aid, and every passing time was akin to ripping it off as I scanned every crowd for a familiar, ridiculously tall boy. I wondered if I would ever be able to act like a normal person around him again. My heart was branded with his initials.

The last period of the day, I walked into AP World History, and there he was. How had I forgotten that we had the class together?

I almost walked into him. He was waiting by the door, probably for everyone else to take their assigned seats before the teacher found one available for him. "Oh!" I said, looking up at him.

"Hi," he said. It was soft and low and not unfriendly and sounded like the most profound statement of the century. He reached toward me, saying "West . . ." quiet as a prayer.

Before he could touch me, I took a step back, still staring, my throat blazingly hot beneath my collar.

I turned around and left not only the classroom but the school itself, completely unable to control the mix of fear, guilt, sadness, and desire that was storming my heart.

"Gordon, it's West," I said as I stood in his Legacy House door-way. "Can I come in?"

"Westie! Yes, of course, of course. Come in, please. Shouldn't you be in school?"

I sat on the same couch as I had the last time I had been there with both Laurel and Silas. "I guess so," I said. "Do you want me to leave?"

"Don't be silly. How are you?" he asked, looking sad in his rocking chair. "I heard the news."

"You did?" I asked.

"I did. How are you?" he repeated. His voice was tender, concerned.

It broke me, and the tears came again. Whatever plug had been preventing them in the hours after Laurel's death had certainly been pulled. Now I couldn't seem to stop. Gordon let me cry.

"Gordon, he thinks it's our fault that she's gone," I finally managed.

"I know," he said. "It's not."

"You know?" I asked, though what I was really clinging to was the "it's not."

"He stopped in."

"Silas came to see you?" I wiped the tears onto my sleeve.

"He did."

"What did he say to you?" When Gordon didn't answer, I changed my question. "What did you say to him?"

"I told him that his sister was finally at peace." His calmness reached out to me across the room like a steadying hand. My disquieted heart didn't lose its agitation, but it felt grateful to have such serene company.

"No matter—no matter how she died? Even if she—?"

"Yes," he said.

"Can you . . . make sure Silas knows? Knows that you think that? I mean, if he—if he comes back to see you?"

Gordon nodded.

He lit his pipe and then reached for the jar of water that usually sat on his coffee table. He moved his hands tentatively around the table, not finding it. He blew out the match as it burned low toward his fingers.

"Hold on," I said. "It's on the table; I'll get it."

I retrieved it, set it in front of him.

He puffed on his pipe, and we sat in silence. Finally, I asked, "How is he doing?"

"He has questions in him, ones that have no answers, but he's clawing his heart out looking for them anyway. He's a broken boy—a broken man—right now, Westie, and struggling with intense guilt, feeling every emotion like a bomb inside him."

I tried to hold back another onslaught of tears.

"He cares about you, West," Gordon said. "Deeply."

"No, he doesn't," I said.

"He does," said Gordon simply.

"No. You should have seen his face, Gordon."

"Unfortunately," said Gordon, with considerable kindness, "I don't have the luxury of seeing people's faces, which forces me to see their hearts."

Soon, the trees around town were shocked into oranges and reds and yellows, preparing to fall like autumn confetti. Elliot won homecoming king, and Ashley Kuiper was queen; I went to coronation but not to the dance. Trudy spent her evenings mostly with Ami Nissweller, and though sometimes they'd invite me along, I felt like a third wheel, a tire slashed open by sorrows and secrets, slowing everyone else down. Silas joined the cross-country team and even broke several individual course records. From what I observed at school, he didn't seem to care.

About anything, really.

I wanted to plumb Gordon for details, but I couldn't bring myself to ask, knowing he'd told me all he wanted. His genuine grief over Laurel's death, though he had barely known her, touched me. I kept thinking of the two of them talking about a dancing God. The thoughtful look on her face had been nearly identical to her brother's as he had taken in Gordon's ideas on dry water, on a black sun, saying they were impossible for those who love God, just illusions.

It made me think of Silas's poem—"Darkness destroyed by the glory of dawn"—how true those words had felt when I'd said them in the lifeguard stand that night, how they'd felt like this mystery I could own, or like a narrative I could crawl inside and be safe. I'd wanted it all that night. I still did.

Dad had had a persistent migraine since Laurel's funeral, and when it was bearable, he and Ed, the associate pastor, spent a lot of time with the Harts. Grief counseling. The tiniest part of me thought that Silas might call again, but my phone was quiet.

I was swamped in regret: Laurel, Silas, Dad, Whit, Trudy, even Elliot. I was like a ghost; all my blurry lines had reappeared, any definition I'd gained over the summer smeared like pencil lead rubbed with a malicious thumb. I wanted to matter to *someone*, someone who could lift my head above the grief.

One evening, I came out of my bedroom and looked down the stairs to where Dad was kissing Mom on the cheek as he slipped on his shoes. "I'm running over to the Harts'," he said to me, and Mom returned to her scrapbooking materials.

Sitting on the top step, I stared down at him. I liked having the whole family home for once, was somehow buoyed by this feeling that if we were all together in our home, then we were safe. It was a small and false comfort, but I'd take anything these days.

"Dad," I said, calmly, chillingly, "please—don't go tonight."

"Honey, I have to be over there. It's part of my job. We'll talk when I get back if you want, okay?" He reached for the doorknob.

"Please stay," I said. *Please just understand.*

"It's going to have to wait, Westlin."

"Have Ed go instead."

My mom looked up from her scrapbooking at the table. My dad hesitated.

"Dad," I said, my voice rising in desperation and anger, "you jump through hoops for everyone but us. How come we never matter—me and Libby and Shea?—and Mom! You're always running off to comfort or console or counsel or study or anything except spend some time with your goddamn family. And we need you."

I *need you.*

"Shea doesn't even . . . and Libby . . ." I was starting to ramble. Annoyed, I released my next words like a harpoon. "I'm so *sick* of hearing what a good man my father is. I don't even know you anymore."

Dad stood motionless as if I'd just backhanded him. "Wink—" he started.

"Don't call me that!" Anger slammed into me, and without thinking, I stood up, pointed an accusing finger at him. "I slept with him, Dad! I *slept* with him, and he dumped me. And you never asked about any of it. *Any of it.* You're so busy saving Green Lake that you don't even realize that your own family is falling apart . . . that *I* am falling apart! You never asked where we were the night that Laurel died. We were in the church bell tower having *sex.* Did you hear me—*Silas and I had sex.* Now why don't you run off to his house and comfort *him*?" I gave him a look of disgust then stormed back into my bedroom, which looked like a disaster zone, overdue library books and dirty laundry everywhere, much of which had been lying around for the last month.

The linen romper. His finger hooking in my belt loop.

The lacy dress. My blood pulsing to the beat of the orchestra.

Her pink pin-tucked button-up. His hands, shaking but determined.

The scent still lingered on the shirt, even a month later: sweat and sandalwood, like leather and cedar and musk and *him*. I dragged it into bed with me, overwhelmed and ashamed and thinking about a thousand things at once: the disturbing lack of skid marks, Silas's body pressed heavily against mine, Laurel's swan song, my calculus exam coming up on Friday, Elliot holding me while I cried, the bridge, the coffin, the harsh suspicion that Trudy's and my friendship was not built to last, Libby's torn paper dolls, Whit's only tie, and how desperately I missed my dad, who I'd once believed could solve any problem. Then I started to cry—big, quiet tears that felt like the only living things coming out of the deadness in me.

And then my dad was kneeling beside my bed, silent, but his hand on my back was like the hand of God.

thirty-four

Dad and I went to Mikey's for ice cream soon after my breakdown.

"I'm going to come back to church on Sunday," I told him.

"Yeah?" he asked, and there was no judgment in his voice.

Staying away had been a failed power play against my parents anyway, and since I now had their attention, there seemed no reason to avoid a community I was feeling more drawn to than ever before.

"I think I—I think I might love God," I admitted. I felt a mix of surprise and acceptance as I vocalized what I'd been processing since the night of my birthday. The mystery of it all had been sinking into my heart like a barb, one I'd reluctantly welcomed. "I don't really know him very well, but I love him. I'm angry at him too. *Really* angry. Do you think that's weird?"

"Not at all. Anger and love aren't mutually exclusive."

It was true. I had learned that lesson from the Hart twins.

Mikey's smelled like cinnamon rolls and burned hash browns and greasy fries.

"I don't want you to hate Silas," I told him.

He looked surprised. "I don't hate him, West! Why would you think that?"

I blushed. "You know."

Dad smiled as he took a bite of his rocky road. He licked some melted ice cream off his finger. He looked tired—really tired—and I wondered if he'd told Teresa and Glen about our secret.

"How is he?" I asked.

"Silas? He's still—what's the word?—reeling, can't seem to find solid footing."

"Lost," I summarized.

"Yeah."

"I wish I could do something for him."

My dad was quiet for a moment, then said, "You know, Laurel Hart used to come alive during Holy Communion. And communion celebrates death. Something to think about, eh?"

"Tell him that, Dad. Please. Find a good way to say it."

"I will."

My ice cream tasted cool and creamy and refreshing, and I had the briefest of insights that things *might* be okay in a million years. It was a lot of responsibility for one cone.

"Can we go on some college visits this fall?" I asked, switching subjects.

"Sure we can, kiddo."

"I don't want to go to Tellham and Barr University. Or anywhere in North Dakota."

He laughed. "Okay."

"I want to be a history major." I hadn't known I was going to say it, yet it made perfect sense: there was nothing I loved more than a good story. And right now, more than anything, I needed the stories to be true. I needed them to keep me—keep us all—from becoming madmen.

Dad smiled again. "That sounds great," he said, then breathed in and exhaled dramatically. "Ahhh, a plan."

I nodded, just a little, then stared intently at my cone. "Part of me still feels *pending*. Till the police report comes out, you know? With some answers?"

When I looked up at my dad, his sad smile sobered my heart, and just that easily, I realized there were no answers forthcoming, no resolution on its way for us.

"We're never going to know what happened that night, are we?" I whispered.

"I . . . wouldn't count on it, West."

I had pinned so many hopes on the police report—as if it would somehow magically decode Laurel's last evening, as if it would be our sanctuary, a safe house that would absolve our guilt—but this was real life, full of uncertainties and ambiguity.

"You gonna be okay, Wink?" Dad asked.

I closed my eyes to the illusory black sun.

Even though it felt as if the ground had been taken out from beneath me, I shouldered myself to believe that was an illusion too. Never before had I thought I could *choose* what to believe—and maybe I didn't think that even now. I only knew that I would fight anyone, including myself, to hold on to the idea that rescue was still happening all around me.

"I think so," I said, my voice flickering like a candle.

I started to take long walks alone—around town, stopping to see Gordon at Legacy House, and sometimes around the lake, despite the chilly air that came across the water. I'd think about Laurel as I stared out across the waves, which were ashy gray in the cloudy weather we'd had lately. And since I saw failure every direction I looked, sometimes I prayed.

I wanted to ask Silas, *Was God in control of Laurel's death too?* Not to be cruel—I honestly wanted to know what he thought about it. I wanted to hear him say yes, to say that God knew what he was doing when she died, to say that it wasn't our fault but God's. But when I heard myself reason it out—caught myself trying to assign blame—I had this strong feeling that I was still on the outside of something large, that it wasn't *about* blame.

It all felt new and overwhelming: instead of processing everything with Trudy or Dad or Gordon or Silas, I was opening up my chest and letting God make sense of the mess. It was a new thing for me to step out alone—although, I guess the point was that I *wasn't* alone. I'd let the wind blow my hair, even as I zipped the collar of my jacket up to the top. The word that was always trying to burrow into my heart was "healing." It was like a question I asked every single minute.

There were no answers—not really—except for this one strange feeling that reminded me of when Trudy and I were kids. One of us would lie on the driveway cement while the other outlined the first's body with chalk, down the slope of the shoulder, in between the fingers, sweeping wide around the head like a halo. We'd color them in with chalk, drawing faces and clothes and hair.

And while I sat and prayed, I had the same sensation—that I was being outlined, defined, and that the definition didn't come from me.

I was trying to hold so many things—but this one thing was holding me.

I still hurt. Every day. But somehow routine managed to creep in like an anesthetic.

At school, I ate lunch with Bridget and Marcy and Trudy—and Ami Nissweller, who was actually pretty cool. It turned out Trudy never slept with either Adam or Alex Germaine. "But the condoms didn't go to waste," Ami said with an amused grin. "The campers *loved* the 'weird water balloons' they found." My laugh was so unexpected that milk came out my nose and I started coughing, and Trudy had to thump me on the back while the lunch attendants glared at us.

"What'd you do with yours?" Trudy asked when I could breathe again.

"I'll never tell," I said slyly—though maybe I would, later, just to her. Or maybe not. I held those memories in a guarded fist I might never uncurl.

"So, Mom and Paul finally noticed the booze disappearing," Whit said to me and Elliot one evening after most people had left the movie theater. He stared at the credits scrolling on the screen. "There was a bit of . . . an intervention." His eyes flicked toward me.

"Were they mad?" I asked.

He shook his head. "No, actually. Mom cried a lot, which sucked. But they started me in weekly therapy—'long overdue,' Mom said—and are going with me to AA meetings at the Catholic church in Shaw."

"Whit," I said softly, then found it was all I had to say.

"And this asshole"—here Whit nodded toward Elliot—"makes me go *running* with him."

I laughed, then Elliot added, "Silas came with us too. Just once. He asked about you." The screen went dark. "God, I can't believe I'm saying this . . . but you need to talk to him, West," he said, to which I replied, "Maybe."

★ ★ ★

And then there was my family.

We started to eat dinner together, during which we took the phone off the hook. Afterward, Shea and Dad played Battleship while Libby and I worked on homework and Mom fussed with my scrapbook to a soundtrack of Chuck Justice.

One evening after dinner, the phone rang. Libby turned down the music while Dad took the call.

"So . . . it's not an emergency," he said when he hung up. "He's *fine*," he stressed, looking in my direction, "but Gordon had a little accident tonight."

My heart sped up. "What do you mean? What happened? What sort of accident?"

"He's *fine*," Dad repeated, "but from what I understand, he misplaced the little jar of water where he dips his used matches. He dropped the match on the coffee table. It set off the Legacy House fire alarm and left a crater in the table and he burned his hand, but apparently it's a minor burn and will heal just fine."

"He's going to have to leave his apartment, isn't he?" I asked. "And move to the other side of the building?"

"His children think that's a good idea."

"Are you going up to see him, Dad?" Shea asked.

"Nope," said my father, sitting back down across from Shea. "You didn't peek at where my ships are, did you, Shea?"

Shea let out a guilty giggle. "Maybe."

"Let's go to the hospital, Dad," I said. "I want to see Gordon."

"He'll be back in Green Lake tomorrow," Dad said. "At

most, the day after." He was trying so hard to make the right decision, I knew. I hated to confuse him.

"Let's all go," said Libby. "Together."

Everyone looked at her.

"Okay?" she said.

After a pause, "Okay," said Dad.

So we did.

"How are you?" I asked when I made my way to Gordon's apartment the next week. It still smelled of smoke and was mostly empty, though a few boxes were stacked against the wall.

He smiled a little sadly and held up his bandaged fingers. "I'm all right. My daughter and Betsy came over to help me pack up—and downsize." He led me into the living room, which still had his rocker. "I can get you a chair," he said.

"No need," I said, taking a seat on the floor and thinking how apt it was for me to sit at the feet of my favorite teacher. I glanced around the room at the empty walls. "Your books!"

"No space for them in the new room," he explained. "And—it was time."

"Did you sell them?" I asked.

He shook his head. "Gave the whole lot to Betsy. She'll take good care of them."

"I'm glad," I said.

"All but one," he corrected. He reached beside his chair, picked up the book that rested there, and held out his copy of *Collier*.

"For me?" I squeaked out, taking it from him.

"No one understands wielding story as a weapon the way you do, dear. Now tell me: How are *you*?"

"I don't know," I admitted, running my hands over the book cover. "I don't understand how one part of me can be healing so well while another still aches."

"Growing pains."

"Yeah, a certain kind."

"Yes," he agreed.

It was quiet then, and I was grateful that Gordon allowed there to be silence between us and that it wasn't uncomfortable. I flipped open the cover of the book; inside, it was signed by Donovan Trick. There was also an inscription from Gordon to his late wife.

Mavis, my heart,

I present to you my favorite story besides ours, both such august arms.

Love, Gordy

My eyes pricked with tears. It had actually been *her* book.

"I've always thought of myself as sort of blurry," I choked out. "It feels silly now."

Gordon's silence asked the question.

I answered, "It was never my job—or Silas's—or Dad's—to define me. The lines were always there. I just didn't know where to look, how to see." I felt a little bashful saying this, even though this was Gordon, and I knew he knew what I meant. Probably even better than I knew myself.

"The police report came out," I said. "Inconclusive."

He pressed his lips together.

"Is it always this way?" I asked.

"What way?" Gordon asked back.

"Does life always have more questions than answers?"

"Oh yes," he said. "At least that's my experience. And actually, the older I get, the more questions I have."

"It seems so backward," I said.

Gordon laughed a little. "Does it really surprise you, Westie? Faith and uncertainty are accomplices."

I nodded. He was right.

I thought about Laurel, about the night we watched the fireworks, when she felt she was going to corkscrew into the universe. I'd feel the same way except my prayers these days were so simple, so stark, so "please-just-keep-me-in-one-piece" that they worked like weights in my shoes. Silas once told me that God's message to him was to *abide*. I needed help with even that.

Gordon's—no, Mavis's—copy of *Collier* sat in my lap. *Stories are our most august arms against the darkness.*

The promise sat in my stomach like a hearty stew, or like truth.

thirty-five

I'd intended to head home after talking with Gordon—the autumn evenings were starting earlier and earlier—but I found my steps compelled toward the beach, the cold air working into all my gaps as I realized it was about time to break out the winter scarf and mittens. I tucked *Collier* beneath my arm and blew on my hands to keep them warm.

My steps grew quick with purpose I didn't understand. Until I saw there was someone in the lifeguard stand, and knew without a doubt that it was him. His posture, though, was bankrupt. Ghosts moved across the semifrozen waters, keeping my feet from retreat. He hadn't seen me yet; I could still slip away unnoticed. But I knew that I wouldn't. Or couldn't.

I could barely breathe as I approached the lifeguard stand. And though I was not at all surprised to see Silas Hart, he was surprised to see me.

"Hi," I said.

"Hi," he said, barely a whisper.

"Can I join you?"

He was still staring at me, and I couldn't interpret the look on his face. He looked tired and somehow older—especially his eyes—but *good*. He needed a haircut. He nodded, almost imperceptibly, and I climbed up into the chair, sat beside him, our legs extended in front of us, not touching. My heart was racing. Neither of us spoke.

"How's school?" he finally asked.

A tiny laugh escaped me. It was the last thing I expected him to say after all these weeks of silence, but he grinned at my giggle. "It's fine," I said. "It's *school*. How do you like it?"

Silas shrugged. He was wearing no jacket, only a sweatshirt—I wondered if the cold Alaskan winters had ruined him for Minnesotan ones. The shirt said, "G.I. José: A Real Mexican Hero," and I was tempted to giggle again, but I figured it was mostly nerves.

"It's all right. It's so small. I feel like everyone's in my business."

"They *are*."

We were quiet again. I heard my pulse pounding in my ears, loud like a storm only I could hear. All I could think of was how clean he smelled, how near he was, how if I only turned my head, I could see him up close for the first time in months. But I only stared ahead.

"Did you read the new Donovan Trick?" I asked, feebly brandishing *Collier*.

"Yeah, it was good."

"Yeah, I liked it too."

Another long pause.

Then, "West." It was so soft. It sounded like a different name, like a brand-new way to pronounce it. I chanced a glance at him and saw that he was looking at his feet. "Look, I'm sorry for how I reacted after Laurel died. I didn't mean to drive you off like that." His words were composed, thoughtful.

I wanted to let myself be folded into his words, but I was new now, different, guarded. "You said I was a distraction," I said back.

This time he turned and looked directly in my eyes. "Now, *that*—that is true."

Ouch. I looked away.

"I get so mad, you know?" he said, and his voice was louder than before, full of pent-up anger and frustration. No wonder his cross-country season went so well, I thought. "Sometimes it feels like I'm being asked to choose between you and Laurel—or actually, like I did choose this summer, and like I failed my sister. I know it's not like that—not exactly like that—but I regret things and I don't. Does that make any sense?"

Not really. And since confusion was a language I'd become fluent in, I nodded.

"I dreamed about her," he said softly.

"Yeah?"

Silas was quiet; then he finally said, "I don't think I'm ready to talk about it yet."

"Okay."

Silence once more.

It was so disarming to be near him again. Even if it hurt, I was glad for this, glad he was here beside me, no matter how long it would take to recover from this tiny interaction. My chest started to ache at the thought. This was Silas Hart, who had seen me naked and had walked away, and I felt bashful.

"I tried to call you," he said.

"I saw that."

"I looked for you after the funeral. You were gone."

"I'm sorry."

"No." The word was stern, causing me to look at him. "You have nothing to apologize for," he said. "Not to me. Not when . . ." His voice faded out, and for a moment, I thought he might cry. He looked so terribly defeated, so lost in regret. Together, we looked out at the lake, its slate-colored waters choppy from the wind. It was curious, not cruel, when he asked softly, "Why are you here?"

I paused for a moment, then said, "To find you, I think."

He seemed confused. "You—you knew I'd be here?"

I shook my head no; that wasn't what I meant. I swallowed and said, "Remember your poem? 'Truest'?" I quoted,

"'Darkness destroyed by the glory of dawn.'"

My heart was thumping in the silence that stretched in the space after I spoke.

"Yes," he said.

After that, I didn't say anything; there was a lump in my throat, and when I found I couldn't swallow, I started to cry. I wasn't even sure why I was crying—except for the whole mess of everything—and for the tone of Silas's "yes," which sounded like a boon, like a pardon. I chided myself for the unbidden tears, but I couldn't stop them.

It might have been habit or instinct, but Silas looked like maybe he wanted to reach for me.

"Silas." I continued to cry. "I don't know how to say this without upsetting you. You have to know my heart in saying this, okay? You *know* me."

He stared at me, wetted his dry lips. I couldn't tell what he was thinking, and what I was about to say might destroy any chance for reconciliation between us. I didn't want to say it.

But I had to.

"You know me," I repeated. "You know I'm not being off-hand when I say this."

This time, he nodded.

I willed my voice to come out calm, steady, and slow: "It's just this. You told once me that—that things might *never* make sense—but that doesn't mean you stop trusting that the world is being rescued. These last couple months have been . . . there's been nothing to *stand* on, you know? Except for this. It's . . . it's like *bedrock*, like you said. Climax before resolution. Darkness destroyed by dawn."

My words washed over him, and I tasted the salt in my silent tears and begged him to understand what I was saying: the mystery, the goodness, the sovereignty. My tears came harder. I was desperate for him to understand that I was not shrugging off his sister's death. I was only trying to pull him onto solid ground so that he could look at all the questions.

His eyes looked sad . . . but purposeful. There was light in them.

"I know you said it was our fault," I whispered, the words seeming to scratch my throat as they left. "And what we did was a mistake; you said so yourself."

The sound of our breathing matched the rhythm of the waves.

Finally, he decided to speak. "*We* weren't a mistake, West. I—I miss you. So damn much, sometimes I think it's going to kill me."

My heart was not even in my chest cavity. It had launched and was out flying over the lake, celebrating, and I wanted to call it back, wanted to make it stop, wanted to tell it that it was too soon to be happy—Laurel's grave was still too fresh, Silas had not finished speaking, and life had more questions than answers.

But then he touched me, put his hand beneath my face,

and gently moved my chin to look at him. "Do you hate me?" he asked. "For what I did to you? I understand if you do. I know why you're with Elliot."

My throat ached, and my heart barreled back into my chest in a damaging sort of way. I closed my eyes, my eyelashes thick with tears, and shook my head. "I don't hate you," I muttered. "I thought *you* hated *me*." Then what he said registered. "Wait—with *Elliot? What?*"

"I saw you at the movies," he said, eyes wide. "More than once. I mean, it's not like I've been . . . stalking you," he spluttered. "I just . . . Are you not with Elliot?"

What I wanted to say was, *No, you have ruined me for other loves*. But I thought of myself kissing Elliot in his new car. I was the fool, not Silas. "No, I'm not with Elliot," I mumbled.

Silas looked out at the lake, letting this sink in. When he looked back at me, his eyes were so deep, so dark. "I just—when I saw you, I felt guilty. For everything—that last night in the bell tower, for Laurel, for hurting you. And then I saw you with Elliot, and you looked so happy. I was actually glad for you for like five minutes—honestly wished to God you hadn't had to deal with any of my family's shit this summer." He was quiet, then he said, calmly, clearly, "But *after* five minutes, I felt just as lost as I did after Laurel died." He swallowed. "I miss you, West. I miss my best friend. I miss you *every single day*. I meant what I said—you're a distraction for me—the most perfect, beautiful distraction I can imagine."

The tears came again. I was like a human irrigator tonight. His words ran in circles around my mind: *I miss my best friend. . . . the most perfect, beautiful distraction.* I glanced over at him through tear-filled eyes. He stared at his shoes.

"It won't be the same," I said. My nose was starting to run, but I didn't care.

He released a bitter, humorless laugh. "You think I don't know that?" he asked. "Laurel's death cracked my life like a fault line." He looked at me. "West? Say the word, and I'll leave you alone. It's just, you're my match; do you know what I mean? I need a girl who reads like a fiend, who isn't embarrassed by my dancing. A girl who knows how to be silly, who wants to explore life and books and ideas—you know, a Brian major." He offered me a hopeful glance.

I didn't say anything, couldn't say anything, couldn't even look at him. It was all so different now—*I* was so different now.

Silas breathed in deeply and let it all out, eyes closed, a long, labored exhalation as the silence stretched between us like a great bay of separation. "Okay," he said. "Okay. It's okay." Then, with effort heavy as regret, he climbed down from the stand and started to walk away.

I sniffled. "I'm going to be a history major," I called out after him, wiping my nose on my sleeve. "Like Gordon was."

At that, he turned around and beamed at me—a wide Silas-grin that seemed like a promise, or like heaven opened up. "Even better."

He helped me down, and after he did, he didn't let go of my hand. There was no intimation that it would happen anytime soon; his grip was stronger than ever before. We paused; the swans on the lake spread their massive wings then and launched powerfully into the sky, creating a white *V* above us that flew southward until they were just gray specks on the cold horizon.

acknowledgments

Thank you to Jesus Christ, for rescuing me twice and daily—and for making me a writer.

I'm forever indebted to my amazing agent, Steven Chudney, who plucked *Truest* out of obscurity and gave it a chance. And to my phenomenal editor, Jill Davis, who championed my story and its characters from the moment she met them. Jill, you pushed me past the brink of my own talent and made this novel more than I could have ever imagined. Thank you too to Laurel Symonds for so much help along the way, and to everyone at Katherine Tegen Books and HarperCollins, including Kelsey Horton, Lauren Flower, Ro Romanello, and Alana Whitman. Thank you to Jenna Stempel for the beautiful jacket and to Alexei Esikoff for her careful copyedits and proofreading.

I'm inexplicably grateful to my beta readers: Stacey Anderson, Elyse Kallgren, Tracy Lair, Rachel Larson, Megan Rapp, Mary Roach, Brienna and Melody Rossiter, and Ashley Thorman.

Truest would not be the story it is without Cindy Woerner and Kristin Luehr. You two helped so tremendously that I—who am rarely without words—have none with which to truly express my gratitude. There's a reason this book is dedicated to you.

Thank you to my parents, Tom and Ronda Sommers, who never batted an eye when I said I wanted to be a writer! Dad and Mom, your support means the world to me. And thank you to Kristin and Kevin, my siblings, for everything: the stories, the laughs, the prayers.

I'm so grateful for my friends—my *team*—for being my sanity, my backbone, my sounding board, and for giving me a tether from our friendships into plenty of space to write. My team includes many of those whose names I've already listed, along with Erica Davis, Desiree Anderson, Brittane Turner, Jessica Willman, Brooke Jameson, Caitlin Leimbach, Dora Von Wald, Chelsea Pederson, and my Voye "sisters," Emily, Rachel, and Abby.

Thank you to my Northwestern friends for celebrating every step with me—especially Josh Wielgus, Erick Klein, and my "Think Tank" peeps, Matt Anderson, Steve Mattson, Whitney Gerdes, and Sam Fredin. Kyle and Janine Marxhausen, you were two of my biggest encouragers on this crazy journey. Robyn Frank was my prayer warrior, which got me through some anxious weeks. Judy Hougen, Betsy Grams, and Deb Schmidt, you cultivated my love for words and stories, and I'm forever indebted to you.

And, finally, thank you to everyone who reads this novel. It's a gift from my heart to yours.